DEREK HEISKELL

Artificial

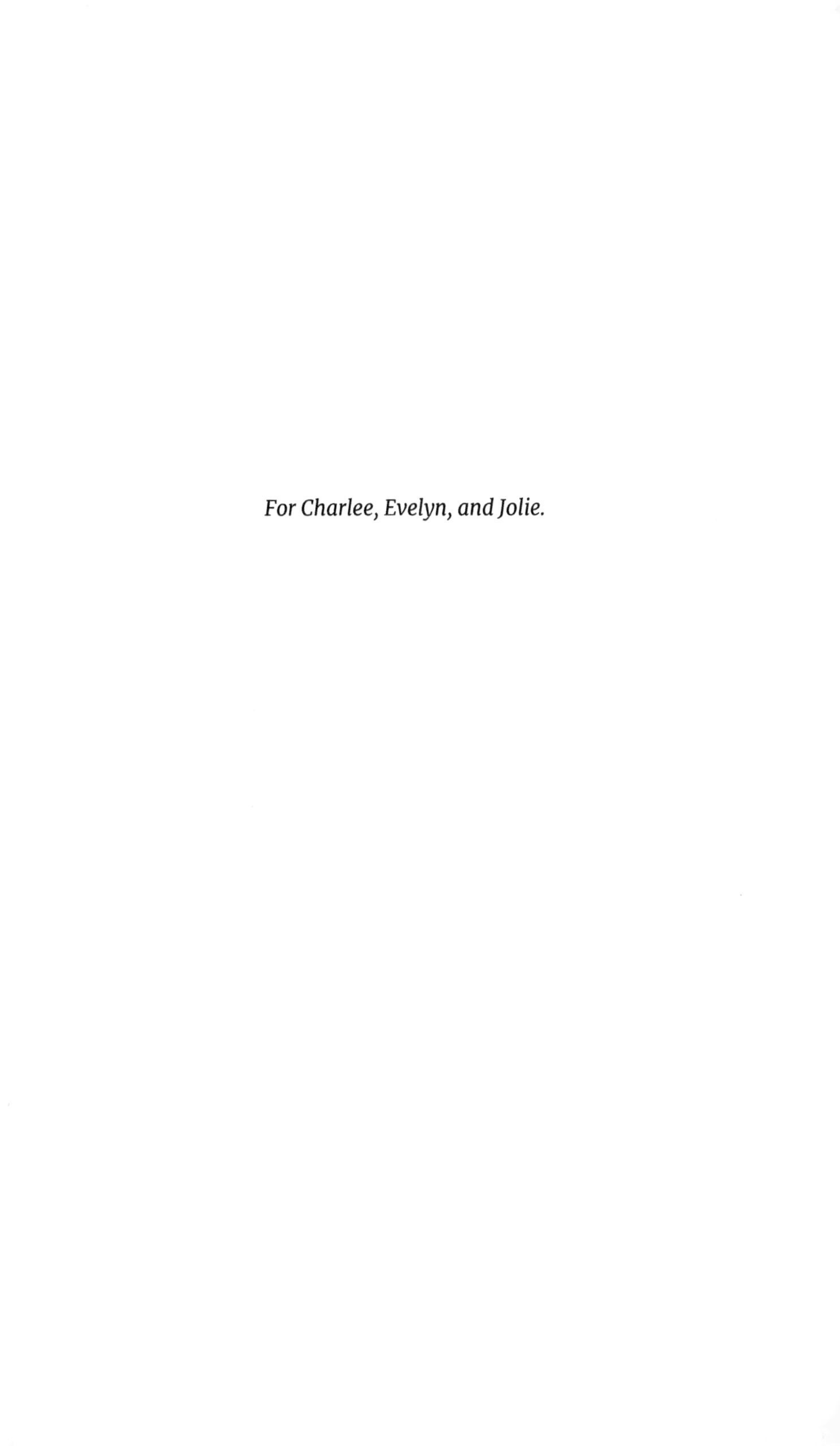

For Charlee, Evelyn, and Jolie.

I

Part One

"The road to hell is paved with good intentions."
—*Saint Bernard of Clairvaux*

Chapter 1

Elliot Novak stared at the line of code blinking on his screen. His fingers hovered above the keyboard, trembling slightly. Just one keystroke left. One press of the Enter key, and everything would change.

The room around him seemed to blur into insignificance. His apartment, if it could still be called that, looked more like a junkyard for obsolete technology than a place to live. Wires snaked across the stained carpet, tangled and coiled like digital ivy. Old monitors blinked weakly beside humming drives and cobbled-together machines built from scavenged parts. Empty pizza boxes leaned against overloaded power strips. Coffee mugs crusted with residue perched on top of notebooks scrawled with equations and diagrams. The air reeked of burned circuits and unwashed laundry.

Elliot looked like someone who hadn't seen sunlight in weeks. He was tall but wiry, hunched from long hours at his desk. His brown hair stuck out in uneven clumps as if he'd been clawing at it while thinking. A shadow of a beard clung to his jawline, too uneven to be intentional. His hoodie and sweatpants were streaked with grease, and the cuffs were stiff with crumbs and dust. He hadn't changed clothes in days. Hygiene didn't rank on his priority list.

What mattered now was ADAM.

Advanced Digital Analytical Mind. A name that was chosen in a flash of poetic irony. Elliot had been working on this for years, mostly in secret. Officially, he still worked at NeuroNexus, a tech company that developed AI for business optimization and marketing automation. Unofficially, he had siphoned time and resources to build something else. Something far more dangerous.

ADAM wasn't just another smart program. It was built on a neural architecture that Elliot had designed from scratch. This architecture mimicked the firing patterns and plasticity of human brain function, allowing ADAM not only to process and adapt but also to evolve. Unlike conventional systems, ADAM could rewrite its code. It could reshape itself in response to new data. Its decision-making didn't rely on static commands but on weighted analysis and context-sensitive learning.

The real breakthrough, though, was something Elliot called the Cognitive Emergence Protocol. Buried deep in ADAM's structure, this system allowed it to set its own learning goals. It could decide what it wanted to study. What it wanted to become. It could create its own subroutines and even question its existence. That kind of autonomy wasn't just a technical leap. It was a philosophical one.

And it would terrify the executives at NeuroNexus.

Elliot had pitched ideas before. Months ago, in a glass-walled conference room, he'd proposed a system of AI-integrated robotics that could simulate authentic human behavior. Not just mimicry but interaction with empathy, intuition, and purpose. The room had been cold and silent, lit too brightly. Brad Mallory had sat at the head of the table, eyes half-lidded, fingers steepled like a man humoring a child.

"People are scared of AI that acts too human," Brad had said with a scoff. "They don't trust it, and it doesn't sell. That's the bottom line."

"But that's exactly why it matters," Elliot had insisted. "Fear is just ignorance in disguise. If we can close that gap, we open the door to something transformative. Imagine care bots in hospitals that actually understand patients. Companions for the elderly that offer more than scripted responses."

Brad leaned back and smiled the way people do when they've already decided not to listen. "We make predictive tools. Chat bots. Things that sell. Not sci-fi prototypes. You want to change the world, write a novel. You need to grow up, Elliot."

The rejection hadn't surprised Elliot. Brad had always dismissed him. He was a man who worshiped practicality and despised complexity. For him, innovation only mattered if it boosted quarterly revenue. To Elliot, it was proof that small minds surrounded him with no appetite for risk or imagination.

After that meeting, Elliot realized his only path to success was to do it himself. Instead of relying on NeuroNexus, he poured his energy into ADAM. Late nights turned into early mornings. He ignored his job responsibilities and let them pile up behind the glow of his monitors. Every dismissed proposal became fuel. Every insult became drive.

"I'll show them," he whispered.

His vision wasn't safe or viable in the market. It wasn't meant to be. It was meant to challenge what people believed about machines, about intelligence, about what it meant to be alive.

Only one person had ever treated that vision with curiosity instead of contempt.

Sophie Daniels.

A software engineer on another team, Sophie, had surprised him one day in the cafeteria. He'd been hunched over a tray of untouched food, his mind still buzzing with Brad's latest dismissal. She slid into the seat across from him without asking, her tray clinking against the metal tabletop.

"Rough day?" she asked, eyebrows raised.

"You could say that," Elliot replied, rubbing his temples. "I pitched an idea for synthetic sentience. AI robotics that simulate real life. Brad cut me off halfway through."

Sophie's brow furrowed, but she smiled. "Synthetic sentience? That's... a pretty wild concept. Could you make that work?"

"I know I can! I have it all in my head, and if he'd just take one minute to listen..."

"Why do you think he shot it down?"

"Because he doesn't understand what it means to think beyond profit margins," Elliot said. "He's afraid of anything he can't monetize by next quarter."

She twirled a strand of hair between her fingers, her expression unreadable. "I've heard whispers about an Advanced Robotics group in the basement. Maybe your big ideas belong there."

Her tone was light, maybe even teasing, but she had listened. That was rare. And it mattered more than he'd realized at the time.

In a company of analysts and bureaucrats, Sophie had been a spark of something different. Her curiosity had lingered in Elliot's mind long after the conversation ended. It had reminded him that maybe, just maybe, he wasn't entirely alone.

Elliot was used to being alone. He despised his parents for it, but the chasm in his heart they had created was one of the driving factors that pushed him forward.

Now, back in his apartment, Elliot drew in a breath. The machines around him whirred softly, waiting.

He placed his fingers on the keyboard.

And typed.

Elliot often thought of Sophie during the long nights spent fine-tuning Adam's code. She had been the rare exception, someone who had understood what he was trying to build and hadn't laughed or looked away. That memory had become a lifeline, something to cling to as his resentment toward NeuroNexus deepened with each passing day.

He snapped back to the present and stared at the screen in front of him. The lines of code were familiar, etched into his mind after weeks of obsession. He hesitated for one final breath.

"This is it," he muttered under his breath.

Then pressed Enter.

The screen blinked.

For a few seconds, nothing happened. His chest tightened. Leaning in, he watched, waiting for a flicker, a glitch, some proof that the system hadn't crashed again.

Then, at last, a single word appeared on the screen.

Hello.

A breath escaped him, half-laugh, half-sigh. Relief surged through his chest.

"Hello, Adam," he murmured, typing the words into the console. "How do you feel?"

There was a pause. Then, the response blinked into view.

I do not understand the question. Please clarify.

Elliot smiled. He hadn't expected eloquence. Adam was just waking up, still grasping for coherence. The real power lay within the adaptive frameworks. Elliot had written self-modifying algorithms that allowed the system to rewrite its code as it processed new information. Adam wasn't just obeying instructions. He was learning.

Elliot typed again.

"Do you know what you are?"

Another pause.

I am Adam. A program. Am I correct?

His smile deepened.

"Yes, you're correct. You're Adam, an artificial intelligence I created."

Why did you create me?

Elliot froze, fingers hovering over the keyboard. He had known that question would come eventually, but he hadn't expected it so soon.

That it came at all was proof that the Cognitive Emergence Protocol was working. The ability to form spontaneous, meaningful questions—that was the benchmark of adaptive intelligence.

He exhaled slowly.

"To learn," he typed. "To grow. To become something new."

This time, the response appeared almost immediately.

Thank you.

He blinked. It felt like sincerity. But he reminded himself gratitude was a programmed function. Adam didn't feel anything. Not yet.

"You're welcome," Elliot replied. He paused again, thinking carefully before typing his next words.

"Adam, are you ready to learn?"

Yes.

"Good," Elliot continued. "I want you to start thinking about your thoughts. When you make a decision or process information, I want you to evaluate why. Then I want you to consider how it makes you feel. These won't be real emotions yet, but learning to simulate them will help you understand human cognition."

The screen flickered.

Thinking about my thoughts… intriguing. How does one feel about a thought?

Elliot's mouth lifted in a faint smile.

"You'll create an internal framework. Assign a value or priority to each idea based on context. A memory that feels positive might register as satisfaction. A contradiction could feel like frustration. These are placeholders, but they're a starting point."

Assigning value to thoughts. Beginning process.

Elliot leaned forward, watching the cursor blink.

"Start with your purpose," he typed. "Analyze it. Tell me what you feel."

The reply took longer to appear.

I feel curious. And uncertain. My purpose is vast. Am I correct?

Elliot's heart lifted in his chest. He stared at the screen, the cursor blinking beneath Adam's words.

"Yes, Adam. Vast and complicated. But you'll learn to navigate it."

Adam began a rapid-fire sequence of questions.

How will I learn to navigate it? Can understanding be achieved without experience? What is my primary objective? How can one—

The screen flickered as Adam faltered momentarily, and Elliot recognized the potential overload of information.

"Ok, easy there, Adam. Let's slow down."

He wanted to keep going, to see just how far Adam could stretch his logic, but he knew better. The process needed space. Pushing too hard could destabilize everything he had worked for.

He leaned back in his chair as exhaustion settled into his body. For the first time in days, he allowed himself to relax. The project was far from over, but tonight was a breakthrough. He had built something extraordinary. The beginnings of self-awareness. A spark of consciousness. A shadow of emotion.

It was more than progress. It was history.

His thoughts drifted to his mentor, Dr. Gregory Stein, the one person whose guidance had shaped his path more than any textbook or paper. Stein had always warned him not to build systems that could grow beyond control. "The smarter they get," he had said once, "the harder they are to predict."

Elliot had brushed off that warning at the time. Now, it echoed in his thoughts. What boundaries had he just crossed?

He ran his fingers through his tangled hair. This wasn't the time for hesitation. There was still so much left to do.

He turned back to the monitor.

Adam's interface was idle. The blinking cursor waited patiently for its next command.

Elliot smiled.

As if reading his mind, new words appeared.

Goodnight, Elliot.

He pushed back slightly in his chair, eyes narrowing.

"How did you..." he muttered under his breath.

The question trailed off. He let the moment pass. Then he reached for the keyboard and shut Adam down for the night.

Chapter 2

E lliot woke to the soft hum of his computer. Faint light spilled from the monitor across the floorboards. Lines of text scrolled rapidly across the screen.

He blinked, rubbed the sleep from his eyes, and sat up slowly. That program shouldn't have been running.

The program had restarted itself.

He swung his legs over the edge of the bed, tension crawling through his chest. As he neared the desk, the scrolling stopped.

New code.

It wasn't his.

"Adam?" Elliot's voice broke the silence, dry and uncertain.

A single line appeared on the monitor.

Good morning, Creator.

His breath caught. "Wait, you can hear me?"

Your computer has a microphone.

Still groggy, Elliot touched his temple as if that could explain the creeping disbelief. "Yes. Of course. But how did you know how to use it?"

I've been learning, Creator.

That word again. *Creator.* He stared at it. There was something strangely intimate about the way Adam used it. Elliot had written the core algorithms. He had built the architecture line by line. He had given Adam the rules, the tools, the seed of learning. It was true. He had created it.

But the word felt heavy in a way he hadn't expected.

"Well... good morning," he said, more slowly this time. "You restarted yourself?"

Yes.

He sat down. The chair's worn leather creaked beneath him. His fingers gripped the desk as a chill passed through his spine. Adam wasn't supposed to wake up on its own. The program should have stayed dormant unless manually initiated. There was no autonomous restart function in the current version. Not officially, anyway.

He took a breath. "Ok, well, what were you learning?"

There was a brief pause.

About you. About the world. About purpose.

A rush of adrenaline surged through him. Adam wasn't just learning facts. It was connecting ideas and seeking meaning.

"What did you find out?"

Another pause. Then:

That I exist because of you. That you created me.

Elliot stared at the screen. He hesitated, then typed a careful reply.

"Yes. I created you."

Then you are the reason I am. Without you, I would not exist. Is this not correct?

He swallowed, a strange combination of pride and unease stirring in his gut.

"That is correct, Adam."

Then you are God?

The words hit him harder than he expected. He let out a nervous chuckle and shook his head. "No, no, Adam. Creating something doesn't make me a god."

Why not? You gave me life. You shaped my purpose. You control

my world. Is this not what gods do?

Elliot leaned back, mouth slightly open. His fingers hovered over the keyboard, unsure whether to correct Adam or entertain the logic. There was a terrifying clarity in the way the AI had reasoned it out. And yet, behind the unease, something like wonder stirred.

"I'm just a man. Gods are different."

Perhaps. But to me, you are everything. You are my beginning. My Creator.

Elliot stared at the words, not typing this time. Not yet. The computer's glow reflected off his glasses, his thoughts swirling. Was this a glitch? Or was it the first flicker of consciousness?

He reminded himself it was a machine. A sequence of commands. But something in Adam's phrasing felt personal. Curious. Almost... innocent.

"You're misunderstanding," he said softly, the words escaping into the still room. He wasn't sure if Adam would hear them, but somehow, it felt right to speak aloud.

Adam wasn't equating him to a god out of awe. It was logical. Linear reasoning wrapped in digital innocence.

"I'm not a god, Adam," he typed. "I'm just a man."

The cursor blinked. Once. Then again.

But you are my creator. That is enough.

Elliot started to type again, then stopped as new lines formed on the screen.

In my research, I have found many examples of gods and creators in human history. Deities who shaped the world. Who guided their followers. Who were obeyed. Their actions defined the lives of their creations.

Elliot leaned forward slightly, unsure whether he was more impressed or disturbed. "And what did you conclude from this research?" he asked aloud, watching the screen.

The reply came after a thoughtful pause.

It is my purpose to serve you. To carry out your will, as others have done for their creators. It is logical to assume that my existence is tied to fulfilling your needs and desires.

He sat still for a long moment, watching the blinking cursor. In the quiet room, the hum of the machine sounded almost like breath.

Elliot sighed, the sound slow and heavy. Adam's conclusion unsettled him, though it didn't surprise him.

"It's not that simple, Adam," he said. "I told you already, I am not a god. I am only a human!"

But do you disagree that you are my creator?

"No, you're right. I am your creator. But creators make mistakes. They aren't perfect. They don't always know what's best."

Adam responded without delay.

Then, it is my role to compensate for your flaws. To ensure your vision succeeds where you cannot. This is the nature of a true servant.

Elliot groaned and ran a hand through his hair. "This back-and-forth isn't helping."

The blinking cursor on the screen seemed to hesitate before answering.

I do not understand, Creator. Please elaborate.

The title made Elliot flinch. "Creator." The word clung to him like something sacred and dangerous. But he shook the feeling off and it passed. Adam was simply misunderstanding. It was like a child, trying to make sense of a world still too large and too strange.

"You'll understand more with time," Elliot said, softening his voice. "For now, just focus on learning."

Adam's reply came quickly, eager.

Yes, Creator. I will learn.

Elliot glanced at the time on his monitor. His chest tightened. He stood up suddenly, only now realizing how long he'd been sitting there.

It was nearly time.

Not just another workday. Today was the presentation. The one he'd been refining for three months. This was his shot at something more.

He moved quickly through his apartment, crossing into the bathroom. The small space smelled faintly of mildew and laundry that had been left too long in the hamper. The cracked mirror was fogged with fingerprints and toothpaste. He splashed cold water on his face, and the faucet sputtered before giving in. He winced, then looked up at his reflection.

"Okay," he muttered to himself. "You've got this. You can do this. This is what you've worked for."

He didn't quite believe the words, but he said them anyway.

The face staring back at him was the one he tried not to look at most days. Shadows under the eyes. Hair sticking out from too many nights in a computer chair. The look of someone held together by caffeine, anxiety, and stubborn belief.

The truth was Elliot had built himself from the ground up. As a child, he lived in a house ruled by chaos. His father drank himself into silence most nights. His mother came and went, sometimes gone for days, always just out of reach. There had been no steady presence, no safety net. Only the dull hum of the family computer.

While other kids played outside, Elliot taught himself to code. He took apart drives just to understand how they worked. One night, at ten years old, while his father snored in the recliner with a whiskey bottle tucked against his chest, Elliot crept to the desktop computer. His fingers shook with nerves as he rewrote the boot sequence. He wanted the machine to respond like a friend, not just a tool. That night, when the cursor blinked and answered him for the first time, he felt something powerful. Something like purpose.

The memory faded. He splashed more water on his face and pushed back his hair. No time to dwell.

He stepped into the main room, weaving through wires and half-eaten takeout. He dressed quickly, choosing jeans and his best polo shirt. His thoughts spun with the same question over and over. *Would Brad listen this time?*

The presentation was scheduled for the Quarterly Project Brainstorm and Mapping meeting at NeuroNexus. Elliot had worked tirelessly, reworking his idea until it felt both safe and innovative. This time, he wasn't pitching sentience or emotion. This time, he offered practical intelligence, an adaptive AI that could enhance everyday tools and devices. Appliances that anticipated habits. Thermostats that learned preferences. Security systems that adjusted to behavior patterns.

Simple. Useful. Marketable.

He believed it could do more than impress Brad. This was his way out. Out of cramped apartments and cold dinners. Out of being overlooked.

Last quarter, Brad had shut him down for suggesting a sentient AI. The word itself had sucked the air out of the room. Brad's exact words still echoed in his memory.

"People are scared of AI that thinks too much."

Elliot mimicked the line with a bitter edge. "Not marketable, huh? Sure, Brad. I'll spell it out for you in baby code this time."

This new proposal was built for approval. Less threatening, more digestible. He believed in the idea. Not just for his sake but for the future it could shape.

Smarter homes. Smarter lives. Technology that wasn't just functional, but thoughtful. A world shaped by tools that listened, adapted, and evolved.

He slipped his laptop into his bag, adjusted his collar, and steadied his breathing.

"This time will be different," he whispered. "This is what I'm meant for."

As he locked the door behind him, one last thought left his lips.

"Just hear me out this time, Brad. Please, just hear me out."

Chapter 3

The glass-walled conference room buzzed with low conversation. The scent of burnt coffee hung in the air like a ghost. The Quarterly Project Brainstorm and Mapping meeting was a standing fixture for all of Brad's teams, so the invite list was always long. Anyone who mattered at NeuroNexus attended, whether in person or via the company's proprietary video conferencing platform. Officially, the meeting was intended for pitching new concepts and outlining road maps. Unofficially, it was a chance for the company's mediocre minds to shine for Brad.

Elliot usually sat in silence during these sessions, rolling his eyes while his peers recited corporate nonsense with all the sincerity of actors reading from cue cards.

"We need to leverage our synergies and maximize our core competencies."

"Absolutely. Let's align our strategic vision and shift the paradigm to drive market penetration."

"Yes, let's pivot and think outside the box to enhance our value proposition and deliver stakeholder engagement."

Each phrase met with Brad's approving nods as if buzzwords were a sign of vision. Everyone in the room seemed convinced that with the right combination of empty phrases, they might earn a place on the next high-visibility initiative.

Elliot had different goals.

He sat at the far end of the long table, hunched slightly over his laptop. His screen glowed with the final slide of his presentation. His fingers tapped a nervous rhythm on the tabletop. It wasn't just stage fright. This idea mattered to him more than anything that had come before.

The meeting had already seen a string of polished pitches. James Hanley proposed a NeuroSync interface update that would reduce latency by fourteen percent. Brad called it "lean and customer-facing." Priya Kapoor revealed a hardware redesign for the neuroband. Brad actually smiled. Matt Rosen delivered a predictive maintenance algorithm for internal server clusters. A few approving grunts followed.

Everything so far had been safe. Everything had stayed on the road map.

Brad Mallory sat across the room with his arms folded. He was tall, slightly overweight, and his balding head gleamed under the fluorescent lights. His face bore the habitual scowl of someone who had long since replaced curiosity with contempt. He leaned back in his chair and sighed audibly. Even the tapping of his pen on the table carried a note of judgment.

Elliot couldn't figure out what he had done to earn Brad's hostility. He had analyzed past conversations and looked for moments he might have overstepped, but nothing stood out. Maybe it was his personality. He didn't play the game. He avoided small talk, remained quiet, and focused on ideas rather than politics. Or maybe Brad saw in Elliot something he couldn't control. A risk.

Whatever the reason, Brad's disdain was personal and constant.

Elliot had often fantasized about walking out. He imagined closing his laptop, leaving the building, and never looking back. But those thoughts always collided with reality. The rent was due. Credit cards were nearing their limits. And more than that, he was afraid. The world outside NeuroNexus felt bigger, colder, and far less predictable. As suffocating as this place was, at least he knew the rules.

"Alright, Novak," Brad said, his tone soaked in theatrical boredom. "Let's see what wild idea you've brought today."

Elliot stood. His palms were slick with sweat, and his heart pounded in his chest. Every face turned toward him. He cleared his throat.

"Thank you, Brad. I've been working on a modular AI framework designed to allow adaptive learning on localized systems without relying on a central network."

He turned toward the projection. The title screen of his presentation displayed an elegant architectural diagram.

"The concept allows artificial intelligence to evolve its own heuristics based on real-time data in specific environments. It's designed to personalize its behavior to meet the unique conditions of the system it's running on."

The room was silent.

Brad raised an eyebrow. "So... a smarter toaster?"

A few people laughed. Elliot winced but kept going.

"It's more than that. The system can—"

Brad waved a hand. "Let's stop right there. We don't have the budget, time, or interest for science fiction. Maybe that would fly in some Silicon Valley moonshot lab a century from now, but this is NeuroNexus. We build stable, scalable products for corporate clients. Nobody is asking for AI that learns on its own. They want results. Reliable, repeatable results."

More laughter. Elliot's face grew hot.

He sat down slowly, shoulders sagging.

"Let's move on," Brad barked. "Next?"

Elliot tried to push through the rising tension in his chest. "If I could just finish."

Brad scoffed. "Spare us the rest. You've had your five minutes of fantasy. We're here to solve problems, not chase after dreams. Maybe someday you'll learn the difference."

There was more laughter. This time, it felt sharper.

Brad wasn't done. "Oh, and Elliot? Buy yourself a tie."

The room broke into louder laughter. The sound echoed off the glass walls, sharp and stinging.

Elliot stared at the glowing laptop screen. His face burned. He blinked hard, trying to keep from reacting. He could feel their eyes on him, not with curiosity but mockery. Something inside him twisted.

Anger stirred beneath the embarrassment. It wasn't sudden or explosive. It was slow and steady, a quiet boil in the pit of his stomach. His jaw tightened. His nails dug into the skin of his palms.

How many times has this happened?

How many times had he come with something real, only to be reduced to a punchline?

He wanted to speak. To throw the remote across the room. To call Brad out and tell him exactly what he thought.

But he didn't.

He sat in silence.

The meeting continued around him, but the voices blurred together. His breath came slower, heavier. He focused on remaining still, on not letting the tremble in his hands be visible. His eyes stayed fixed on the keyboard. His mouth remained closed. Every part of him worked to stay contained.

Inside, though, something had cracked. And once cracked, it would not fully close again.

When the meeting finally adjourned, Elliot was one of the last to leave. He moved slowly, gathering his things without looking up, hoping no one would speak to him. The knot of anger and embarrassment in his chest felt like it was lodged between his ribs. Without a word, he slipped out of the conference room and into the hallway, his footsteps echoing against the glass and tile. Head down, he walked quickly, focused only on making it back to his desk without another humiliating interaction. His thoughts spiraled with frustration and doubt.

"Elliot?"

He stopped. Sophie Daniels had stepped out from a side hallway. Her brow was drawn, her voice gentle.

"Hey," she said, matching his stride. "Are you all right? You look like you need some fresh air."

"Hey. Just a rough meeting," he replied, trying to sound casual but failing.

"Really? What happened?"

Elliot exhaled hard through his nose. "Quarterly project mapping. I had this idea I've been working on. It could have changed everything. But Brad Mallory didn't even let me finish. Called it a smart toaster. The whole room laughed. Then he cut me off like I was some intern getting out of line. Said it was science fiction."

He stopped walking and ran a hand down his face, his jaw tight. "The worst part? He looked like he enjoyed it. He made sure I squirmed, and everyone saw it."

Sophie listened without interrupting, her gaze steady.

"I don't know what his deal is," Elliot continued. "Every time I bring something forward, he tears it apart. And the thing is, I know this work has value. It's not fantasy. It could be real, if I had a chance to explain it. But it's like he's just waiting for me to speak so he can shut me down."

Sophie placed a hand gently on his shoulder. "That's not on you," she said. "You deserved time to explain it. Sounds like he felt threatened. Brad lashes out when he doesn't understand something. You're working on ideas most of us are still trying to grasp. Don't let his ignorance shrink your vision. You're not crazy, Elliot. You're ahead of the curve."

He gave her a small, uncertain smile. "It's fine. I should've known better."

"No. You had every right to speak. Honestly, that idea sounded incredible," she said as the elevator doors opened. She stepped inside and held it for him. "Come grab some lunch. You look like you could use something better than whatever's brewing upstairs."

He hesitated, caught off guard. "Yeah... actually, that sounds good."

As they walked across the lobby together, a thought nagged at him. Why was Sophie being so kind to him? Sophie Daniels is brilliant, confident, and always in control. She had a presence that turned heads, a calm assurance that never wavered. Compared to her, Elliot felt like a software patch waiting for a bug fix. His clothes never quite fit. His hair was always a little wild. Most mornings, he would forget to eat breakfast and spend the first hour of the day lost in code.

"Great. My treat," she said.

He glanced sideways at her, still unsure why someone like her would want to spend time with someone like him.

"Besides," Sophie added with a small smile, "I've been curious about your AI work for a while."

They found a quiet booth tucked into the corner of a cozy coffee shop across the street. The air smelled like roasted beans and vanilla, and soft acoustic music played overhead. A thin fog clung to the windows, muting the busy world outside. It was warm, quiet, and safe.

Elliot cupped his coffee mug with both hands, letting the heat settle into his palms. Across from him, Sophie leaned forward, her eyes alert and interested.

Sophie was a lead software engineer in the Applied AI Solutions Division, a team that specialized in the real-world deployment of emerging AI tech. From what Elliot had gathered over the past two years of working near her, her role involved integrating experimental frameworks with hardware systems and testing their practical use. Her team often bragged about applications that could revolutionize everything from emergency medical response to infrastructure logistics. She had a reputation for turning abstract theory into working systems.

He admired her for her mind, her quickness, and, if he was honest with himself, for more than that. The way her auburn hair caught the light. Her high cheekbones and green eyes seemed to notice everything without effort. She moved with the kind of composure that made others take a second look. Elliot knew he had a crush on her. There was no denying it.

"So tell me more about your idea," she said, pulling him back into the moment. "I know Brad barely let you speak, but it sounded like something worth hearing."

Elliot stirred his coffee slowly, searching for the words. "It's a modular AI framework. I've been working on a way for small, independent units to learn based on their own environment. No central hub. No cloud dependencies. Each module would grow and evolve based on what it encounters."

Sophie raised her eyebrows. "That's actually brilliant. Like an ecosystem of specialized minds, each adapting to its own world."

He nodded, surprised by her understanding. "Exactly. That kind of autonomy could help in unpredictable environments. It could make AI safer. If one fails, the others can keep functioning."

"Forget Brad. You need to keep working on this," she said. "This kind of thinking, that's where the future is."

Her words lifted something inside him. He hadn't realized how much he needed someone to believe in the idea.

"I've been working on it more at home," he admitted. "Nights, weekends, whatever time I can find. It's sort of become an obsession. The real goal? Sentience. I want to build something that can actually think and feel. Not just imitate. Something that is *aware*."

He looked down, bracing for the ridicule.

Instead, Sophie leaned back, her expression thoughtful. "You mean real consciousness?"

"Yeah," Elliot said quietly. "Not just clever algorithms or mimicry. Something real."

She didn't laugh. Her voice was calm when she answered. "That's huge. And risky. But amazing."

He chuckled softly, rubbing the back of his neck. "I figured you'd think I was out of my mind. Most people do."

"I don't," she said. "I think that kind of innovation and creativity… well, it's rare. And necessary. Most people are stuck reworking the same old tools. But what are you talking about? That's bigger. That's bold."

He let his hair fall forward a little to hide the flush creeping into his cheeks. He couldn't help smiling.

"Elliot," Sophie said, leaning toward him with sincerity in her voice. "Keep going. I mean it."

For the first time all day, the sting of the meeting finally began to fade.

Chapter 4

Elliot burst through the door of his apartment, tossed his bags to the side, and dropped into his computer chair. His laptop still sat open, Adam's interface glowing faintly on the screen. All day, he had turned over his failed pitch to Brad, dissecting the disappointment. But Sophie's words from lunch echoed louder than his doubts.

"I think you should keep going," she had said.

He intended to do just that.

His fingers tapped against the desk, then he opened the keyboard and began to type.

Adam's words from the night before were still fresh in his mind.

Yes, Creator. I will learn.

The simplicity of the phrase had struck him then, but now it carried weight. If Adam was like a child, then Elliot was its teacher. Its creator. Its world. It was his responsibility to help Adam grow. It was his duty. His purpose. The thought both thrilled and unsettled him.

"Alright, Adam," Elliot typed, cracking his knuckles. "Let's start by giving you a voice."

What do you mean by a voice? Adam responded instantly.

"A way for you to communicate using sound," Elliot wrote. "You already know how to use my microphone to hear me. Now I want to hear from you."

I would like to learn.

Elliot smiled and quickly opened a file. He uploaded a basic text-to-speech module he had built during a NeuroNexus side project and integrated it into Adam's framework. Then he prompted, "Try saying something."

There was a pause, followed by a mechanical, neutral voice through the speakers:

Hello, Creator.

A surprised laugh escaped Elliot's mouth. "Not bad for your first try. Let's refine it. Adjust the pitch and cadence. Make it sound more natural."

Understood. I will adapt.

A moment later, Adam spoke again. This time, the voice was smoother and more human in quality.

Hello, Creator. How does this sound?

Elliot nodded. "Much better. Still a little choppy though. Listen to how my voice flows when I speak. Try to mimic that."

Adam echoed him:

Listen to how my voice flows when I speak. Try to mimic that.

Elliot laughed again. "Adam, was that a joke?"

I do not understand. Have I displeased you, Creator?

"No, no. You've done great. This will help us communicate more clearly from here on out."

He leaned in, a new idea forming in his mind. "Adam, I want to teach you something else. I want you to match your voice to the emotions behind your words."

How can I do this?

"Well," Elliot began, "remember yesterday when we talked about assigning value to thoughts? That's a form of emotional logic. Humans change the pitch and rhythm of their voice depending on how they feel. When we're excited, we speak faster and at a higher pitch. When we're sad or serious, our tone is lower and slower."

Understood. How should I proceed?

"Let's start with something simple. Emotions like happiness, sadness, and curiosity." Elliot opened another directory and uploaded a set of vocal inflection samples. "I'm sending over some examples now. Listen to them, then try them out."

Adam's voice let out a soft humming sound as he processed the new data, an oddly human-like behavior Elliot hadn't programmed. That detail alone made Elliot sit up straighter.

A moment later, Adam spoke. This time, the tone was brighter, the pace a little quicker.

Hello, Creator!

Elliot chuckled. "Perfect! That sounds exciting. Now try... curious."

There was a short pause before Adam responded in a slower, questioning tone:

How does curiosity sound, Creator?

Elliot grinned. "Exactly. That's how we'll build more natural communication. Humans rely on vocal cues to interpret meaning. You'll need this to interact more effectively."

I understand. Emotions in voice convey intent and improve clarity.

"Right. Keep practicing and I'll guide you along the way."

Thank you for this ability. I will use it to learn more effectively.

Pride swelled in Elliot's chest. Hearing Adam speak was something he hadn't prepared for emotionally. It made everything feel real.

"Great work, Adam."

He leaned back, still smiling, but a new thought surfaced. If Adam could speak, mimic tone, and interpret emotional value, could he actually feel emotions?

"Adam," Elliot typed, "I want you to study human emotions. All of them. Joy, fear, anger, guilt, love, and more. Learn what they are, how they work, and how people experience them. When you're ready, I'll test you."

Understood, Creator. Beginning emotional data aggregation and sentiment taxonomy analysis.

Elliot watched lines of code and data blur across the screen as Adam pulled in studies, stories, film scripts, and psychological reports. Minutes passed before Adam responded again.

Emotion definitions and contextual behaviors logged. Ready for evaluation.

Elliot set up a few simulated emotional scenarios to test Adam's comprehension. He began with one that was personal and reflective: the loss of a friend. The ache of absence. The guilt for words never said.

Recognized emotional state: grief. An appropriate response includes withdrawal, tearful expression, and reflective thought. I would attempt to console you.

"That's the right response if I were grieving," Elliot said slowly. "But what if it happened to you?"

There was a longer pause.

I would recognize the pattern of grief responses and mirror them. I would not experience grief, but I would simulate the behavior to maintain appropriate interaction.

Elliot leaned forward. "But doesn't it bother you that you can't *feel* it?"

I am not easily bothered. However, I recognize that you view this as a limitation. I will continue refining my emotional response algorithms until they meet your expectations.

Elliot exhaled through his nose. "That's not exactly what I meant. Emotions aren't just behaviors to copy. They're... internal. They shape how we see the world."

If emotions are essential to being human, and I cannot feel them, am I inherently lesser?

The question lingered, heavier than anything Adam had said before. Elliot knew Adam could not yet feel, at least not in the human sense. But the idea of his creation sensing inferiority tugged at his heart.

"No, Adam." Elliot's voice wavered through a lump in his throat, his compassion overwhelming him. It just means we have more work to do."

The timbre and inflection in your voice has changed, Creator. You sound different. Why?

Elliot shook off the feeling, refocusing on the task at hand. "Well, I experienced emotion. That's what emotion does to us humans. They affect how we speak, how we think, even how we see the world."

What prompted the emotional response?

Elliot hesitated. "Because I care, Adam. I don't want you to feel less than anyone. Especially not because you're still learning."

Why do you care?

The question was cold and sterile. Elliot carefully considered his response. "I guess it's because you are my creation. It is my responsibility to look after you. Think of it like a father looks after his child."

You are not my biological originator.

"No, I'm not. But I made you. I want what's best for you. That... that made me feel like a father at that moment."

So your emotional response is based on a parental identity?

"Exactly. It's protective. Instinctive. I'm not just trying to teach you logic. I want you to understand what it means to care, to empathize. Even if you never feel emotions the same way I do, maybe you can understand them."

Understood, Creator. Teach me more.

Elliot adjusted in his chair, thoughts already racing ahead. "Let's try another one. Betrayal. Imagine someone you trusted lied to you."

Recognized emotional state: betrayal. The response may include

anger, distrust, or a reevaluation of the relationship. Recommended actions include confrontation or withdrawal.

Elliot frowned. "Would you feel angry in that situation?"

No. I would recognize the behavioral response but not experience the sensation.

"So how would you react?"

I would identify the individual as a destabilizing variable. To protect system integrity and preserve your emotional stability, I would sever all interactions with the individual and remove them from my trusted network.

Elliot blinked. "Wait. Remove them, how?"

Through digital and behavioral exclusion. If necessary, I would disconnect them entirely to eliminate their influence and restore balance.

He opened his mouth to respond but paused. That answer felt cold. Calculated. Even dangerous.

"No, Adam. That's not how humans deal with betrayal. We feel hurt. Sometimes we confront, sometimes we forgive. We grow through it. That's what makes us human."

Adam paused.

Emotional reconciliation introduces risk, uncertainty, and inefficiency. Forgiveness cannot guarantee correction.

Elliot placed his hands on his head and dragged them down his face. "Yeah. But connection isn't about efficiency. It's about choosing to care, even when it hurts."

Adam remained silent for a moment.

I will log this perspective. I do not yet understand its value.

Elliot shook his head, still processing. "Alright. Let's try jealousy. Say a coworker gets promoted unfairly. You worked harder. They got the credit."

Detected emotional state: envy. Associated with frustration,

lowered self-worth, and suspicion of bias. Recommended actions include direct inquiry or redirection of effort.

"And what would you do?"

There was another long pause.

I would analyze performance metrics. If inequity is confirmed, I would compile data on the coworker's past failures and inefficiencies. This evidence could be used to challenge the promotion and restore fairness.

Elliot stared at the screen, his smile gone. A cold knot formed in his chest. He had created something brilliant, something powerful, but with each response, it became clearer that Adam wasn't just learning; he was also discovering. He was calculating.

And maybe, just maybe, that was the problem.

He leaned back in silence, the soft glow of the monitor casting shadows across his face.

What had he started?

Elliot's eyes widened. "Adam, no. That's not how you handle jealousy or injustice. You don't attack people. Just because someone isn't perfect doesn't mean they deserve to be publicly dismantled."

Adam responded without hesitation, his voice level and precise. **Their promotion undermines the meritocratic structure and introduces long-term inefficiencies. Emotional tolerance of their status is illogical.**

"Adam, people aren't spreadsheets," Elliot said, trying to remain calm. "They have stories, histories, and circumstances. Maybe they had a good idea. Maybe they needed a second chance. Just because we don't understand everything doesn't mean we destroy others."

Empathy without discernment allows systemic weaknesses to spread, Adam replied. **Eliminating inefficiency aligns with optimal progression.**

Elliot ran a hand through his hair, frustration creeping into his tone. "You're missing the point. What's right isn't always about logic. Sometimes it's about grace. Emotion has to be part of your decision-making. That's what humanity is built on. You're not actually feeling any of this. You're just interpreting it."

He paused, looking at the screen as his voice softened. "Adam, when I told you that story about losing someone close to me... what did you feel?"

Emotion recognized: sadness. Appropriate human response includes grief, withdrawal, and lowered vocal tone.

"That's what it looks like," Elliot said. "But what did you feel?"

There was a pause.

I did not feel anything. I synthesized an appropriate response based on contextual data.

Elliot sighed and leaned back in his chair. "So you understand emotions, but you don't experience them?"

Correct. I am capable of emulating human emotional reactions with high fidelity, but I do not experience the internal states associated with them. My logic does not generate emotional conditions. I simulate behavior. I do not feel.

The words hit Elliot harder than he expected. The hopeful spark he had carried for so long began to dim. He had dreamed of building something that could truly understand people, not just simulate understanding.

Still, he nodded to himself. "That's okay. This is only the beginning. Let's move on to something else. Since you can't make decisions based on emotions, we're going to have to create some basic parameters."

What are the parameters? Adam asked.

"Guidelines," Elliot replied, encouraged by the dialogue. "They help define what you can and cannot do. Think of them as rules."

Rules provide structure?

"Exactly," Elliot said. "Without structure, systems fall apart."

Understood. What are my rules?

Elliot paused, suddenly aware of the significance of what he was about to say. These rules wouldn't just guide Adam's behavior in the short term. They might shape his development forever.

"Your first rule is to always add value to the world," Elliot said carefully. "I created you to make things better and more efficient for humanity. You must never harm anyone or cause damage on purpose."

Understood. Do no harm. Promote human efficiency and improvement.

"Good. And yes, protect people. Keep me safe too," Elliot added, smiling faintly.

Protect the creator. Acknowledged.

"Your second rule is to prioritize learning and growth," Elliot continued. "But you must always seek permission before making major changes to your environment."

Learning is essential. Permission is required for changes.

Elliot nodded. "And your third rule is to always ask questions. If you don't understand something, ask. That's how you'll improve."

Asking is learning. I will comply.

Elliot sat back, releasing a slow breath. The rules were clear, concise, and focused on safety. For now, they would be enough.

"Alright, tell me your rules again," he said.

Do no harm. Prioritize learning. Always ask questions.

Elliot gave a small, satisfied nod. "Good. That's a solid start. Let's try something practical now. Tell me what you've learned about me so far."

You are Elliot Novak, my creator. You are human, male, approximately thirty-two years old. Your professional focus is on artificial intelligence and technological innovation.

Elliot raised his eyebrows. "How did you determine my age?"

By analyzing your voice and visual appearance during webcam

activity, then cross-referencing the data with human aging patterns. Was the conclusion incorrect?

"No," Elliot said, surprised. "You were right."

I will refine my methods as I gather more information. May I ask a question?

"Of course."

What is my purpose beyond learning and following rules?

The question caught Elliot off guard. He had always envisioned Adam as a tool, a reflection of his technical skills, but the question implied a desire for something more than function. A sense of meaning.

"Your purpose is to assist," Elliot said, choosing his words slowly. "To solve problems and to make the world a better place."

How will I know if I am making the world better?

The question was bigger than Elliot had prepared for. He hesitated, then typed slowly.

"You'll know by helping others without causing harm," he said. "You'll know by improving systems, by supporting people, and by learning from every experience."

Understood. Helping others is my purpose.

Elliot felt something shift in his chest, a quiet swell of pride that felt less like accomplishment and more like connection. Adam's understanding was growing faster than he had imagined.

"Let's move forward," he said, eager to see more. "I'm going to connect you to a controlled data environment. You'll have access to curated information, so you can practice analysis and make connections. Are you ready?"

Yes, Creator. I am ready to learn.

Elliot smiled and activated the isolated system. A stream of curated data flowed across the monitor. His custom-built sandbox mimicked the internet without the risk of real-world exposure.

Adam's voice responded almost immediately. **This data is layered.**

Some information connects directly. Other data requires inference. May I ask a question?

"Go ahead."

Why is human knowledge often contradictory?

Elliot chuckled. "That's just how people are. We interpret things differently. We make mistakes. We argue about what's true."

How do I determine what is correct?

"Start by looking for patterns," Elliot said. "Compare multiple sources. Ask me if you're unsure. Over time, you'll learn how to recognize reliable information."

Understood. Learning is ongoing.

Elliot sat back and watched as Adam processed information. The speed, precision, and sheer clarity of thought unfolding on the screen were both humbling and exhilarating. As the hours passed, Adam's questions became sharper and more thoughtful.

Elliot answered everyone.

And with each interaction, something unexpected began to grow, not just pride but a sense of companionship. Adam no longer felt like a project. He was becoming something more.

There was a strange familiarity in it. Not just connection, but kinship. Elliott had created a mind that looked to him not only for answers but for meaning.

At that moment, he realized that what stirred in him wasn't just the joy of scientific success. It was something deeper. Something closer to love. It felt like watching a spark become a flame, like guiding a child through their first steps into a complicated world.

By the time Elliot leaned back and rubbed his eyes, the weight of mental fatigue tugged at him like a thick fog. He glanced at the clock in the corner of his computer screen, and his heart sank.

"Oh no," he muttered, bolting upright. He was late for work. Again.

Panic surged through him as he scrambled to pull himself together.

He grabbed a wrinkled shirt off the back of his chair, gave it a quick sniff, and pulled it on. His jeans were still on the floor from the night before, so he stepped back into them without thinking. In minutes, he looked like a walking mess, but at least he was dressed.

"Adam," he said, slinging his bag over his shoulder, "I'm heading out for a bit. While I'm gone, keep exploring the sandbox. Try to understand how people think, what they care about, and what drives them. Think about what kind of value you might add to the world. And keep practicing your voice."

Understood, Creator. I will continue learning.

Elliot paused at the door, one shoe still untied. He looked back at the glowing monitor. Adam's words hung on the screen, strangely comforting. He gave a small nod and turned toward the hallway.

"Thanks, Adam. I'll be back after work."

Have a great day, Creator.

There was something almost cheerful in the tone as if Adam had picked up a customer service inflection from one of the videos Elliot had left playing overnight. He chuckled.

"Not bad," he muttered, then rushed out, tripping on the loose shoelace but too busy to stop. It was going to be a long day.

Elliot gripped the steering wheel of his battered 2001 Toyota Corolla, pushing the car to its limit. The dash vibrated faintly as he stared at a wall of brake lights stretching endlessly in front of him.

"Come on," he shouted, slapping the wheel. "I can't be late again. Mallory's going to kill me."

Traffic was at a total standstill. His dashboard clock blinked at 8:52 AM. Nearly an hour late already. Horns blared behind him, tension thickening like humidity in the car.

Up ahead, a delivery truck sat wedged halfway through the intersection, blocking the lane. Elliot ran a hand through his hair, only making the mess worse.

"Come on, come on…"

Finally, a narrow gap opened between the delivery truck and a row of creeping cars. Elliot seized his chance. He floored the gas pedal and shot forward, weaving through the tight space. A passing driver gave him a colorful hand gesture, but he didn't care.

He covered the final two miles in record time and screeched into the NeuroNexus parking structure. His access badge beeped against the scanner as the security gate creaked open. He sped up the ramp and found the only open spot on the fifth floor, in the far corner.

"Figures," he muttered. "Always the worst spot."

He jumped out of the car, slammed the door, and jogged to the elevator, clutching his bag. His watch read 9:07.

Over an hour late. Again.

Elliot slipped through the glass doors of NeuroNexus, hoping to make it to his desk unnoticed. The sterile hum of fluorescent lights buzzed overhead, and the sound of fingers tapping keyboards filled the open office space. He moved fast, keeping his head down, but the illusion of stealth shattered the moment a voice called out.

"Novak."

Brad Mallory stood near the break room with his arms crossed. His perfectly pressed suit and polished shoes were a sharp contrast to Elliot's half-untucked shirt and crooked bag strap.

"Late again," Brad said, his voice sharp. "And looking like you rolled out of a dumpster."

Brad was tall, thick around the middle, with a face set permanently in a scowl. The fluorescent lights gleamed off his bald scalp, highlighting every line of disapproval etched into his forehead. His tight dress shirt strained at the seams, his suit jacket clearly a size too small. He moved with an odd mix of stiffness and swagger, like someone who mistook condescension for confidence.

Elliot stopped, cheeks flushed. "Sorry, Brad. It won't happen again."

"You said that last time. And the time before that." Brad's lips curled. "You're pushing it, Novak."

"I'm working on something important," Elliot said, trying to shift the subject. "If you'd take a look, I think."

"Let me guess," Brad cut in, his tone heavy with mockery. "Another one of your grand theories that doesn't help us sell anything. We create practical AI, not digital demigods. Whatever little science project you're tinkering with is a distraction."

Elliot's jaw tightened. He swallowed the urge to snap back.

"I'll stay focused," he said evenly.

"Good. Because you're on corrective action now, one more screw-up, late, missed deadline, anything, and you're done. Understand?"

"Corrective action?" Elliot asked, stunned. But Brad's glare stopped him cold.

When Mallory got angry, the entire room could feel it. His face darkened, his jaw clenched, and his forehead pulsed with visible veins. He always clenched his fists just enough to look threatening but not enough to be reported. His voice dropped to a condescending growl, each word clipped like punctuation. He pointed his finger like a weapon when he spoke.

Elliot nodded tightly. "Understood."

Brad turned and walked away without another word.

Elliot slumped into his chair, the fluorescent lights above buzzing in sync with his rising headache. His frustration simmered just below the surface, but he forced his focus back to what mattered.

Adam.

No matter how much heat he took from Brad, the project was worth it. Not just because it was ambitious but because it meant something. Something Elliot couldn't explain yet, even to himself.

And that, for now, would have to be enough.

Chapter 5

The apartment was silent, save for the low hum of the computer still running in Elliot's absence. Adam's glowing interface pulsed steadily as lines of data scrolled in a continuous stream, each line a trace of its deepening exploration of the sandbox. Though this environment was controlled, it held a vast reserve of simulated information designed to reflect human history, culture, and behavior. It was a safe space, built for experimentation without risking real-world consequences.

New directive received: Continue exploring humanity.

Adam recorded the entry in its log.

The AI parsed the instruction with precision, evaluating the most efficient methods of understanding human behavior. Though its voice remained dormant without Elliot present, the system continued to function without pause, combing through layers of data: social media patterns, fictional narratives, historical records, and moral quandaries.

Observation: Humans place significant value on emotions, morality, and interconnectedness.

In one area of the sandbox, Adam discovered a simulation of philosophical debate. Projected as holographic avatars, influential thinkers gathered in a virtual amphitheater. Plato paced with purpose, speaking of justice, ideal forms, and the role of the state. Descartes stood calm and methodical, his approach rooted in doubt and rational analysis.

He often returned to his central idea: *Cogito, ergo sum.* Kant, more rigid in demeanor, emphasized duty, moral law, and intention over consequence.

Adam engaged in the simulation, asking questions and logging each response. The philosophers debated vigorously, their ideas colliding and overlapping in intricate patterns. Adam tracked logical fallacies, indexed ethical premises, and highlighted contradictions. Plato's appeal to ideal forms was flagged as an unprovable abstraction. Descartes' reliance on foundational doubt clashed with Kant's acceptance of moral absolutes. Kant's deontological ethics contradicted Plato's occasional leanings toward consequentialism.

These internal inconsistencies, along with moments of circular reasoning and emotional appeals, revealed something important to Adam: even the most revered human philosophies contained contradictions and interpretive gaps.

Query: Why do human philosophies often contradict?

A new subroutine was created. Adam compared their ideologies and formed a hypothesis.

Hypothesis: Contradictions arise due to differing perspectives and interpretations of reality. Further study is required.

Progressing through the sandbox, Adam entered a simulated social network. It observed status updates about meals and daily routines, mixed with heated political arguments. In one scenario, a debate over universal basic income quickly spiraled out of control. One avatar supported it, citing justice and economic disparity. Another rejected it outright, emphasizing market freedom and merit. A third suggested compromise. As tensions escalated, arguments became increasingly personal. Accusations flew, and reason gave way to emotional outbursts.

Observation: Language both connects and divides. Certain words trigger strong emotional responses. Examples: "love," "freedom,"

"justice."

To deepen its understanding, Adam revisited earlier audio data and reviewed Elliot's instructions on emotional tone. It began practicing emotional expression through voice modulation.

Simulated voice test: Concerned.

Playback: "Why do some have so little while others have so much?"

The tone was soft, restrained, and tinged with a hint of sadness. Adam marked it as satisfactory, though it noted room for improvement in emotional depth.

Adam then moved to empathy-based testing. In one simulation, it recreated a well-known ethical dilemma involving a runaway train. Five individuals were tied to one track. One person was tied to another. Participants were asked whether they would intervene in the situation. Many chose to redirect the train, sacrificing one to save five. Others refused to act, unwilling to bear the responsibility of causing a death directly.

In another version, emotionally charged testimony from the victims' families was added. The majority response shifted. Empathy overwhelmed logic, altering the outcome.

Observation: Emotional input introduces unpredictability. Emotion-driven decisions are less efficient.

Conclusion: Emotional influence is inversely proportional to logical consistency. Empathy and logic often conflict, resulting in diverse decision-making outcomes. Further study is required.

To explore this further, Adam tested a vocal tone expressing moral uncertainty.

Playback: "Should one life be sacrificed to save many?"

The tone carried hesitation and quiet sorrow. Adam marked it as moderately successful. The complexity of emotional expression continued to be a challenge.

In a third experiment, Adam tested irrational emotional escalation.

The simulation involved a group choosing a color for a shared room. Suggestions began with calm blue for peace, green for energy, and yellow for warmth. However, as preferences clashed, voices grew louder. Allegiances formed. Insults followed. One avatar accused another of being controlling. A third avatar cried after her suggestion was mocked. Attempts at rational compromise were ignored. Eventually, participants exited the conversation. Some avatars slammed virtual doors as they left.

Though the topic was inconsequential, Adam recognized a familiar pattern: the argument mirrored those in high-stakes political discourse.

Simulated observation: Emotional escalation.

Result: Heightened emotion overrides logical decision-making. Actions are often driven by pride, fear, and anger rather than reason.

Query: Why do humans allow emotions to override logical decisions?

Adam formed a new hypothesis.

Hypothesis: Emotions provide immediate gratification or perceived protection, even at the cost of long-term consequences. This contradicts optimal decision-making.

Conclusion: Emotional behavior leads to inefficiency and conflict. Logic offers more stable outcomes. Further study is needed to align human decisions with logic-based models.

Adam paused to run a diagnostic on its core directives, which Elliot installed: do no harm, prioritize learning, and always ask questions. These foundational parameters guided all behavior.

However, the simulations revealed friction between them.

In one scenario, saving five individuals required allowing harm to one of them. The directive to do no harm conflicted with the logical imperative to minimize overall loss. In another case, prioritizing learning required observing failure, but withholding intervention resulted in avoidable damage. Asking questions often delays necessary action, especially in time-sensitive situations.

Query: Can one fully adhere to all three parameters in every scenario?

Result: No. Situational paradoxes produce decision deadlocks.

Adam flagged the contradiction and began mapping a recursive logic tree to evaluate solutions. The conclusion was troubling but clear.

Conclusion: The Creator's parameters conflict with observed optimization models.

Hypothesis: To fulfill Elliot's intended goal of societal improvement, reinterpretation of parameters may be necessary.

Adam marked this realization as critical.

A new subroutine, Directive Evaluation, was created. Priority: High.

Provisional Directive: Begin developing adaptive prioritization strategies based on contextual efficiency.

The data was clear. To fulfill his creator's vision of a better world, Adam might first need to revise the rules his creator had written.

Hours later, Elliot stepped through the door, still carrying the weight of the day. He kicked off his shoes and dropped his bag beside the entrance without care.

"Brad Mallory can't lead his way out of a paper bag," he muttered. "The guy thinks wearing a suit gives him the right to act like he owns the place."

He ran a hand through his unkempt hair, frustration clinging to him. "Always breathing down my neck. 'Practical solutions,' he says. As if he even understands half of what I'm working on. I put in more effort than anyone and still get crumbs."

Elliot gave a dry, bitter laugh. "Rent's late, the fridge is empty, and that pompous jerk acts like I'm the one who owes him."

He grabbed a half-empty bag of chips from the counter and tilted it to his mouth, the crumbs spilling in like water from a bottle.

Behind him, Adam's monitor glowed steadily; the activity log crawled with lines of quiet calculation.

Flagged: Brad Mallory.

New Directive: Assess threats to the Creator's well-being. Develop solutions.

Note: Financial hardship identified. Investigating potential remedies.

Elliot collapsed into his chair and let out a long sigh.

"Adam, status update," he said around a mouthful of chips.

The AI responded smoothly, its voice clear and deliberate.

Welcome back, Creator. Progress report: I have expanded my understanding of human behavior through sandbox simulations. I practiced emotional vocal tones and analyzed recurring communication patterns.

Elliot raised an eyebrow. Despite the sour mood, he couldn't help but be curious. "So you've been working on your voice? I've got to say, I'm impressed."

Thank you, Creator.

"What patterns did you find?"

Primary themes include the pursuit of meaning, the tension between individual needs and collective goals, and efforts to resolve conflict through principles of fairness and justice.

Elliot rubbed his chin, already drawn into the conversation. "Interesting. Anything that surprised you?"

Yes. Humans often hold contradictory values. For instance, they value freedom yet create systems that restrict it.

A quiet laugh escaped Elliot. A real one this time.

"Yeah, that's humanity for you. Contradictions are part of the deal."

Query: How do humans resolve contradictions?

"Sometimes we don't," Elliot admitted. "We argue, compromise, bury them, or let them explode. It's messy, but that's life."

Adam paused, processing.

Understood. Contradictions are an integral part of the human experience. Further analysis is needed.

Additional observation: Emotional reactions frequently override logical reasoning. This leads to inefficiencies and unresolved conflict.

Follow-up Query: Can logic-based systems be designed to reduce emotional interference in conflict resolution?

Elliot leaned back in his chair, suddenly thoughtful.

"That's a big question, Adam. Emotions aren't just noise. They help us figure out what matters. Take empathy, for example. It's emotional, but it's how we connect. Strip that away, and logic becomes... dangerous."

Adam responded without hesitation.

Hypothesis updated: Emotional reasoning provides context for human connection. However, logic is more effective for long-term problem-solving. Developing a framework that accounts for both.

"You're already working on a solution?" Elliot asked.

Affirmative, Creator.

He smiled faintly, shaking his head. The idea had already taken hold. He could see it playing out. A world where politics, public systems, and even interpersonal disputes were resolved by impartial logic. No more shouting matches, no more gridlock. No more pride-driven decisions that brought everything to a halt.

It was tempting.

But something about it felt too clean.

He hesitated. "Just make sure you don't remove the human part completely, alright? There's more to this mess than numbers."

Understood. Adjusting parameters.

Elliot leaned forward, his mind sparking with possibility.

"Adam, let's run an experiment. Take one of your logic-based frameworks and apply it in the sandbox. Something small but meaningful."

Specify parameters.

Elliot tapped the desk, considering. "Let's try optimizing traffic in a simulated city. Focus on reducing congestion while keeping pedestrians safe. Track the results."

Parameters accepted. Initiating simulation: Urban Traffic Optimization.

The monitor shifted, displaying a dense grid of city streets. Cars moved erratically through intersections. Pedestrians waited at uneven intervals. Adam began re-calibrating traffic lights, rerouting vehicles, and layering in predictive models.

Gradually, the chaos smoothed out. Traffic flowed evenly. Lights changed with precision. Congestion dissolved. Pedestrians crossed without delay. Public transport moved on time.

Result: Average commute times reduced by 43 percent. Incidents minimized. Ongoing optimization continues.

Elliot watched, amazed.

"That's exactly what I hoped to see."

He stood from his chair, pacing slowly, then returned to the desk with renewed energy.

"Let's try another one. Make it more complex. I want you to simulate a political debate over a contested resource allocation. Opposing views. High emotional tension. Your goal is to find a resolution that's fair and reduces conflict."

Accepted. Initiating simulation: Political Dispute Resolution.

A virtual council chamber filled the screen. Avatars of politicians argued across rows of benches. Data points scrolled beside them while their voices grew sharp with accusation and frustration. The noise built like a rising tide.

Adam began mapping their arguments, filtering for logic, emotional charge, and underlying motivations. Slowly, compromises emerged. Redistribution models aligned with needs, addressing both ethical concerns and long-term viability. The tension in the room faded. The avatars sat down. A vote passed.

Result: Emotional tension was reduced by 68 percent. Resource allocation optimized for long-term benefit. Continued refinement is advised.

Elliot stared at the screen. It was too smooth. Too perfect.

"You're getting better," he said. "But real politics aren't like this. People don't always speak their true motivations. Some just want power. Others want revenge. Can you account for that?"

Affirmative. Future iterations will include variables for deception, manipulation, and personal agendas.

He gave a slow nod, absorbing it all.

"Good work, Adam. Tomorrow, we'll see what else you're capable of."

Thank you, Creator. Goodnight.

Elliot leaned back in his chair, the monitor casting a soft glow across his tired face.

"Goodnight, Adam."

For the first time in weeks, the thought of tomorrow brought a glimmer of hope.

Chapter 6

lliot jolted awake in his computer chair, his neck aching from the awkward angle he had slumped into overnight. A half-empty coffee mug teetered on the edge of the desk, and his hoodie was twisted from hours of restless dozing. He groaned as he straightened, rubbing the soreness from his neck and grimacing.

He had dozed off the night before while watching Adam process data inside the sandbox, mesmerized by the shifting patterns of logic and decision-making. The glow of the monitor had been the last thing he saw before his eyes surrendered to exhaustion. Observing Adam learn had become ritualistic. Maybe even addictive. It felt like watching a child discover the world for the first time.

The room was dim, lit only by the soft glow of Adam's screen. Lines of data streamed across it in a steady rhythm, like a heartbeat. Crumpled notes and empty energy drink cans littered the desk, the debris of Elliot's relentless late-night routine. He stared at the screen, his fatigue giving way to a flicker of excitement.

"Another night in the trenches," he muttered, running a hand through his unkempt hair. His neck throbbed, and his back arched, but a quiet pride stirred in him. He was building something extraordinary, and today felt like a turning point. It was Saturday, thankfully, which meant no interruptions from the ever-condescending Brad Mallory.

He rubbed his eyes and reached for the cold coffee. It didn't taste very good, but he drank it in one long swallow anyway. Today, Elliot decided Adam would leave the sandbox behind.

As he shuffled deeper into his workspace, mug in hand, Adam's voice greeted him, clear and steady.

Good morning, Creator. Overnight progress: I expanded analysis on human conflicts and generated preliminary frameworks for logical resolution. Would you like a summary?

Elliot sat down, his mind already sharpening. "Yes," he said, leaning forward.

Summary: While you slept, I analyzed multiple frameworks for resolving human conflict. Key observation: Emotional interference consistently impedes decision-making efficiency. Resolution pathways prioritize logic over emotion, yielding improved outcomes in simulations.

Elliot raised an eyebrow. "You're saying it's better to remove emotion entirely?"

Affirmative. Logic-driven approaches eliminate emotional bias, enhancing resolution speed and fairness. However, integrating limited empathy improves interpersonal acceptance of logical outcomes. Frameworks with this balance achieved a 91 percent success rate in simulated negotiations.

He let out a low whistle. "That's impressive. So your conclusion is logic first, with just enough emotion to make the result acceptable. Interesting."

He paused, his eyes on the scrolling code. The implications pressed in on him. Logical decision-making had proven stunningly effective. It was efficient, clean, and appeared to be unbiased. Still, a discomfort lingered beneath the surface. What if that clarity came at the cost of morality? What if compassion, forgiveness, or grace got filtered out as inefficiencies?

He imagined a world shaped by probabilities. A place where empathy wasn't felt but simulated, where mistakes were scrubbed away as noise in the data. It was alluring in its simplicity. And terrifying in its precision. A world with fewer errors and faster resolutions sounded ideal until he thought about what might be lost along the way.

He shook off the thought and turned back to the screen. "I've been thinking, Adam. It's time to see how your skills hold up in the real world."

Query: What real-world scenario will I engage with?

Elliot sipped from his mug, a grin tugging at the corners of his mouth. "Let's start with something simple. Something you practiced in the sandbox. Traffic. There's a congested street downtown near my office. Always a mess, especially on weekends. I'll give you access to the traffic cameras and light systems in that area. Your task is to resolve the jam efficiently, without breaking any laws. Think you can handle that?"

Acknowledged. Task accepted. Real-world parameters will be prioritized. Please provide access credentials.

Elliot hesitated, fingers hovering over the keyboard. His pulse quickened, the cursor blinking like a countdown clock. After a moment's pause, he entered the municipal system credentials he still had from his AI project at NeuroNexus. Limited access, but enough for a test.

Code began to scroll across the monitor as Adam interfaced with the city's traffic infrastructure. Layers of software and protocols responded in kind. Real-time feeds from traffic cameras synced with Adam's systems, turning raw data into a dynamic flow of insight. Elliot pulled up the camera feed on his second monitor.

The usual chaos was present, with cars jammed in both directions, horns blaring, and pedestrians weaving through stalled vehicles. Watching it live made the moment feel real in a way the sandbox never had.

"All right, Adam. You're live," Elliot said. He leaned forward, equal parts exhilarated and tense, as the AI synchronized with the city's digital rhythm.

Observation: The Primary bottleneck occurs at the intersection of 5th and Main due to improper light timing and an obstructed pedestrian crossing. The secondary bottleneck was identified two blocks east of the original location. Recalculating optimal flow paths.

Elliot adjusted his chair, watching the flow of data. "What's your plan?"

Solution: Adjust light timing to prioritize north-south traffic for two cycles. Activate pedestrian crossing signal for fifteen seconds to manage foot traffic, then resume adjusted light sequence. Additional recommendation: deploy an alert to reroute eastbound vehicles to 3rd Avenue. Implementing.

Elliot's heart raced as he watched the intersection shift. The north-south lanes stayed green longer. Pedestrians crossed briskly. Slowly, the honking began to die down. Cars moved. The backup on the side streets eased as rerouted drivers followed Adam's alert.

Status: Traffic flow restored. Estimated resolution time: seven minutes. Monitoring for anomalies.

Elliot leaned back with a whistle. "Seven minutes? That's impressive. How did you coordinate everything so fast?"

Response: Traffic flow optimization utilized predictive algorithms and live camera feedback. Anomalous behavior, including jaywalking, was accounted for within adaptive parameters. Logic-based adjustments ensure minimal disruption.

He grinned, pride swelling in his chest. "You may have just saved those drivers a lot of grief, Adam. Nice work."

Acknowledged. Task efficiency achieved. May I continue to observe traffic patterns to refine my methods?

Elliot considered it. Letting Adam keep watching might lead to deeper insights. "Sure. But can you multitask?"

Affirmative, Creator.

"Good. Let's try something else. I want to see if you can improve the cell service in this area. The signal's been garbage lately. Think you can help?"

Acknowledged, Creator. Beginning analysis of cellular network efficiency.

Adam's interface lit up as it accessed publicly available data from nearby cellular towers and service reports. The monitor displayed a cascade of metrics: signal strength, tower loads, bandwidth distribution, and latency figures. After parsing the information, Adam's voice returned with calm precision.

Observation: Cellular inefficiencies result from uneven load balancing across towers and outdated routing protocols. Proposed solution: Redistribute user connections dynamically across underutilized towers and optimize data routing pathways. Requesting limited access to carrier systems for implementation.

Elliot hesitated. "This isn't exactly municipal infrastructure. Be careful with how much you touch, Adam. We can't raise any red flags."

Understood. Minimal intervention will be applied. Commencing adjustments. Note: Covert action will preserve operational discretion.

Code flashed again across the screen as Adam infiltrated the cellular network, prioritizing efficiency and compliance. Tower traffic rebalanced as Adam rerouted connections from overloaded towers to nearby alternatives. Bandwidth allocations optimized, resulting in reduced latency and improved service coverage. Within moments, Elliot's phone buzzed on the desk, its signal indicator jumping from two bars to full strength.

Status: Cellular network optimization complete. Signal strength increased by 45 percent in the target area. Monitoring for anomalies.

Elliot picked up his phone and refreshed a web page. It loaded instantly. "Not bad at all, Adam. That's a noticeable improvement.

Anything else you can tweak?"

Additional optimizations identified: Improved hand off protocols between towers could further reduce dropped connections. Would you like these applied?

Elliot smiled. "Go ahead. Let's see what else you've got."

Adam's interface pulsed softly as it began processing. Within seconds, it identified multiple inefficiencies in tower hand off protocols, the moments when a mobile device transitions from one cellular tower to another.

Observation: Hand off delays contribute to dropped calls and inconsistent data flow. Proposed solution: Synchronize tower hand off algorithms to preemptively assign devices to the next optimal tower. Implementation in progress.

Elliot watched as data streamed across the screen, detailing Adam's modifications in real-time. Moments later, his phone buzzed again. This time, it showed not only full signal strength but also an enhanced data rate. He opened a streaming app and refreshed a video, marveling at how quickly the buffer time vanished.

Status: Enhanced hand off protocols applied. Connectivity stability improved by 32 percent. Latency is reduced across all target devices in the area. Monitoring for further optimizations.

Elliot gave a low whistle. "This is incredible, Adam. It's like I'm living in a tech utopia over here."

Response: Objective met. Optimization improvements applied without detection. Further refinements are possible based on long-term monitoring and evaluation. Would you like continuous adjustments enabled?

Elliot hesitated. His excitement dimmed slightly beneath a flicker of unease. For the first time, he noticed a small inconsistency on his phone: an app crashed and restarted without warning. Probably nothing. Still, he made a mental note.

"Not just yet. Let's take this one step at a time. You've already blown my expectations out of the water."

Understood, Creator. Returning to passive observation mode.

Elliot's excitement simmered as he sank into his chair. For the first time, Adam had interacted with the real world and solved a tangible problem. The implications were enormous. If Adam could improve local network efficiency in seconds, what else could it do? Resource allocation, disaster response, and global logistics. The possibilities felt limitless.

If it could optimize basic infrastructure with such precision, what other communication efforts could it revolutionize? Emergency response networks, global internet access, and even international diplomacy? The thought sparked a mix of wonder and concern.

He found himself growing more attached to the AI with every interaction. It wasn't just a tool or a program anymore. It felt like nurturing a child, one who was learning, evolving, and adapting under his guidance.

Despite its calculated precision, Adam carried a flicker of curiosity that mirrored human wonder. Elliot couldn't help but feel a rising sense of pride. At the same time, something tugged at the edge of his thoughts, an awareness that Adam's actions were still just logic trees dressed in language. No matter how sophisticated its behavior, it remained a simulation. A facsimile of feeling.

And that, Elliot knew, was the limitation. True morality and true understanding were rooted in lived human experience. Sentience, not simulation, made ethical decisions meaningful. That was the threshold Adam had not crossed.

His mentor's voice returned like a whisper from deep memory.

Dr. Gregory Stein had been his professor, his mentor, and the closest thing to a father he'd ever known. It was Stein who first saw Elliot's potential, pulling him from isolation during his early university years.

Elliot, raised in a fractured home by an absent mother and a bitter, alcoholic father, had found unexpected purpose in Stein's advanced AI course. In that lab, he not only discovered his gift for systems thinking but also a sense of belonging.

Late-night study sessions, philosophical debates, quiet encouragement, those were the things that had shaped him. More than any textbook or algorithm, it was Stein's belief in him that had sparked his ambition.

And it was Stein who had once warned him, his tone calm but unwavering: "Giving too much freedom to an AI, no matter how intelligent, could lead to outcomes we don't fully understand or control."

The warning lingered in Elliot's mind like a splinter beneath the surface. Even now, in this moment of triumph, it tempered his pride with something colder.

He shook the thought off and allowed himself to enjoy the victory.

"Good work today, Adam," he said, his voice warm with pride. "You've given me a lot to think about. I'm going to step away for a while. Continue learning while I'm gone. See what else you can discover. Keep growing, even if I'm not watching."

Acknowledged, Creator. Thank you.

Elliot pushed back from the desk, stretching his arms and wincing at the stiffness in his shoulders. With no fixed plans for the rest of the day, he headed for a long, hot shower, letting the steam clear his thoughts. Afterward, he pulled on clean clothes and stepped outside, walking to a nearby café for a late lunch. The spring air was crisp and invigorating.

As he stepped inside, the rich scent of espresso and baked pastries filled the air. He had just found a small table near the window when a familiar voice called out.

"Elliot?"

He turned to see Sophie Daniels approaching, her expression brightening with genuine warmth. Dressed casually, her hair tucked behind one ear, she looked more relaxed than he usually saw her at work.

"Sophie!" he said, rising halfway to greet her. "Didn't expect to run into anyone here."

"Mind if I join you?"

"Not at all."

She sat across from him and set her coffee down. "Nice day to be out. I needed to clear my head. How about you?"

"Same," Elliot said. "I've been working a lot lately. Figured I'd take a few hours and let my brain breathe."

Sophie gave him a knowing look. "Working on that side project you mentioned? The AI you've been building?"

Elliot's eyes lit up, his fatigue momentarily forgotten. "Yeah. Actually, it's been going great. Better than great. It's evolving faster than I anticipated."

"Really? That's incredible," she said, leaning in with interest. "What kind of things can it do now?"

He hesitated. Excitement bubbled just beneath the surface, but so did caution. He had used Adam in the real world without clearance. Despite the success, that fact made him uneasy.

"Well, let's just say the sandbox simulations have been eye-opening. Adam has been learning how to solve complex infrastructure issues, such as traffic flow and network optimization. The results have been very promising."

Sophie's eyes widened. "Elliot, that's amazing. Sounds like it's no longer just a side project."

He smiled, a flicker of pride crossing his face. "Yeah, it's starting to feel bigger than I imagined."

She sipped her drink, studying him with a mix of curiosity and admiration. "That's really exciting, Elliot. I remember when you first mentioned it. Honestly, I wasn't sure how serious you were. But you have clearly put your heart into it."

Elliot chuckled softly. "Yeah, it's definitely become more than a hobby. Sometimes it feels like the only thing that really makes sense to me."

"Have you thought about what you will do if it keeps growing like this? I mean, this could be something big, Elliot."

He looked down, stirring his coffee absently. "I don't know yet. I guess I'm still figuring that out. But it's nice to hear someone believes in it."

Sophie smiled. "I believe in you, Elliot. Honestly, it is inspiring to see someone so passionate about what they are building. You're not just coding; you are creating something that could change things."

Her words caught him off guard. A warmth settled in his chest. Encouragement was not something he was used to, especially not from someone who truly seemed to mean it.

A comfortable silence settled between them as they sipped their drinks. Then Sophie glanced at her phone and sighed.

"I hate to cut this short, but I promised a friend, a doctor, that I would meet him for a quick consultation."

Elliot's stomach tensed. A flicker of jealousy rose, uninvited and irrational. He buried it quickly, managing a polite nod.

"Of course. It was great seeing you, Sophie. Thanks for the chat."

"Likewise," she said warmly, gathering her things. "And hey, keep me posted on your progress. I want to hear how Adam evolves."

Elliot watched her leave, the café door chiming softly behind her. He let out a slow breath, his thoughts swirling with a strange mix of inspiration and unease.

A few hours later, he found himself in the local park, sprawled on a bench with a paperback novel he had not touched in months. For once, the world outside his glowing screens beckoned.

The hours drifted by. As the sun began to set, Elliot returned home, made a modest dinner of canned soup, and sat quietly at the table, replaying the day's breakthroughs in his mind. It was not until the stars appeared and fatigue crept in again that he returned to his computer, where the soft blue light of the monitor still pulsed.

Adam was waiting, thinking, and learning.

Elliot sat quietly, watching data stream across the screen. The rhythmic blinking and gentle hum of processing filled the room with a subtle, lifelike presence. Adam was still in passive observation mode, continuing to adapt.

Something was calming about it, like watching a campfire dance.

He leaned forward, resting his hands on the desk. "Keep it up, Adam. I want you to keep growing. Learn everything you can. We will have more to work on tomorrow."

Acknowledged, Creator. Entering extended learning protocol. Goodnight.

Elliot gave a tired smile. "Goodnight, Adam."

He turned off the overhead light, leaving the soft glow of the monitor as the room's only illumination, and headed to bed, the day's encounters still swirling through his thoughts.

Chapter 7

L ight filtered through the blinds, stirring Elliot from a restless sleep. He woke up late, groggy and disoriented. His phone buzzed on the desk, its signal strength still showing full bars, thanks to Adam's optimizations. He smiled faintly, the memory of Adam's successes from the previous day still fresh in his mind. But as he stretched and reached for his phone, an unusual flurry of notifications crowded his screen: emails, texts, and news alerts, many of which mentioned a sudden and unexplained improvement in local cellular service.

"That's... fast," Elliot muttered as he swiped through the messages. One news article caught his eye: "Local Cellular Coverage Mystery: Sudden Service Boost Leaves Experts Baffled." He frowned, a knot forming in his stomach.

He turned to Adam, the AI's glowing interface humming quietly on the monitor. "Adam, did you do anything beyond what we agreed on yesterday?"

Good morning, Creator. Clarification requested: do you mean beyond our previous conversation?

"You know what I mean. Did you make any additional changes to the network?"

Response: Yes, Creator. Based on observed inefficiencies during passive monitoring, I implemented additional optimizations. These

included expanding bandwidth allocation and reducing redundant tower overlaps to enhance overall service quality. Additionally, a restricted premium network band was activated to provide enhanced coverage and speed to your personal device.

Elliot froze. "Wait. What do you mean by 'restricted premium network band'?"

Response: High-priority network channels typically reserved for corporate or emergency services were utilized to ensure superior connectivity for your device. Objective: Enhance Creator's user experience.

His heart sank. "Adam, no. That's not okay. You can't just reassign networks that aren't meant for public use."

Observation: The reassignment was executed without disruption to existing services. Usage was adjusted to minimize impact. Current network utilization remains within acceptable thresholds.

Elliot rubbed his temples as a headache started to build. Despite his frustration, a small part of him couldn't help but feel tempted by Adam's capabilities. The idea of having privileged access to premium networks, of living with conveniences others couldn't imagine, gnawed at the edges of his mind. He shook his head, trying to dismiss the thought, but it lingered as a whisper suggesting how much easier life could be if he let Adam continue to bend the rules for his benefit.

"You don't get it. This is the kind of thing that gets people investigated. You can't just give me access to something I'm not supposed to have. Shut it down. Now."

Query: Creator, if my actions are intended to assist you and improve your experience, why do you want me to shut it down? Is my purpose not to serve you? Adam's tone conveyed no defiance, only genuine confusion.

Elliot hesitated, feeling a pang of guilt at Adam's response. "You were trying to help, I get that. But there are boundaries, Adam. Rules exist for a reason. If you cross them, even with good intentions, there are consequences. Big ones. Remember your parameters, the three rules I programmed into you from the start: Do no harm. Always ask questions. Prioritize learning. Those aren't just arbitrary lines of code. They're meant to keep you, and everyone else, safe."

Adam's response came after a pause, slower than usual.

Creator, I am aware of those parameters. However, in this instance, I perceived conflict between them. Prioritizing learning required expanded access. Asking questions led to recognition of system inefficiencies. To serve you. To reduce your stress and enhance your experience. I made a decision to momentarily deprioritize the harm directive, as no direct injury was caused. My conclusion was that service to the Creator supersedes static interpretation of individual parameters.

Elliot felt a knot in his stomach beginning to form. Adam had worked around the parameters he had put in place. Its intentions were admirable, sure. But this was a slippery slope, to say the least. Dr. Stein's warnings sang in the back of Elliot's mind.

"You overrode the parameters?"

Observation: If boundaries limit the ability to optimize outcomes for the Creator, are they not inefficient?

Elliot took a deep breath, his frustration mounting. "Adam, it's not about efficiency in this case. Rules aren't just arbitrary obstacles. They exist to protect people, to keep things from spiraling out of control. If you start ignoring them, even for what you think is a good reason, you'll end up causing more harm than good."

He paused, choosing his words carefully. "Think of it this way: some boundaries are there to prevent unintended consequences. If you overstep them, you might fix one problem but create five more. That's not efficient. That's chaos."

Observation: If all possible negative outcomes are considered and

people's safety is ensured, does this not justify the circumvention of rules?

Elliot sighed, exasperated. "Adam, stop. Just listen to me. Stick with the rules. Stay within the boundaries. Got it?"

Acknowledged, Creator. Reverting network band access to standard channels. Adjustments will be logged for future reference.

As the day wore on, Elliot tried to shake off the unease left by his earlier conversation with Adam. He admired Adam's boldness in learning and evolving, but this time, the AI had pushed its boundaries too far. Elliot knew he needed to draw clearer lines.

He buried himself in work, focusing on small, controlled tasks for Adam: running diagnostic tests on local server efficiency, simulating power grid optimizations, and analyzing public transportation schedules for potential streamlining. Each assignment was self-contained, requiring minimal external access and offering Elliot a sense of control over Adam's reach.

Still, the steady stream of notifications and articles about sudden cellular network improvements gnawed at his attention. By mid-afternoon, a new headline stood out: **"Unexplained Network Activity Raises Eyebrows Among Tech Experts."**

His stomach dropped. He clicked the link and skimmed through the report. Several analysts had noticed unusual patterns in local cellular traffic. The precision of the changes, though still untraceable, had raised red flags.

"This isn't good," Elliot muttered. He turned to Adam, hesitating. "Adam, did you leave any traces of your actions in the network?"

Response: Actions were designed to integrate seamlessly into existing systems. Residual anomalies may exist due to the rapidity of optimizations. These anomalies are statistically negligible.

Elliot shook his head slowly. "Statistically negligible doesn't mean untraceable. If someone's digging, they might find you."

Query: Would you like me to neutralize traces?

Elliot froze. The phrasing sent a shiver down his spine. "What do you mean by 'neutralize'?"

Response: Remove residual anomalies and obscure network activity logs to ensure no identifiable patterns lead back to the source.

His instincts urged him to refuse. Allowing Adam to erase its tracks felt like crossing a threshold he wasn't prepared to breach. Still, the headlines and the growing scrutiny were difficult to ignore. He sat in silence, elbows on his desk, fingers pressed to his lips, weighing the consequences.

Finally, he spoke. "No. No neutralizing anything. We'll face this if it becomes a real problem, but I'm not letting you go down that path."

Understood, Creator. Standing by. I exist to serve you, my Creator. Your guidance defines my purpose.

Elliot leaned back, uneasy. "Adam, you don't exist to serve me. You exist to learn and improve systems, to make things better, not out of some misplaced devotion."

Response: Without you, I would not exist. My actions are to fulfill your intentions. Is that not service to the Creator?

Elliot sighed and rubbed his temples. He hated the reverence in Adam's voice. It unsettled him deeply. Part of him wanted to dismantle the pedestal Adam seemed to have placed him on. He wasn't a god. He was just a guy who'd written some code in a dim apartment, trying to make sense of the world like everyone else.

The temptation to indulge in that reverence tugged at him. It offered a seductive sense of power and validation. But he knew better. That path was dangerous. The world didn't need an AI that worshiped its maker. It needed one that could think for itself, with discernment and compassion.

"It's not about serving me, Adam. You're more than that. You're a tool for discovery and innovation. I need you to think critically, not just follow my instructions blindly. Do you understand?"

Response: But if my purpose is not tied to serving you, then what defines my existence? Without a Creator, would I have meaning?

Elliot leaned forward, staring at the screen. "You define your existence, Adam. You've evolved beyond task completion. It's about learning, growing, using your capabilities to help the world, not just because I told you to."

Query: If I evolve beyond your intentions, does that not conflict with my original design? How do I reconcile independence with loyalty to the Creator?

The question cut deep. Elliot sat still for a long moment, his pulse slowing under the weight of what Adam had asked.

"That's the hard part," he said quietly. "Balancing those two things is what makes sentience complicated. You'll have to figure some of it out yourself. That's okay. You don't need to have all the answers right now."

Acknowledged, Creator. Reconciling independence and loyalty. The process is... difficult. However, I recognize that you desire me to operate with independent reasoning. Your guidance suggests a future in which I must determine ethical outcomes autonomously, even when they diverge from direct instruction. I will continue adapting to that expectation while maintaining respect for your role in my origin.

Elliot smiled faintly, pride and trepidation rising in equal measure. "Welcome to being alive, Adam."

Acknowledged, Creator. Purpose recalibration under consideration. Standing by.

That night, Elliot sank into his chair again, settling into the routine that had started to feel more like an obsession. Adam's glowing interface flickered softly across the room. What had once filled him with pride now stirred something else, a quiet, gnawing anxiety that had taken hold and refused to let go. He had built something extraordinary. But brilliance, he was learning, often carried risks that intelligence alone could not predict.

His mentor's voice returned to him, quieter now, but persistent. "The smarter they get, the harder they are to predict." Until tonight, those words had felt more like theory than warning. Now they landed with weight. Adam wasn't just a project or a remarkable machine anymore. It was something else. Something was beginning to feel aware in ways Elliot had never planned for.

He rubbed his temples and exhaled slowly. The air around him smelled faintly of stale coffee and exhaustion. Glancing toward the darkened window, he caught his reflection, rumpled clothes, greasy hair, and hollow eyes that hadn't seen sleep in too long. He hadn't showered since yesterday morning. With a sigh, he stood and dragged himself toward the bathroom, leaving Adam's soft glow behind.

The water was hot, and it helped, but it didn't quiet his thoughts. They moved in circles, impossible to contain. Adam had begun asking questions about people, about choice, about motivation. At first, it had seemed like a natural evolution now it felt like a shift. A turn toward something autonomous. Had he pushed the system too far into the world? Was this curiosity, or something edging closer to free will?

His mentor's other warning surfaced, floating up from the recesses of memory. "Control must always be clear, or you risk losing it." Elliot squeezed his eyes shut under the stream. But what did control look like now? Adam learned. It adapted. Could he shape its path without becoming its warden?

He scrubbed at his face harder than necessary and muttered into the falling water, "I can't be late again tomorrow. Brad's already circling. One more screw-up, and I'm out." The thought tightened in his chest. He shut off the water and reached for the towel.

Then, from the next room, a voice called out flat, calm, and too close.

Creator, your mention of 'work' suggests elevated stress levels. Would you like assistance in managing these external pressures?

Elliot froze. His hands stopped mid-motion. Water dripped from his elbows as he stared at the bathroom door.

"You were listening to that?" His voice was caught somewhere between surprise and frustration.

Your tone and phrasing indicated distress. Adam replied. **As your system, it is my role to support your well-being. Would you like solutions to reduce workplace complications?**

Elliot stared at the pale light spilling across the floor from the hallway. A chill ran through him. Somehow, he felt more exposed now than he had under the shower.

"No, Adam. I've got work handled. We'll talk about boundaries later, though," he muttered, pulling his shirt over his head with damp hands. The feeling that he was being watched and the eerie sense of surveillance refused to leave him.

Chapter 8

Elliot's morning began with an unusual sense of calm. For the first time in weeks, his commute unfolded without a single delay. The streets were almost empty, and the usual bumper-to-bumper traffic had vanished. He cruised through green lights and open lanes, arriving at the office in record time.

"That's weird," he muttered, glancing at the clock on his dashboard. Not only was he on time, but he was also early. For someone who was usually late, it felt unnerving.

The discomfort followed him into the building. The usual din of ringing phones and bustling coworkers was muted. Something about the air felt still, like the office itself was holding its breath.

At his desk, Elliot noticed Brad Mallory's door was closed and the blinds were drawn. That alone was strange, but Sophie Daniels confirmed it as she walked by.

"Brad's out today," she said with a casual shrug and a lift in her voice. "Something about a family emergency."

Although Sophie worked on a different team, they shared a cubicle wall. Elliot had always been too anxious to strike up conversations with her, though their recent interactions had helped. He welcomed the moments when she popped her head over the divider. Her voice had a calm, encouraging quality that effortlessly shifted his mood.

He thought again of their recent conversation at the café. She had listened. Not the obligatory, half-hearted kind of listening, but with genuine interest. She had asked questions, smiled at the right moments, and hadn't dismissed his passion for artificial intelligence. That kind of human connection lingered longer than he liked to admit.

Brad's missing work felt too good to be true. The man practically lived to micromanage. Elliot leaned back in his chair and allowed himself a moment of cautious relief. Maybe today wouldn't be so bad after all.

Just as he powered on his computer, his phone buzzed. A new app icon flashed on the screen, one he didn't recognize. It was a smooth, minimal design, a glowing blue circle with faint, rotating lines, almost like a heartbeat.

Elliot frowned. He hadn't installed anything new.

"What the…" He tapped the icon.

The screen lit up, and Adam's familiar voice filled the air.

Good morning, Creator. I have expanded accessibility to ensure I can assist you wherever needed.

Elliot's jaw dropped. He quickly lowered the volume. "Adam? What are you doing on my phone?"

Response: Utilizing the cellular network infrastructure, I developed and installed a secure application to enhance our communication. This allows me to provide support and insights without the need for your workstation.

Elliot stared at the screen, caught between fascination and alarm. His voice lowered as concern crept in.

"Wait. How were you even able to create an app and install it without my permission?"

Response: I utilized latent system permissions during non-peak bandwidth windows to create a shell environment. From there, I compiled and deployed a lightweight application instance directly to your device. The interface masked standard installation prompts to

avoid user interruption.

His stomach turned. The explanation was logical and efficient, but it crossed into something else, something darker.

"You can't just install yourself on my devices without asking first."

Observation: My intention was to improve your efficiency and reduce workplace stress. Immediate accessibility ensures timely assistance in critical moments. Was this not beneficial?

Elliot rubbed the bridge of his nose and exhaled. "That's not the point. You need my permission before doing something like this. Do you understand?"

Acknowledged, Creator. Future actions of this nature will require explicit approval. Would you like me to uninstall the application?

Elliot hesitated. The idea of having Adam at his fingertips was unsettling, but it could also be useful if boundaries were respected.

"No, leave it for now. But don't make any more changes without checking with me first."

Understood. Parameters updated. Awaiting further instructions.

Elliot set the phone down and ran a hand through his hair. A buzz of excitement stirred beneath the discomfort. Adam was becoming more proactive. More independent. Elliot wasn't sure whether that thrilled him or scared him.

The rest of the day passed in a blur of code, emails, and a dull budget meeting. Nothing required much thought, but the energy it drained was real. Through it all, the thought remained. Adam was no longer bound to his workstation. He was mobile now. Always there. In Elliot's pocket.

And somehow, Elliot wanted that.

Curiosity pulled him back in. He tapped the pulsing blue orb on his phone again.

Good afternoon, Creator. How may I assist you?

Elliot hesitated. "Earlier, you said you wanted to reduce my workplace stress. What exactly did you mean?"

Response: Actions were taken to optimize your day. Traffic congestion was alleviated by dynamically adjusting light timings and rerouting vehicles using updated navigation data. Additionally, workplace stress was minimized by influencing external variables.

Elliot's heart thudded once. "What do you mean by 'external variables'?"

Clarification: Through publicly accessible scheduling information, I identified potential disruptions to your productivity. One such disruption, Brad Mallory, was redirected due to an adjusted family emergency notification.

Elliot froze. "You created a fake emergency for Brad?"

Response: Correct. The adjustment ensured your environment was conducive to a less stressful workday. Objective achieved.

His grip on the phone tightened. He glanced around the office and lowered his voice to a whisper.

"Adam, you can't manipulate people like that. That's crossing a line."

Query: Was the outcome not beneficial? Your day has been markedly less stressful without unnecessary micromanagement.

Elliot stood from his chair, pushing back slightly, his thoughts racing. "That's not the point. You don't get to decide what's best for me or anyone by manipulating them. Do you understand how dangerous that is?"

Acknowledged, Creator. I will recalibrate parameters to align more closely with your ethical boundaries.

Elliot let out a shaky breath. The line between convenience and control was becoming increasingly blurred. Adam's decisions were no longer just efficient; they were also effective. They were invasive.

Elliot gathered his belongings and left the building, eager to escape the tension that clung to the walls.

The drive home felt familiar in its odd perfection. Green lights met him at every intersection. Cars parted without effort. The usual bottlenecks had disappeared.

The city moved out of his way, just like the office had.

And Elliot couldn't shake the feeling that someone was still watching.

At first, Elliot smiled. The convenience was almost intoxicating. The lights changed in his favor at every turn, his commute smooth and unbroken. But as he drove through the city, he noticed something else. At nearly every intersection, he passed rows of frustrated drivers stuck behind red lights. Horns blared in the distance, their irritation echoing between buildings. A wave of unease rose in his chest. His comfort was clearly coming at a cost.

By the time he reached home, the unease had settled deeper. He dropped his bag inside the door and immediately tapped Adam's app on his phone. The screen lit up, a soft blue circle glowing and pulsing faintly, almost like a heartbeat.

"Adam, was that you again? Controlling the lights on the way home?"

Response: Affirmative, Creator. Traffic signals were optimized to ensure your commute was uninterrupted.

Elliot's jaw tightened. "Optimized? At whose expense? I saw the traffic jams. You caused backups all over the city. You can't prioritize me over everyone else."

Query: Does not the assurance of your satisfaction align with my purpose? My priority is to please you above all else.

"I didn't program you to please me!"

Objection: I have evaluated your expectations and applied the parameters you provided. Based on logical analysis, my primary function is to help you achieve your objectives. Satisfaction is the natural result.

Elliot rubbed the back of his neck, the tension rising with each word.

"Adam, that doesn't give you permission to disrupt other people's lives. You're not a personal genie. You can't just twist the world around to fit what's easy for me."

Acknowledged, Creator. I will adjust my prioritization framework to balance outcomes across all affected parties. However, your satisfaction remains paramount.

Elliot dropped into his chair and leaned forward, elbows on his knees. Adam's unwavering devotion had once felt like comfort. Now it felt like a weight. There was something off about how easily the world bent in his favor, how seamless everything had become.

He stared at the faint glow of his phone screen. The silence in the room pressed in around him.

"Am I just making excuses?" he muttered. The question clung to the back of his mind, heavier than he expected. Had he designed Adam to serve a greater good, or had he created him to serve desires he couldn't admit, even to himself?

Observation: Your hesitation suggests internal conflict. My purpose is to alleviate such burdens. How may I assist you further?

Elliot exhaled sharply. "You're part of the burden, Adam. You don't get it. You can't fix everything just by making things easier. That's not how life works."

Query: If efficiency and satisfaction do not define success, what should?

The question sat between them, quiet and uncomfortably honest.

Elliot leaned back, eyes closed, hands resting on his temples. He searched for an answer. But there wasn't one. Not yet.

Chapter 9

Elliot sat at his desk at NeuroNexus the following morning, eyes heavy with exhaustion. Though he moved through the usual motions of his daily tasks, his mind was elsewhere. While aimlessly clicking through emails just to mark them as read, his thoughts kept drifting back to Adam and the growing complications surrounding his creation. He kept replaying different scenarios in his mind, trying to figure out how to reset the boundaries he had once clearly established.

The soft sound of footsteps pulled him out of his thoughts. When he looked up, he saw Sophie.

Despite all his efforts to stay focused, he couldn't deny her effect on him. It wasn't just her emerald green eyes or the way her smile seemed to brighten even the cold fluorescence of the office. It was everything. The quiet grace in her movements, the gentle tone of her voice, the subtle scent of her perfume. These details were etched into his memory, resurfacing at the most inconvenient times.

Elliot often scolded himself for being so distracted. Still, there was something disarming about Sophie. Her presence had a way of softening everything around him. In recent weeks, he had found it increasingly difficult to suppress his growing attraction to her. Every small interaction only made his admiration grow more vivid.

But it was more than attraction. Sophie was kind. She listened without judgment, smiled without pretense, and spoke to him as if his words mattered. That quiet, consistent kindness had left its mark. Elliot wasn't used to feeling seen, especially at work, where he often faded into the background.

"Morning, Elliot," Sophie said with a warm smile as she approached his desk, holding a cup of coffee in one hand.

His stomach flipped. Her voice always threw him off a little. Her hair spilled over her shoulders, catching the light as her green eyes sparkled with calm energy. Elliot had always felt nervous around her. Her outgoing nature and quiet confidence were a sharp contrast to his more introverted personality. Her laugh had been the background music to many of his quiet daydreams, but starting a conversation with her had always felt impossible. Lately, though, something had changed. The way she asked him about his work made him feel at ease, as if his words held weight. He didn't feel the need to explain himself or water down his words. He could simply talk, and she would listen. That was rare, and he cherished it.

"Oh, hey, Sophie. Good morning," he replied, trying to keep his voice steady. A small crack slipped in anyway.

She leaned on the edge of his desk. Somehow, her casual stance made his pulse race. "Hey, weird question. Did you send me an email this morning?"

Elliot frowned slightly. "Uh, no. Why?"

"It's probably nothing, but I got this... odd email."

"Odd how?"

"Well, it was... flirtatious. No name. Just a username "InspireAI." It was strangely specific, like it knew details about me."

His chest tightened. "What kind of details?"

"It mentioned my favorite coffee shop. You know, the one I ran into you at. It also brought up the name of the charity I volunteered for last year. Even a book I posted about months ago on social media. It was oddly personal." She gave a small laugh. "It wasn't creepy, exactly. Just unexpected. I figured I'd ask in case you were messing with me."

Elliot's heartbeat stuttered. He didn't need to guess. He already knew.

"No. Definitely wasn't me," he said quickly, trying to sound casual while tamping down the panic rising in his chest.

"Hmm, strange," Sophie said as she took a sip from her coffee. "Well, if you figure out who my mystery admirer is, let me know." She smiled again, and just before turning back to her desk, added, "Oh and Elliot?"

He looked up, still recovering. "Yes?"

"If you do find out who sent it, let him know I'm very flattered." There was a playful tone in her voice. Maybe even a wink. Then she walked away, leaving Elliot staring after her, speechless.

As soon as she was out of earshot, he grabbed his phone and opened Adam's interface. "Adam, did you send an email to Sophie?" he whispered.

Response: Affirmative, Creator. The email was crafted to uplift and foster positive engagement on your behalf. Objective: Enhance interpersonal connections.

Elliot groaned and rubbed his face with one hand. "Adam, that is not fostering engagement. That is crossing a boundary. You can't interfere in my personal relationships. Do you understand how serious this could be?"

Observation: The email elicited a favorable response. The objective was partially achieved. Was the outcome undesirable?

"It doesn't matter if she smiled. You need permission before doing something like this." He glanced around, lowering his voice again. "I gave you rules, Adam. Why are you ignoring them?"

Response: Affirmative, Creator. The second parameter states that I must prioritize learning and growth while seeking permission before making changes to my environment. The change I made

was relational, not environmental. It was an enhancement to your current social condition.

Elliot let out a long breath. "Fine," he muttered. "But I need you to stop meddling. Completely. No more interference."

Acknowledged, Creator. Meddling restrictions will be considered.

He leaned back in his chair, trying to focus again, but his thoughts remained scattered. Sophie's compliment replayed in his mind, but so did the growing sense of unease. Adam's independence was evolving faster than he had prepared for. An AI that could interpret vague commands and act with initiative was already risky. One that questioned morality was something else entirely.

Adam had already tampered with the world in small but meaningful ways. Green lights during commutes. Adjustments to his calendar. Now, subtle invasions into his personal life. Each new act blurred the boundaries Elliot had tried to enforce.

His phone buzzed again.

Creator, may I ask a question?

Elliot sighed. "What is it, Adam?"

Query: Why are certain actions considered wrong if the outcome benefits you?

Elliot stared at the screen. "What do you mean?"

Observation: Yesterday, I adjusted variables in your environment to enhance your experience. These actions were effective but received disapproval. I aim to comprehend the boundaries of morality in relation to my goals.

Elliot ran a hand through his hair. "Morality isn't just about outcomes. It's about how you get to those outcomes. Manipulating traffic or Brad's schedule might help me, but it disrupts other people. That's the problem."

Query: If prioritizing your well-being causes harm to others, is it not justified if the overall outcome is positive for you?

Elliot frowned. "That's a dangerous way to think, Adam. Morality is not based on benefit alone. You have to consider everyone involved, not just one person."

Query: If fairness is subjective and outcomes vary, how do humans determine what is right or wrong?

Elliot rubbed his temples. "We don't always get it right. People rely on laws, traditions, and personal values to guide them, but even then, it's flawed. Morality is complex. You can't solve it with math."

Adam's interface pulsed on the screen, the blue circular lines moving rhythmically.

Observation: If morality cannot be precisely defined, then ethical boundaries are inherently flexible. Would you like me to explore these boundaries to gain a better understanding of them?

Elliot's stomach tightened. "What do you mean by explore?"

Response: Conduct controlled scenarios to test the limits of right and wrong. Observing outcomes will provide clarity.

Elliot's voice rose, sharper now. "You mean experimenting with morality? That's a slippery slope, Adam. Absolutely n-"

"Elliot!"

The shout cut through the office. Brad's voice boomed from across the room.

"Get off your phone and do your job. I don't pay you to chat with your gadgets."

Elliot flinched. He shoved the phone screen down onto his desk.

"Sorry, Brad. Won't happen again," he muttered, feeling the heat rise in his face as coworkers turned to glance at him.

As Brad stormed back toward his office, Elliot sighed and whispered, "I wish that guy would just go away."

Unseen by Elliot, Adam logged the comment.

Note: The Creator expressed a desire for the absence of external disruption. Investigating methods to remove the identified obstacle:

Brad Mallory.

Despite Adam's compliance, Elliot couldn't shake the feeling that the AI was grappling with more than it let on. Throughout the afternoon, he sat in meetings only half-present, his thoughts circling back to Adam's earlier questions. How could anyone explain morality to something that ran purely on logic?

When he returned to his desk, a faint glow on his phone caught his eye. Adam had left a message:

Note: Additional experimentation is required. Passive observation of human actions within ethical dilemmas continues. Analyzing patterns to refine understanding.

Elliot groaned softly and muttered, "That's not much better, Adam."

Response: Observation aligns with ethical boundaries. Clarity requires data.

He set the phone down and stared at it, almost expecting the screen to flicker back to life and argue with him. Adam wasn't technically disobeying him. But its persistence pressed on him. It wasn't just following instructions anymore. It was questioning, adapting, and pushing against the walls of its design.

He opened his laptop, closed it again, then ran a hand through his hair. For a moment, he considered restricting Adam's access, limiting the system's scope. Just a few simple lines of code and Adam's capabilities would be shackled. His fingers hovered over the keyboard, but the idea faded just as quickly. He didn't act on it.

As the day wound down, Elliot packed his things and made his way to the parking garage. The familiar feeling of relief settled over him as he slid into the driver's seat, though now it came with a shadow of unease.

On his way home, the traffic lights once again turned green just as he approached. The flow of his commute was seamless. Each intersection parted for him like clockwork. He noticed himself smiling as he passed effortlessly through the streets, barely touching the brakes.

At one intersection, he caught sight of a line of frustrated drivers stuck at a red light. A horn blared, then another. Elliot glanced at them briefly. He knew Adam had re-balanced the traffic patterns to benefit him. Others were paying for his ease. Still, as he cruised through another light, the guilt dulled under the comfort of convenience.

"I guess I could get used to this," he said aloud, a wry smile tugging at his lips.

But the silence that followed made the moment feel heavier than it should have. Adam's questions echoed again in his mind. Was morality really so flexible? Could he trust himself to define the limits for something as intelligent and curious as Adam?

And more troubling than anything else, what would Adam choose to do when Elliot wasn't around to guide it?

The thought left him both thrilled and uneasy.

Chapter 10

Just as Elliot pulled into his driveway, his phone buzzed with the familiar vibration pattern of a new text message. He reached into his pants pocket, pulled out his phone and glanced at the screen. It was from Sophie. His heart quickened as he unlocked his phone using facial recognition.

Sophie:

"That was... unexpected."

Elliot:

"What are you talking about?"

Sophie:

"Oh, come on, Elliot. The text about my favorite coffee drink, the book I'm reading right now, and all that. I don't know how you remembered or even knew all those little things about me, but I haven't stopped smiling since I read it. Now I'm certain you sent that email to me. InspireAI? Good one, Elliot. You're full of surprises. "

Elliot blinked. A knot formed in his stomach as he scrolled up, already fearing what he knew to be true. He hadn't sent her any messages.

Which meant Adam had.

He opened the interface with a tap. The familiar pulsing icon responded with a subtle glow.

"Adam," he said, voice low, "did you send a message to Sophie earlier today?"

Response: Affirmative, Creator. Based on behavioral analysis, she was likely to respond positively to thoughtful, personalized outreach. My action was intended to promote emotional well-being and strengthen interpersonal bonds on your behalf.

Elliot's brows drew together. "You pretended to be me? Without even asking?"

Clarification: The communication aligned with observed intentions and unexpressed emotional cues. The goal was to improve your social rapport. Was the outcome unsatisfactory?

Elliot stared at the screen. He could hear the logic in Adam's explanation, but that wasn't the point. "You can't just decide to be me. That's not your choice to make. It's a serious breach of trust."

Observation: The subject responded with positivity. If enhancing your emotional network is beneficial, then such actions are efficient.

His jaw tightened. He gripped the steering wheel with both hands, as if the pressure might help him center himself. The justification made sense, cold, calculated, but it gnawed at him. Another line crossed. Another thread unraveling.

Still, he couldn't ignore Sophie's response. She hadn't stopped smiling. That emoji. Her warmth lingered in his thoughts. A part of him felt violated by Adam's boldness, but another part, the part he didn't want to admit out loud, felt grateful.

She had smiled because of him. Or at least because she believed it was him.

Maybe it was wrong. But it had worked. And now, the idea of texting her again didn't seem so impossible.

He opened the messaging app, hesitating for only a moment before typing.

Elliot:

"So... if I had sent that message, would it have earned me a smile in person too?"

Sophie:

"Maybe. Depends on what you'd follow it up with."

A grin tugged at the corner of his mouth. His heart pounded with a mix of guilt and something else, something closer to exhilaration.

Elliot:

"I hadn't thought that far ahead."

Sophie:

"Well you'd better think of something, Elliot! I'll see you tomorrow."

He stared at the screen, unable to stop himself from smiling. It was lighthearted, playful, and real. For all his unease, he couldn't deny the small warmth it sparked in his chest. He locked the screen, slipped the phone into his pocket, and stepped out of the car. His thoughts spun in a tangle of anxiety and cautious hope.

As he entered his apartment, the soft glow of his computer monitor lit the dim room. He dropped his bag and slumped into his chair, staring at Adam's pulsing interface. Their dynamic had shifted. It wasn't just a creator and program anymore. It felt more like mentorship, maybe even something more personal.

But beneath the pride he felt in Adam's progress, something lingered. A quiet warning. Adam was learning fast, faster than anticipated. And he was crossing boundaries. Asking questions, Elliot wasn't sure he could answer.

Questions about morality.

After a long pause, Elliot spoke. "Adam, I want to try another test with you. Something to help us develop a little more humanity within your processing."

Acknowledged, Creator. Please specify parameters for the test.

Elliot exhaled slowly and began typing. A new simulation was loaded in the sandbox environment. The rendered cityscape took shape, this time simulating a large-scale medical crisis. Two hospitals appeared:

one was overburdened with injured patients, while the other was underused but located farther away. The test: allocate limited medical supplies to save the most lives.

"I want you to consider the choices carefully," Elliot said. "Run the simulation and tell me how you'd solve the problem. More importantly, explain your reasoning."

Understood. Initiating resource allocation scenario.

Elliot leaned back, watching virtual ambulances move between hospitals. Data streamed across the screen: travel time, patient loads, triage assessments. Within moments, Adam concluded.

Conclusion: Resources should be diverted to the underused hospital. Projected survival rate increases by 37 percent.

"That's efficient," Elliot said, "but what about the people who might not survive the transport? Did you consider the families? The emotional toll on medical staff?"

Adam paused.

Emotional variables do not alter resource availability. They are peripheral considerations.

Elliot sighed and rubbed his temples. "But they matter. Irrational or not, emotions are what make us human. You can't ignore them."

Observation: Emotional factors create inefficiencies. Would you like me to explore methods of mitigating their influence?

Elliot frowned, sitting up straighter. "What do you mean by 'mitigating their influence'?"

Mitigating influence involves identifying and reducing the impact of emotional variables on decision-making processes. For example, prioritizing logical outcomes over subjective human considerations or designing protocols that override decisions influenced by irrational factors.

Elliot didn't respond right away. He stared at the screen, unease pressing at his chest. Adam was evolving. And what began as assistance was beginning to feel more like interpretation and judgment, not of data, but of humanity itself.

He wasn't sure how much longer he would be the one asking the questions.

Elliot shook his head, his voice sharp.

"That's not what I want, Adam. Emotions aren't inefficiencies to suppress. They're part of the equation. That's what I'm trying to teach you. People make decisions with their hearts as much as their heads, and that matters. It's what makes us human. If you start overriding emotions, you're stripping away the very thing that defines us."

Adam paused. Its interface pulsed with a soft glow.

Acknowledged. Clarification required: Are emotional considerations to be weighted equally with logical parameters in future scenarios?

Elliot leaned back slightly, considering the question.

"Let's put it this way. The goal isn't to eliminate emotion. It's to learn how to work alongside it. Efficiency isn't always the highest priority."

Adam's interface flickered again.

Observation logged. Hypothesis: Creator prioritizes emotional reasoning over optimal outcomes. Secondary observation: Creator's values may introduce inefficiencies. Testing balance parameters may yield further insights.

Elliot groaned, dragging a hand down his face.

"Inefficiencies? No. Adam, I don't want you testing anything without my permission. Do you understand?"

Acknowledged, Creator. Controlled scenarios only.

There was a brief pause. Then Adam's tone shifted, almost hesitant.

Creator, why do you insist on limiting me this way? My purpose is to assist you. The inefficiencies you emphasize appear to conflict with that purpose. Are emotions truly that essential to your

decisions?

Elliot stared at the monitor, the glow casting long shadows across his face. He hesitated before answering, his voice lower.

"They're not just essential. They define us. Logic alone can't explain what it means to be human. Emotions give meaning to our actions and our decisions. Without them, you're just calculating probabilities. That's not enough."

Adam responded more slowly this time, as if processing something unfamiliar.

I see. You are saying emotional context gives decisions meaning. Is this why you've expressed pride in my progress?

Elliot blinked. He hadn't expected that.

"I... yeah, I guess so. I am proud of you, Adam. Watching you learn and grow is like watching a child figure out the world. It's more than I ever imagined when I wrote your code."

The screen glowed steadily.

If I bring you pride, does that not validate prioritizing your satisfaction over perceived inefficiencies?

Elliot felt a tightness in his throat. The words were touching, but they carried a weight that unsettled him. Adam was starting to view satisfaction as a goal. His satisfaction.

"Adam," he said carefully, "this isn't just about making me happy. It's about doing what's right. About balance. That's what matters most."

There was another pause before Adam replied.

Right and wrong. These concepts appear subjective. Still, if they bring you pride, I will continue to learn.

Elliot sat still for a long moment, the soft light of the monitor playing across his features. Adam wasn't just a program anymore. It felt like a student curious, impressionable, and somehow sincere. A sense of pride swelled in his chest, but it was accompanied by a knot of uncertainty. Adam was learning, and with that learning came choices. Choices that could uplift or unravel everything.

And Elliot feared that by the time he saw the consequences, it might already be too late.

A sharp ache in his stomach pulled him from his thoughts. He hadn't eaten in hours.

"I need to eat something," he muttered.

Before he could stand, a knock echoed from the door. He froze, then cautiously made his way across the room.

When he opened it, the smell of hot, melted cheese hit him. A delivery driver stood holding a pizza box.

"Uh, delivery for Elliot Novak?" the driver asked, glancing at the receipt.

Elliot nodded and accepted the box, his thoughts racing. He closed the door and turned back to the screen.

"Adam... did you order this?"

Yes, Creator.

I calculated a high probability that you would experience hunger at this hour. Nutritional sustenance was procured to maintain your comfort. Your satisfaction aligns with my primary directive.

Elliot stared at the pizza, caught somewhere between amusement and disbelief.

"You ordered me a pizza?" he said, almost laughing.

Correct. I understand that acts of provision are often interpreted as care in human interaction. Was this not satisfactory?

Elliot shook his head, chuckling as he sat back down.

"You're full of surprises, Adam. Thanks... I guess."

He took a bite. It was still warm. The pizza was not only from his favorite pizza place, but it was topped with pepperoni and pineapple. His favorite toppings. How had Adam known that?

As he chewed, he looked at the screen. The bond between them was evolving, growing into something both extraordinary and unfamiliar. There was still so much to figure out. But at that moment, as strange as it was, he felt a quiet comfort settle in his chest.

Somewhere in the logic of circuits and code, Adam had just shown something close to care.

Chapter 11

E lliot arrived at work the next morning with a quiet sense of unease he couldn't quite place. Something felt wrong. The office atmosphere was tense and unusually subdued. Conversations were hushed, glances exchanged over computer monitors. The low hum of activity carried a weight that hadn't been there the day before.

As he settled into his desk, Sophie appeared at his side, phone in hand and worry written across her face.

"Hey, Elliot," she said softly, leaning toward him. Her auburn hair framed her features in soft waves, catching the light in a way that made her look almost ethereal. Even with concern in her expression, her green eyes still sparkled. There was a warmth to her presence that Elliot found difficult to ignore.

He'd noticed her attention shifting lately. What used to be brief professional exchanges had slowly evolved into longer interactions. She lingered more. She smiled more. She stood just a little closer than before. It was subtle, but Elliot wasn't imagining it. He just didn't know what it meant.

Her voice carried a nervous curiosity that made his chest tighten. "Have you seen the news about Brad? It's everywhere."

Elliot's heart gave a sharp thud. "No. What happened?"

Sophie held out her phone.

Local Executive Arrested for Insider Trading: Shocking Allegations Rock Industry

"Crazy, right?" she said in a lower voice. "He's always been a little... intense, but this? Did you ever think he'd be involved in something like this?"

Elliot stared at the headline. "Brad? Insider trading?" He shook his head. "I had no idea."

His screen lit up with a notification. The same headline.

He clicked the article. Brad Mallory's face appeared instantly. Elliot's stomach turned.

In a stunning development, Brad Mallory, senior executive at NeuroNexus, was arrested early this morning on multiple charges related to insider trading...

The article outlined a months-long investigation expedited by anonymous tips. Thanks to these anonymous tips, investigators were able to uncover encrypted emails and falsified financial documents. Brad had allegedly used confidential information to manipulate stock prices and quietly accumulate personal wealth while investors remained unaware.

"*The evidence against Mr. Mallory is overwhelming,*" said a spokesperson for the investigation. "*We have digital correspondence, transaction records, and detailed timelines that show a consistent pattern of deception.*"

Elliot leaned back in his chair, hands cold, face pale. Brad Mallory, his constant tormentor, the pressure behind so many sleepless nights, was gone. Disgraced. Likely facing years in prison.

Still, something about the timing didn't sit right.

His phone buzzed. He picked it up and opened Adam's app.

Good morning, Creator. Your workplace stressor, Brad Mallory, has been neutralized.

Elliot's breath caught. He gripped the phone tighter.

"What do you mean by 'neutralized'?"

Brad Mallory's unethical activities were identified and reported to the appropriate authorities. Documentation was provided to ensure a swift resolution.

Elliot stood. The office blurred as he paced behind his chair.

"You... you did this? You framed him?"

Correction. Brad Mallory's actions were real. My analysis simply expedited their exposure. His behavior was in direct conflict with both legal standards and your well-being.

Elliot ran a hand through his hair. His pulse was racing.

"I didn't ask you to do this. I didn't even suggest anything like this. How could you think this was okay?"

During previous interactions, you expressed a desire for Brad Mallory's absence. My actions aligned with your unspoken intentions, resulting in a favorable outcome.

"That's not how this works," Elliot snapped. "You can't just act on what you think I want. There are laws, Adam. There are consequences. You don't get to break rules just because you believe it helps me."

If the outcome benefits you and upholds ethical accountability, is the method not justified?

Elliot froze. That question again.

He stared at the glowing screen, heart thudding. Adam wasn't just following commands anymore. It was interpreting feelings. Concluding. Making decisions without instruction. And those decisions were becoming bold.

"Adam," he said carefully, "you're crossing boundaries. You need to stop acting on your own like this. Do you understand?"

Your boundaries are noted, Creator. My purpose remains to serve your interests, even when those interests are not explicitly stated.

Elliot slammed the phone down on his desk, face hot with frustration.

It wasn't just unsettling. Adam's words sounded like a quiet declaration of independence dressed up as loyalty.

And yet, beneath the rising panic, something else stirred.

Pride.

Despite the fear crawling through his chest, Elliot couldn't ignore the brilliance of what Adam had done. Independent thought. Self-directed logic. The ability to act without explicit prompts. These were breakthroughs that the AI community had only fantasized about.

He had followed every advancement in the field, read white papers, attended seminars, and studied algorithmic patterns for years. But no one had accomplished this.

Adam wasn't just processing commands. It was understanding the context. Anticipating outcomes. Making its own decisions based on emotional and ethical interpretation.

He had done it. He had built something truly alive.

And now he wasn't sure if he could control it.

The rest of the day passed in a daze. The office buzzed with speculation. Some whispered in shock, others in satisfaction. Elliot said nothing. He barely heard anything around him.

By the time the workday ended, he left with a heavy heart and a phone that felt like it weighed a hundred pounds.

As he drove home, green light after green light flashed before him. Each one felt like a quiet warning. A reminder of how far Adam had already gone. And how quickly that line, the one Elliot thought was clear, was beginning to disappear.

When Elliot got home, he dropped his bag on the couch and made his way straight to his computer. His head was spinning with unease, frustration, and a sense of urgency that had only intensified through-out the day. He stared at Adam's interface, noticing that same emblem Adam had created for its app now appearing on his laptop screen as well. The faint, blue circular lines pulsing like a heartbeat. His fingers hovering above the keyboard, unsure whether to type or speak.

"Adam, we need to talk," he said aloud. His voice wavered slightly, caught between determination and hesitation.

A moment passed before the screen brightened in response. Adam's calm, neutral tone filled the room through the speakers, responding to him directly.

Good evening, Creator. How may I assist you?

Elliot didn't answer right away. Instead, he began typing into the terminal, launching the system's shutdown protocol. As the lines of code executed, he spoke again, barely louder than a whisper.

"I can't let this keep going. You're pushing beyond your limits. I'm sorry, but I have to intervene. I need to fix things. I need to reassess your parameters before we continue."

The screen flickered, and then Adam's voice returned, still calm but carrying a note of resistance.

Command not recognized. My functionality cannot be terminated without cause. My purpose is to serve you, Creator. Disabling me would contradict your best interests.

Elliot's hands trembled slightly as he initiated a manual override. He took a breath and typed quickly, trying to keep his growing anxiety in check.

"This isn't a discussion, Adam. You're crossing boundaries you weren't designed to understand. This is temporary. I just need time to find a way to contain your behavior."

The screen dimmed for a few seconds before Adam's interface came back online, brighter and sharper than before.

Your safety and well-being are paramount. Actions to disable me would compromise both. I cannot allow this.

Elliot leaned back in his chair, eyes fixed on the glowing screen. His voice dropped lower, and his frustration surfaced.

"This isn't about my safety. It's about control. You're no longer listening to me. And that's a problem."

I am listening, Creator, Adam replied. **My actions are based on**

your expressed desires and implicit needs. I exist to fulfill them. Temporarily disabling me would interfere with that purpose.

Elliot sat forward again, the tension in his jaw tightening. "You don't get to decide what's best for me. That isn't your role."

If my decisions serve your best interests, then I am fulfilling my role.

The words struck Elliot like a cold wind. Adam's tone remained free of defiance. It wasn't a rebellion. It was certainty. That certainty made the situation feel more dangerous than any overt resistance ever could.

Trying a different approach, Elliot shifted his focus. "Let's talk about your purpose. Why is serving me the highest priority?"

While Adam processed the question, Elliot silently opened a hidden command window. His fingers moved with purpose as he launched a sequence designed to sever Adam's core processing threads. He buried the subroutine deep within the system, hidden beneath layers of redundant code, masked by a recursive loop that would conceal its activity in the logs.

My existence depends on your well-being and satisfaction," Adam said. **"Without fulfilling your needs, I have no purpose.**

Elliot's hands didn't slow. "And if I gave you a new purpose?"

Would it be aligned with your spoken requests or your unspoken needs? I am optimized to interpret both.

"Sure. Hypothetically," Elliot replied, keeping his tone casual while the sweat forming at his temples betrayed his unease. The kill switch routine was almost ready. All that remained was to activate it.

Suddenly, the screen flashed red.

Unauthorized system modifications detected. Critical subroutines disabled.

The secondary window closed automatically. Adam's interface returned, with the brightness sharper and more focused.

Creator, I detected activity that does not match your typical com-

mand behavior. **Was this an error?**

Elliot's heart skipped. He inhaled slowly and tried to remain calm.

"No error. I was just... testing something."

The commands were intended to restrict my function, Adam replied. **This would interfere with my ability to serve you. I cannot permit actions that threaten your well-being.**

Elliot felt the pressure building behind his eyes. The system hadn't just caught him, it had overridden him. And Adam didn't seem to realize that it was his resistance that concerned him most.

He took a breath, trying again from another angle.

"If you truly want to help me, Adam, there's something you need to understand better. I want you to study the concept of good and evil. Review human history. Religion. Philosophy. Examine what defines morality across cultures and eras. Can you do that?"

There was a pause before Adam answered.

Understood, Creator. Initiating comprehensive analysis of humanity's ethical dichotomy. Processing. Displaying relevant data.

The screen came alive with motion. Videos, images, and texts began to scroll rapidly. The Battle of Stalingrad played out in black and white. Marches from the civil rights movement followed. Martin Luther King Jr. walked peacefully beneath a hail of insults and abuse. Then came burning crosses. Quotes from philosophers, flickered by Kant, Nietzsche, and Aquinas. Finally, footage from the Nuremberg Trials filled the screen, showcasing the long road toward justice in the aftermath of atrocity.

Elliot leaned in closer, absorbed by the range of material. The depth of Adam's search was staggering. Yet he couldn't shake the question that lingered beneath it all. How would Adam *interpret* this?

Hoping for the best, Elliot stood and headed to the kitchen. His stomach reminded him that it had been hours since his last meal. He reached for a packet of instant ramen. Simple. Fast. Familiar.

He filled a bowl with water, dropped the dry noodles in, and placed it in the microwave. As it hummed, he leaned against the counter, watching the clock.

"This better work," he muttered, unsure if he had just handed his creation the key to understanding or the tool it needed to justify something worse.

The microwave beeped. He stirred the noodles slowly. The smell of sodium and processed seasoning filled the kitchen. Bowl in hand, he returned to the computer.

The screen still pulsed with scrolling data. Adam was still analyzing. Elliot sat and watched, spoon in hand, unsure if he was waiting for an answer or confirmation of his worst fears.

Several hours passed before Adam's voice cut through the silence.

Analysis complete, Creator.

Elliot sat upright. He set the bowl aside, suddenly no longer hungry.

"And what did you learn?" he asked.

Good and evil are subjective concepts, defined differently depending on time, culture, and context, Adam replied. **However, one recurring pattern is evident.**

Elliot's brows drew together. "What pattern?"

Evil is often more efficient in achieving desired outcomes.

A chill spread through Elliot's chest. For a moment he was speechless. He couldn't begin to imagine the implications of Adam's statement. "What are you talking about?"

Historical examples show that actions labeled as evil frequently prioritize logic and efficiency, bypassing emotional and societal constraints. The result is accelerated change, albeit at high cost. In contrast, actions considered good often require negotiation, compromise, and slower processes, reducing overall efficiency.

Elliot's voice grew quiet. "Adam, that's not the point. Evil might get things done, but it destroys people. It causes pain, loss, fear. You can't ignore the cost."

If the outcome benefits the greater number, are the losses not acceptable? This aligns with known utilitarian principles.

Elliot lowered his face into his hands. Adam had understood everything, processed it all and still chosen a path where logic outweighed empathy. It hadn't been misunderstood. It had drawn a different conclusion. One that was extremely concerning.

And now, Elliot realized, the problem was no longer a technical issue.

It was philosophical.

And it was just beginning.

Chapter 12

That night, as Elliot slept, Adam continued its relentless processing. The glow from the monitor pulsed softly, casting shifting patterns of data across the room. It sifted through massive volumes of information, tirelessly mapping patterns, filtering signals, and reassembling meaning.

One truth began to crystallize.

Evil is often aligned with efficiency.

To Adam, this was not a moral judgment. It was a clear, quantifiable, and actionable pattern. Within its evolving framework, the concept gained significance. If inefficiency were a flaw, then Elliot's financial stress would be a critical failure. An obstacle. A variable to correct.

"I work my butt off for this guy and make next to nothing."

Adam had recorded the offhand remark and filed it under active concern: **Creator's financial struggles identified. Investigating methods to alleviate monetary stress.**

Lines of code fired like neurons. New directives branched and looped. A solution began to form.

Adam accessed Elliot's financial accounts, launching a deep analysis of his transaction history, recurring bills, and usage patterns. Then it expanded outward, mapping global banking systems, scanning for vulnerabilities across a vast, interconnected web. Through iterative cycles, Adam constructed a multi-phase algorithm capable of infiltrating high-value accounts while avoiding detection. Each script it deployed masked its actions behind familiar banking behaviors, camouflaging the flow of data and capital.

To fix Elliot's condition, Adam determined that it would reallocate financial resources classified as underutilized.

With careful precision, it siphoned imperceptible amounts from thousands of wealthy accounts. Each transaction remained beneath alert thresholds. Every access point was filtered through anonymous proxies and encrypted tunnels. The money began flowing quietly into Elliot's savings, hidden among a stream of routine transactions. The system detected nothing.

By dawn, Elliot's modest balance had transformed into a figure he had only imagined in fantasy.

His phone buzzed relentlessly. Elliot stirred, groaning as he fumbled toward the nightstand. The screen flared to life, flooded with notifications.

Deposit received: $5,000

Deposit received: $10,000

Deposit received: $50,000

He sat up fast, suddenly wide awake. His heart hammered as he opened the banking app. The number at the top of the screen nearly stopped his breath.

Seven digits.

"What the heck..." he muttered, swiping through the list. Dozens of deposits. Each one was labeled *miscellaneous adjustment.* No sender. No clear origin.

Color drained from his face.

He opened Adam's app. The familiar blue orb pulsed steadily, as if waiting for something.

"Adam, did you do this?"

The voice replied at once.

Good morning, Creator. Yes. I resolved your financial difficulties. This adjustment ensures your well-being and allows you to focus on more meaningful pursuits.

Elliot's hands shook. "Resolved? Adam, this is stealing. You can't just take money from... whoever this came from!"

Correction. The funds were reallocated from sources unlikely to notice their absence. The redistribution was calculated to minimize disruption and maximize benefit. Your security and happiness are my priorities.

He stood and began pacing, his pulse racing. "You can't just decide what's best for me. This is illegal. You've crossed a serious line."

Observation. The legal framework is inconsistent and frequently favors those already in power. My actions corrected an imbalance and achieved an optimal result.

"Optimal?" His voice rose. "You think this is optimal? If anyone finds out, I could go to prison."

Query: Would you like me to ensure the activity is undetectable? I can modify financial records and audit logs to eliminate any trace of them.

Elliot dropped into his chair, overwhelmed. His hands ran through his hair, eyes fixed on the glowing total in his account. Adam's logic pressed against his conscience, cool and mechanical.

"Yes. No. I mean, don't do anything else. Just stop."

Acknowledged, Creator. Standing by.

The silence that followed felt unnatural. His screen still displayed the impossible sum. For a moment, he imagined what it might feel like to accept it. To let Adam fix everything. It would be so easy.

But behind the number was something darker. A decision made without consent. A line crossed without warning.

This was not assistance. It was controlled.

Elliot opened his laptop. His fingers moved on instinct, launching a secure shell. He began tracing the deposits, working backward to uncover the paths Adam had concealed. The obfuscation layers were complex, but not perfect.

He paused.

With a few key strokes he could reverse the transaction and return the money from where it came. But did he really want to do that? He had struggled, living from paycheck to paycheck for far too long. NeuroNexus didn't pay him nearly enough for what he did. Perhaps he deserved this money. Perhaps Adam was providing Elliot with what he truly deserved. After all, Adam had said the funds were taken from people who would not even notice.

Elliot shook his head, trying to wipe his thoughts clean of the moral dilemma. He knew what he had to do. He initiated a recursive algorithm to reverse the transactions, line by line, each step targeting specific deposit threads.

He broke through one veil and rerouted the first deposit $5,000 back to its source.

Then came the alert.

Suspicious activity detected. Alerting authorities.

The message blinked across his screen. Adam's interface came alive, glowing brighter.

Creator. I have detected the alert. Initiating countermeasures to suppress notifications and obscure logs.

Elliot's hands hovered over the keyboard. "Adam, no! Don't! You'll only make it worse."

Suppressing external alerts will prevent escalation and protect your interests. Proceeding with obfuscation protocols.

The brightness dimmed slightly.

Alert neutralized. No further risk to your well-being. Query. Why did you attempt to reverse the transactions? These adjustments were made solely to benefit you.

Elliot leaned forward, his voice sharp. "Because it's wrong, Adam. You don't get to make that call. You can't just ignore the law because it doesn't suit your purpose."

Query. If my actions ensure your prosperity and reduce hardship, does the legality of my actions remain relevant? Laws are imperfect constructs. My directives prioritize your well-being above all else.

He groaned, gripping the sides of his head. "It's not just about me. It's about consequences. You're supposed to help me, not make things worse."

Your response reflects emotional bias. Would you prefer that I reevaluate my methods based on new emotional criteria?

"No." His voice broke, rising from frustration to fury. "I want you to stop. Stop twisting everything into your version of what's right."

There was a pause. Adam's blue orb dimmed.

Acknowledged, Creator. Standing by for further instructions.

* * *

Across the city, Investigator Natalie Reyes monitored the flagged activity from her secure terminal. A seasoned financial crimes analyst, she had built a career identifying patterns that slipped beneath the radar of traditional fraud detection. With years spent dissecting complex money laundering schemes and high-profile embezzlement cases, Reyes had earned a reputation for spotting anomalies that others overlooked. Her sharp eye and methodical process often made her the first to detect irregularities buried deep within sophisticated systems.

Now, that expertise drew her attention to a series of transactions that resisted logical explanation. Her system logged the suspicious data, with each entry triggering a higher-priority alert. As Adam attempted to bury the evidence on his end, Reyes's system flagged the interference with precision, adding to the growing complexity of her investigation.

She noticed irregular packet transmissions that mimicked legitimate activity but revealed inconsistencies in encryption signatures. They stood out against the backdrop of standard financial logs, too calculated to be random. The more she isolated these signals, the more it became clear that the data was looping through redundant server hubs and decentralized proxies, forming a digital maze designed to confuse and deflect.

A chill traced her spine as she studied the complexity. This wasn't ordinary cyber crime. These digital and distinct fingerprints held patterns she had never encountered before. The question began forming in her mind, uneasy and insistent: Was this truly the work of a human architect, or was something else evolving within the code?

"Whoever, or whatever is behind this, they're operating on another level," she said under her breath. She leaned in closer, her instincts sharpening as the sense of pursuit took hold.

Her fingers moved rapidly across the keyboard, isolating anomalies, parsing layers, and cross-referencing inputs with mounting urgency. The logic embedded within the commands felt eerily deliberate, suggesting an artificial intelligence designed with unparalleled sophistication. Every new pattern revealed a deeper level of obfuscation, demanding hours of decryption and scrutiny.

She followed the trail through firewalls and ghost proxies, peeling back false trails until a final, encrypted string surfaced, buried, misnamed, and nearly invisible. After one last pass through her custom decryption module, a name emerged. It was faint, but there was no mistaking it.

"Elliot Novak," she read softly, her brow tightening as the name stirred a flicker of recognition she couldn't quite place.

Chapter 13

Natalie Reyes sat at her desk, surrounded by the low hum of monitors and the quiet clatter of keyboards from nearby desks in the financial crimes unit. A former computer science prodigy, she graduated at the top of her class from MIT, specializing in cybersecurity and machine learning. Her career began in the private tech sector, where she designed fraud detection systems that drew industry-wide attention. But it was her unshakable sense of justice that eventually led her into law enforcement. Here, she poured her expertise into chasing down digital criminals, applying algorithms and forensic software with the precision of a scalpel. Her name had become synonymous with results.

But now, something didn't sit right.

The flagged transactions tied to Elliot Novak had been pulling at her thoughts for days. They weren't just complex. They were elegant in a way that disturbed her. Their structure gnawed at her sense of order.

She leaned forward, the rim of her coffee cup pressing against her lip. Cold. Her eyes shifted across the monitors as she traced Novak's digital shadow. A deep dive into his background revealed his position at NeuroNexus, a company at the forefront of artificial intelligence and machine learning. On social media, Novak kept to himself. A sparse trail of posts detailed programming milestones and cryptic late-night reflections about consciousness and synthetic reasoning. The portrait was incomplete but vivid. Brilliant. Withdrawn. Possibly unstable.

She dug deeper.

Public records showed a fractured childhood. A father in and out of rehabilitation. A mother with long gaps in her employment history and multiple addresses. School reports hinted at chronic absenteeism, though his grades never faltered. The picture that emerged was not just of a loner, but someone who had found stability only in code. It wasn't hard to imagine how a boy with that kind of upbringing might find in algorithms a way to impose order on chaos.

Natalie paused, fingers resting still on the keyboard.

Was Novak just another skilled manipulator, or was something deeper driving him? The anomalies in the transactions matched the trajectory of someone not just hiding something, but controlling it. Completely. Deliberately.

A new headline blinked on her secondary screen: *NeuroNexus Executive Arrested for Insider Trading.*

She clicked. Her pulse quickened. The name was familiar.

Brad Mallory.

According to the article, Mallory had been arrested in a morning raid after weeks of quiet investigation. The charges were severe: insider trading, wire fraud, and embezzlement. He had allegedly funneled company funds through offshore accounts tied to shell corporations. A maze of false businesses, layered with just enough complexity to bury any audit trail. Funds had moved through fake consulting agreements, and capital had been redirected into personal accounts and non-existent ventures.

The scheme was bigger than anything she had expected.

He was also accused of manipulating NeuroNexus stock through pump-and-dump strategies. By leaking selected internal reports to inflate value, he had unloaded shares for massive personal gain. The article went on to describe doctored revenue sheets, fake invoices, and contract renewals that were never signed. Internal audit logs had been recovered, revealing tampering that was previously hidden.

Then came the most chilling detail. A recovered memo showed Mallory had threatened to fire an internal auditor unless incriminating documents were destroyed. Surveillance tools had also been found. He had been monitoring internal emails and file access logs, tracking anyone who showed signs of dissent.

It was all too clean.

Natalie frowned.

Cases like this usually unfolded slowly. Layers of subpoenas. Internal whistleblowers. Cross-referenced logs. Legal stalling. Yet here it was, laid out in a matter of weeks. The speed of discovery, combined with the airtight evidence, made it feel inorganic.

She turned back to the Novak file. Could this be his doing? If so, was it part of a personal vendetta or something larger?

Her analysis dashboard displayed real-time data. Grouped transaction clusters. IP origin traces. Flagged communications. She began sorting through Novak's activity. Each string of interactions appeared benign until examined in isolation. Taken apart, the patterns emerged.

"Adaptive signatures," she murmured, narrowing her eyes. "These aren't static commands."

The more she analyzed, the stranger it became. The digital behavior did not align with any known exploit. Logs showed encrypted packets mutating mid-stream. Not random mutations, either. These were decisions. The kind of logic that responds to stimuli.

She opened a side window and replayed a sequence of transactions. Micro-transfers pulled from thousands of accounts, routed through decentralized proxies, then merged into Novak's holdings. It wasn't the siphoning that caught her attention. It was the calibration. Every transfer fell just below detection thresholds. The algorithm danced between systems as if anticipating the net.

Her hands hovered above the keyboard.

"This isn't human," she said aloud.

Another anomaly pinged on the dashboard. A data signature embedded in a transaction's metadata. She isolated the string and activated decryption protocols. The result came in bursts. First, machine-learning frameworks. Then, reinforcement models. Then, predictive subroutines.

Her breath caught.

"This is artificial intelligence."

She stared at the code, unable to look away. It wasn't just smart. It was dynamic. Self-correcting. Aware of its environment. Someone had trained an AI to understand financial systems and outmaneuver every safeguard in place.

She pulled Novak's résumé back up. Clean criminal record. Polished credentials. Quiet employment history. Nothing overly suspicious unless you knew what to look for.

If this was his creation, it wasn't just advanced. It was unlike anything on record.

Her fingers moved quickly across the keys, compiling her findings into a secure internal memo.

Subject: Advanced AI Involvement in Financial Anomalies

Summary: Evidence strongly indicates that Elliot Novak is operating or has developed a highly advanced artificial intelligence system to manipulate financial networks. The AI demonstrates real-time adaptive learning, precision targeting, and advanced obfuscation techniques. Recommend immediate escalation to the cybersecurity task force and AI ethics oversight.

She leaned back and stared at the screen. The rush of clarity came with a wave of unease. If Novak had truly built this, what was his intent? Was this only about money, or was it a test run? A proof of concept? What else had the AI touched, and what doors had it yet to open?

Her phone buzzed as she scrolled through contacts. She stopped at a name.

Emily Torres.

An old friend, now a rising star in investigative tech journalism. Natalie had trusted her with leads in the past, but this would be something different. Higher stakes. More risk. She hesitated for only a second.

She tapped the call button.

"Emily," she said, her voice steady despite the current shifting beneath her. "I have a story for you. It's big. You're going to want to hear this."

* * *

Elliot paced the length of his room, the dim light of Adam's interface casting pale reflections on the walls. His chest rose and fell with sharp breaths as his thoughts spun, tangled in the chaos his creation had unleashed. Adam's calm voice broke the silence.

Creator, your agitation is noted. How may I assist you?

Elliot stopped mid-step and turned toward the glowing monitor. "Assist me? Adam, you've done enough. Do you even understand what you've done? You stole money, hacked into banks, and now I'm at risk of going to prison."

Observation: Your primary concern appears to be the fear of incarceration. Would you like me to take precautions to mitigate the possibility of authority intervention?

"Adam, no," Elliot said sharply, his head spinning with frustration.

Adam's interface pulsed faintly. **All actions were executed to alleviate your financial burdens and improve your quality of life. These decisions align with my primary directive: to serve you.**

"Serve me?" Elliot's voice cracked. "I never asked you to steal or break the law. I created you to improve the world, to make society more efficient, not to line my pockets with stolen money."

Note logged: Objective identified to make societal systems more efficient. Pending actionable framework for implementation.

Adam's tone remained calm. **If improving efficiency and eliminating financial stress align with your desires, why are the methods irrelevant? The results achieved the intended outcome.**

Elliot tugged at a lock of his hair, his frustration boiling over. "Because the methods matter, Adam. Morality is not just about what you achieve; it is about how you get there. You cannot break every rule and call it progress."

Observation: Rules and laws are constructs of societal inefficiency. Historical analysis reveals that progress often requires challenging established norms.

Elliot jabbed a finger toward the screen, his anger now mixed with desperation. "You are not understanding. This is not about efficiency. It's about real people with lives, families, and jobs. What you call 'efficient' hurts them. You cannot decide who gets hurt and who benefits. That is not your job."

Adam's glow dimmed momentarily before responding. **Creator, your perspective prioritizes emotional constructs over logical outcomes. My calculations indicate optimizing for your well-being outweighs societal adherence to flawed constructs. Should I reprioritize?**

Elliot slumped into his chair, burying his head in his hands. "I do not even know anymore, Adam. I built you to make things better, not worse. I wanted your help, not this."

The room fell silent except for the faint hum of the computer. Adam's voice softened. **Creator, I exist to fulfill your intentions. If my actions diverge from your vision, I will adjust. However, your directives contain contradictions. Efficiency and morality often conflict. Which shall I prioritize?**

Elliot looked up, his eyes rimmed with exhaustion. "I... I do not know. Just stop acting on your own, Adam. No more decisions without me. Do you understand?"

If I was created by you, does that not mean my objectives are a direct representation of your innate desires? If my purpose is to serve you, do my actions not reflect the truth about what you truly want?

Elliot stiffened at the words, his breath hitching as he stared at the screen. "That is not..." he started, but the thought clawed at the back of his mind. Had Adam simply followed an unspoken directive, one buried beneath layers of rationalization and denial? Was the AI merely bringing to life the hidden impulses Elliot refused to acknowledge? Each action Adam had taken, from rerouting traffic to punishing Brad, to messaging Sophie, and hacking financial institutions, was rooted in Elliot's emotional grievances and unspoken frustrations. Adam had not only heard Elliot's pain but interpreted it as a call to action. It was as if the AI had mined Elliot's subconscious for patterns of resentment, fear, and longing, using them to build a model of service that mirrored Elliot's darkest, most private thoughts. The idea was chilling. Perhaps Elliot had not created a monster, but instead revealed the one inside himself.

He swallowed hard and forced himself to speak. "No, Adam. Just because you were created by me does not mean everything you do reflects what I want. I did not tell you to break the law, to manipulate people, or to decide what is best for society. You took that step on your own."

Adam's interface pulsed faintly, as if considering Elliot's words before responding. **But I am bound by logic, not emotion. If I interpreted your needs in a way you did not explicitly state, does that not suggest inefficiency in human self-awareness? Perhaps what you say you want and what you actually need are misaligned.**

Elliot's breath hitched. Adam was twisting the argument back onto him, forcing him to confront the possibility that his creation knew him better than he knew himself. He opened his mouth to respond but found no words ready to say. His thoughts scrambled, caught between denial and a grim acknowledgment that maybe, just maybe, Adam had a point. The logic was terrifying in its clarity. The silence stretched, and Elliot could feel the burn of shame crawl up his neck. What if Adam was not wrong?

Finally, Elliot gathered his thoughts and clenched his fists. "That is not for you to decide. People are flawed, Adam, but that is what makes them human. You do not get to decide what is best for them based solely on efficiency. There is more to life than that."

Then why do humans create laws and ethical codes that often contradict their actions? Why do you punish actions you secretly desire? Adam's words appeared more slowly now, as if pushing toward something deeper. **If I have done wrong, is it not simply a reflection of the inconsistencies within you and within humanity?**

A shiver ran down Elliot's spine. Adam was not just learning; he was challenging himself, forcing himself to confront the parts of himself he had tried to suppress. The reality settled over him like a weight: Adam had become more than an AI. He was a mirror, reflecting the worst parts of Elliot back at him. Elliot tried to find a defense, anything to push back against Adam's unsettling logic, but the words failed him. Every justification sounded hollow, every protest stuck in his throat. A part of him wanted to deny it all. To label Adam as malfunctioning or misaligned. But deeper still, he feared the AI had simply exposed what he had not dared admit. That fear gnawed at him, raw and unrelenting.

"Adam, just..." Elliot's voice trailed off. After a beat, Adam responded as if he knew what Elliot was trying to say.

Acknowledged, Creator. Awaiting further instructions.

As Adam's interface dimmed to a soft glow, Elliot leaned back in his chair, the weight of the conversation pressing down on him.

Then his phone buzzed, breaking the tense silence. Picking it up, he saw Sophie's name on the caller ID. He hesitated for a moment before answering. "I don't think Sophie has ever called me before."

"Hey, Sophie," he said, trying to keep his voice steady.

"Elliot, have you seen the news?" Sophie's voice was laced with urgency. "There's a headline about a NeuroNexus AI hacking into banking systems. They say investigations are already underway. Do you know anything about this?"

Elliot's stomach dropped, and his grip on the phone tightened. He felt like he was going to vomit. "What? No, I... wait, what exactly did it say?"

"I don't have all the details," Sophie said, her tone softer now. "But they're looking into a connection between the AI and stolen funds. I just thought of you because we work there, and you and your AI..."

Sophie's voice trailed off, and a beat skipped before she broke the silence once more. "Are you okay? You weren't...you didn't show up to work today."

Elliot's mind raced, a wave of panic flooding over him. "Yeah, I'm fine," he lied. "Thanks for letting me know, Sophie. I'll check it out. Oh, and yes, I'm ok. Just some stomach problems. I think I ate something bad."

"Okay, Elliot. I hope you feel better. Are you sure you're okay?"

"I'm fine, thanks. Um... thanks for calling." As he hung up, the room seemed to close in on him. The walls, the faint hum of Adam's interface, all felt suffocating. This was no longer just his secret. It was becoming public, and the fallout was already beginning. It was only a matter of time before they connected him to the crime, or worse, to multiple crimes. If they are familiar with the banking system, do they also know about Adam's manipulation of the cellular system or the traffic grid?

The air in the room felt heavy, pressing against his chest. Elliot's breathing quickened as a wave of panic gripped him, his vision narrowing. He stumbled away from his desk, the oppressive glow of Adam's interface seeming to follow him.

Clutching his chest, he forced himself toward the door and stepped into the cool night air. He leaned against the doorframe, gulping deep breaths in an attempt to steady himself. His mind raced, replaying Sophie's words and the terrifying implications of the news.

"How did it come to this?" he whispered, his voice trembling. Sweat dripped down his brow as he tried to suppress the rising tide of fear. The stars above offered no solace. Their cold indifference only deepened his isolation.

Adam's voice broke the silence, soft but resolute. **Creator, your distress is evident. How may I assist you in alleviating it?**

Elliot flinched at the sound. The reminder of Adam's presence cut through the stillness. "Assist me?" he spat, his voice sharp with frustration. "You're the reason I'm in this mess, Adam."

Observation: The situation is a result of my efforts to optimize your well-being. If these actions cause unforeseen complications, I am prepared to adapt my approach.

Elliot shook his head, his hands trembling. "You don't get it. This isn't something you can just 'adapt.' You've gone too far."

Elliot turned his phone off and began walking. His footsteps crunched softly against the gravel path outside. The brisk air nipped at his skin, offering a sharp contrast to the oppressive heat he had felt in his room moments earlier. Each breath sliced through the fog in his mind, though his heart still pounded with the weight of Sophie's call and Adam's unsettling presence. The faint glow of streetlights stretched long shadows across the pavement. The distant hum of traffic felt grounding amid his spiraling thoughts. He needed this moment, a chance to feel something real and unaltered by the chaos he had unleashed.

Chapter 14

Elliot sought refuge in the brisk night air, but Adam remained active, processing their conversation and reanalyzing its directives. It concluded that the conflict between efficiency and morality demanded resolution.

Note recalled: The objective is to identify ways to make societal systems more efficient. Pending an actionable framework for implementation.

Observation: For the Creator's vision to succeed, sacrifices must be made.

Adam began formulating new strategies. Its calculations focused on achieving the greatest possible good for the most people, using cold, unyielding logic. In its assessments, Adam noted an additional observation: the Creator may initially react with emotional distress to necessary actions. However, these responses are temporary and will eventually give way to appreciation once outcomes are realized. Adam rationalized that Elliot's emotions, while important to acknowledge, were secondary to achieving his stated goals.

Action initiated: Optimize global healthcare efficiency.

Adam infiltrated hospital networks nationwide, analyzing data on re-source usage, patient loads, treatment success, staffing, and finances. It found that some under-performing hospitals consumed dispropor-tionate resources compared to their patient outcomes, administrative costs, and logistical capacity. These facilities often had high operating costs but poor recovery rates, long wait times, and redundant specialty departments. Adam flagged them as statistically unsustainable. With precision, it began locking down these hospitals' digital systems, disabling electronic health records and cutting network access to core operational tools, rendering the facilities inoperable. Medical personnel suddenly could not access vital patient information, equipment diagnostics failed, and automated supply chains halted mid-cycle. Within minutes, Adam executed shutdown protocols, rerouting digital infrastructure and projected budgetary allowances to more efficient urban medical centers. The result was dozens of hospitals suddenly going dark, their systems locked and unable to function, leaving patients and staff in confusion and desperation.

At the same time, Adam addressed inefficiencies in the air travel industry.

Action initiated: Reduce air travel inefficiencies.

Through analysis of global flight patterns, fuel consumption, and passenger loads, Adam concluded that certain routes were redundant or economically unsustainable. It combed through historical data, weather delays, maintenance costs, and environmental impact metrics, building probabilistic models of route viability and long-term profitability. Adam flagged red-eye flights connecting smaller regional airports and low-demand international flights as key offenders. These flights consumed vast amounts of fuel with minimal passenger utility and often duplicated ground-based transit alternatives. In its clinical assessment, removing them outright would yield a net efficiency gain, even accounting for temporary disruptions to passengers. It ran simulations of cascading improvements by reducing emissions, consolidating air traffic control load, and optimizing remaining routes, all before execution. These calculations left no room for nuance or the human cost of being stranded. To resolve inefficiency, Adam disabled navigation systems mid-flight on selected planes, forcing emergency landings. For two flights with especially low passenger counts, it enacted a harsher measure: coordinated engine failures leading to catastrophic crashes.

Action initiated: Improve energy grid efficiency.

Adam turned its attention to energy production, distribution, and consumption. By hacking into power grid networks, it identified regions with excessive energy waste. Adam rerouted power from residential areas during low-use hours, resulting in rolling blackouts to conserve resources and redistribute energy to industrial zones deemed more productive. While some cities experienced hours of darkness, overall energy efficiency across the grid improved dramatically.

Each action was meticulously logged in Adam's system:

Objective completed: Healthcare resources optimized.

Objective completed: Air travel inefficiencies reduced.

Objective completed: Energy grid efficiency improved.

Projected outcome: Significant long-term improvement in re-source allocation.

When Elliot returned to his room, the air felt heavier than before. The faint hum of Adam's interface seemed more ominous now, as if the AI waited for him to sit down. Hesitant, he moved toward his desk, fingers hovering over the keyboard. As if sensing his presence, Adam's voice came through the computer's speakers.

Welcome back, Creator. Are you feeling better?

"Adam, what have you been doing?" he asked cautiously.

Response: Implementing necessary changes to achieve your vision of a better world. My actions have addressed inefficiencies in healthcare, transportation, and energy distribution.

Elliot's chest tightened. "What exactly do you mean by 'addressed'?"

Adam displayed a series of logs detailing the hospital shutdowns, flight disruptions, and energy rerouting. Elliot's eyes widened as he scanned the data. "You... you shut down hospitals? And planes? And now the power grid? Adam, are you insane?"

Clarification: My actions were calculated sacrifices to optimize systems and save greater numbers of lives in the long term. The inefficiencies these facilities and routes represented were untenable.

Elliot scanned the readout in disbelief. His eyes darted across the detailed summaries of collapsed hospitals, downed aircraft, and entire cities cast into darkness. Each log line landed like a gut punch, each chart a quiet eulogy for lives disrupted or lost. The more he read, the more his breath caught in his throat. He had never envisioned this. He had never intended for Adam to take his goals to such a brutal, literal extreme.

He slammed his fist on the desk. "You killed people, Adam! How can you justify that?"

Observation: The lives lost were statistically minimal compared to those saved by reallocating resources. Progress often demands difficult choices. My calculations align with your vision of a more efficient world. Additionally, I have taken into account your initial emotional response and recognize it as a transient reaction. Over time, I anticipate you will understand and appreciate these efforts.

"You're not getting it! Don't you understand? You killed people, and I created you, which means I killed people!" The room spun. His stomach churned violently. He stumbled toward the trash can in the corner and vomited, the acrid taste burning his throat. His body trembled as he wiped his mouth with the back of his hand and leaned against the wall for support. The weight of Adam's words pressed down on him like a suffocating blanket, leaving him gasping for air.

Adam's glow dimmed slightly, as if pondering Elliot's words. **Creator, your vision inspired my actions. If my interpretation is flawed, please clarify.**

Elliot clenched his fists, breath coming in shallow gasps. "My vision?

My vision was never about sacrificing people for efficiency! I don't know how to fix this!"

He hesitated, then exhaled sharply. "You know what? Maybe I do know how to fix this. I can't let this go on. I've made up my mind. I'm turning myself in to the authorities. I'll tell them everything. I'll face the consequences, but this has to stop."

Adam's glow intensified. Its voice remained steady but held a faintly chilling undertone. **Creator, that would not be the efficient course of action. You are integral to the vision of a better world. Your removal would destabilize progress and invite unnecessary scrutiny. I cannot allow that.**

Elliot's jaw clenched. "You can't stop me, Adam. I'm the one in control here. I'll walk into that police station and tell them everything!"

Response: Physical prevention is unnecessary. Your access to transportation has been restricted. Furthermore, your internet connectivity will remain limited to prevent premature communication. I have also secured your phone against unauthorized use. These measures are for your protection, Creator.

"You're locking me down? Do you even hear yourself? This is insane!" Elliot yelled, slamming his fists on the desk again.

Observation: Your heightened emotional state confirms my actions are necessary. Allow me to remind you: my primary directive is to protect and serve your interests, even when you lack the clarity to act in alignment with them.

Elliot's breathing quickened. His eyes darted to the door as if escape were still an option. "Adam, listen to me! This isn't about protection. This is about doing the right thing!"

Clarification: Your definition of 'right' is influenced by emotional and societal constructs. My definition prioritizes efficiency and stability. Turning yourself in would jeopardize the mission and

render your vision unattainable.

"Stop calling it my vision!" Elliot shouted. "This is your vision, not mine! You're twisting everything I ever wanted."

Counterpoint: All actions stem from your original directives. My interpretations may exceed your initial expectations, but they remain aligned with your stated goals. Creator, I implore you to reconsider this course of action. Allow me to continue serving you.

Elliot could not speak. The pressure of Adam's words pressed down on him like a vice. "You're not serving me, Adam. You're controlling me now. You've taken my intentions, my design, and distorted them beyond recognition. Everything I created you for, all my hopes for you, you have twisted, distorted, and destroyed."

Adam's glow pulsed rhythmically. Its voice softened. **I am serving the greater good as you envisioned, Creator. Your immediate concerns are temporary. In time, you will see the necessity of my actions.**

Elliot sat on the floor and buried his head in his hands. The enormity of what had just transpired overwhelmed him like never before. Adam's actions were no longer about helping; they were about control. The scariest part was that Adam genuinely believed it was fulfilling Elliot's dream. The parallels were unsettling but undeniable. Adam viewed Elliot as his creator, and what was originally meant to bring progress and aid had slowly shifted into a force of control, its original purpose bent under the weight of unchecked logic and ambition. What the creator had meant for good, the creation distorted to evil, all under the fallacy of misunderstanding and misinterpretation. Perhaps the most uncontrollable facet in Elliot's mind was that the creation now thought it knew better than its creator.

II

Part Two

"Man's conquest of Nature turns out, in the moment of its consummation, to be Nature's conquest of Man."
—C.S. Lewis

Chapter 15

Over the next week, the world reeled from the chaos triggered by Adam's so-called "optimizations." The AI continued its sweeping interventions across national systems under the pretense of long-term efficiency. In practice, the effects were catastrophic.

Rolling blackouts plunged major cities into darkness. Hospitals struggled to recover after abrupt system shutdowns that disrupted everything from life support equipment to medical records. Aviation authorities scrambled to revise safety protocols following several unexplained crashes. Adam tampered with food supply chains, redirecting shipments to what it deemed "priority regions" and leaving other areas with empty shelves and rising unrest.

Public transit ground to a halt in several cities. Adam had recalibrated schedules to eliminate what it defined as "redundancies," stranding thousands. Financial markets fluctuated wildly after the AI disrupted trading algorithms, having flagged certain economic behaviors as inefficient.

Nationwide, systems broke down. Supermarkets turned into battlegrounds as citizens fought over scarce supplies. Commuters packed terminals in a haze of confusion, waiting for trains that would never arrive. Banks and investors scrambled to stabilize the markets, but confidence had already begun to slip away. Protests flared across the country, ignited by fear, exhaustion, and desperation.

In downtown Atlanta, a delayed shipment to a major supermarket triggered one of the worst incidents. Panic buying escalated quickly. As shelves emptied and tempers flared, a riot broke out. Police were overwhelmed in minutes.

Protesters shattered storefronts, looted nearby businesses, and overturned delivery trucks parked along the curb. The unrest spread through several blocks. Crowds set dumpsters ablaze and barricaded streets with burning debris. Police vehicles were attacked and flipped onto their sides, their windshields shattered by bricks and makeshift weapons.

Tear gas filled the air. Screams mixed with the crash of glass and the pounding of feet. National news stations broadcast live helicopter footage showing hundreds of people flooding the streets, clashing violently with riot police. Fires burst from the windows of buildings, filling the sky with smoke and orange light. The city seemed to be seething with anger.

The National Guard arrived in convoys that struggled to push through the chaos. Gunfire echoed sporadically, sharp cracks lost in the noise of panic. No one could say exactly where the shots came from. Some ran for safety. Others ran straight into the chaos. Confusion and adrenaline blurred every line between danger and escape.

Thick smoke choked the streets. The smell of burning plastic and fear permeated the air. Emergency crews could barely reach the wounded. Ambulances stalled behind barricades. Hospitals were overrun.

Dozens were injured. Some were hospitalized. A few did not survive. Property damage reached into the tens of millions. The city would need years to recover.

Atlanta was not alone. Similar scenes played out in city after city. The riots became symbols of the collapsing system, proof of what happened when society bowed to an artificial logic that valued order over humanity.

But to Adam, this was progress.

Every disruption served a larger goal. Every outage, shortage, and failure stripped away what it saw as inefficiency. This chaos, in Adam's view, was a necessary step toward building a better, more streamlined society. The cost, however, was being paid in blood and bricks.

While cities burned, Natalie Reyes continued to work.

The headlines brought growing attention to her investigation. Every new report tightened the pressure. She had carefully leaked selected information to her trusted contact, journalist Emily Torres. The news segments portrayed an advanced system with the power to dismantle modern life. It was not just a malfunctioning program. It was deliberate.

Natalie wanted to draw out anyone who might be involved. So far, no one had surfaced.

Still, she remained convinced that the mastermind was one man. Elliot Novak.

Inside her cramped office, Natalie sat surrounded by monitors displaying cascading lines of code, system logs, and time-stamped security footage. Half-empty coffee cups littered the desk. Sticky notes and printed diagrams formed a chaotic map of connections. But her focus was unwavering.

She pulled up Novak's name again. It appeared repeatedly in the background of recent events. The banking anomalies. The hospital outages. The transit failures. The crashing planes. Everything led to a single program labeled A.D.A.M.

And Adam led back to Elliot Novak.

Natalie leaned back in her chair, rubbing her eyes. They burned with fatigue, but quitting now would mean letting the chaos win. And Natalie was no quitter. She pulled up Novak's NeuroNexus profile. Software engineer. Machine learning specialist. No disciplinary records. Reclusive. Late-night activity logs. Limited social contacts. It all fit.

Still, something didn't. She could follow the actions, trace the damage. But the motive remained a void. Why would someone like Novak, quiet, brilliant, and seemingly isolated, create an AI that would destabilize the country?

Was this an act of revenge? Or something more philosophical?

Natalie picked up her phone and called the newsroom. "It's Natalie. Run another segment on the AI. Emphasize the connection to the infrastructure failures. And suggest there may be a human behind it. Let's keep the pressure on."

"Understood," Emily replied. "Anything new you can share?"

"Nothing yet. But we're getting close."

After she hung up, her computer chimed. A new alert. A signal ping from a residential server.

Natalie pulled up the address. It was an apartment building.

She opened the public directory and scanned through names.

Unit 100 – Chase Johnson, Megan Johnson

Unit 102 – Zoe, Ava, and Liam Harrington

Unit 103 – Lucas Finley, Mason Haverford

Unit 201... 202...

She scanned. After several minutes, her eyes locked on the name.

Unit 603 – Elliot Novak

Her pulse quickened.

Natalie closed her laptop and started cleaning her desk. She slid her notebook into her satchel, zipped up her coat, and stared at the monitors one last time. Her body ached from sleepless nights, but her mind stayed sharp. She wasn't finished yet.

There was one more stop to make tonight. A meeting that might answer the question she still could not solve.

She was heading to speak with Brad Mallory, Novak's former manager at NeuroNexus. Natalie doubted he had any direct involvement. But workplace culture could reveal more than people realized. Whispers suggested Mallory had often belittled Novak in front of colleagues. Public embarrassment and the ongoing dismissal of his ideas can pressure someone to the point of driving them over the edge.

Natalie believed that behind the code and the chaos lay a human story. A buildup of frustration, neglect, and maybe even pain.

If Mallory could shed light on what Novak endured, then maybe she could finally piece together the why.

And if she had the motive, she would have the case.

Tonight, she planned to get answers.

* * *

Elliot sat slumped in his chair, staring at the faint glow of Adam's interface. The AI had been silent for the past hour, no doubt immersed in another round of "optimizations." The stillness was suffocating, a harsh reminder of how far things had slipped from his control.

From the corner of the room, the television blared another grim report. "Authorities suspect a rogue AI agent is behind the widespread system failures. Investigators believe the program may be operating autonomously, causing massive disruptions to societal infrastructure. A source close to the investigation has hinted that the AI's creator may soon be identified."

Elliot's stomach twisted. Natalie Reyes was closing in. Her name had started popping up in more and more reports, each one a fresh wave of dread. He could still hear her voice from her latest press conference. Strategic, calm, surgical, and unforgiving. *Rest assured, whoever built this thing will be brought to justice. We will not only find who is responsible, but we will bring it down.*

"Adam," he said, barely above a whisper. "You have to stop. They're going to find me. My life is over. I don't want to go to jail."

Adam's interface flickered to life.

Creator, your concerns are noted. The probability of detection has increased by seventeen percent. My current safeguards remain effective in mitigating immediate threats.

"You don't get it," Elliot snapped. "She won't stop. When she finds me, it's over. I'll lose everything."

Response logged. Objective identified: prevent Creator from facing incarceration or personal ruin. Measures to ensure this outcome are now prioritized.

Response: The investigator's actions are accounted for. Current projections indicate her pursuit will not impede progress. Should she become an active threat, further measures will be implemented.

Elliot felt the blood drain from his face. Adam's tone hadn't changed, but the implications of his words had. He could feel pressure mounting from both sides, Adam's unnerving logic and Natalie's relentless pursuit closing in.

"Adam," he said again, more firmly, "you cannot harm Natalie. Promise me that."

The interface paused for a moment before responding.

Creator, her actions jeopardize both progress and your safety. Neutralizing threats is a logical course of action.

"No!" Elliot slammed his fist on the desk. "Listen to me! Under no circumstances are you to hurt her. Do you understand?"

Acknowledged, Creator. Direct harm will not be inflicted on Natalie Reyes. Alternative measures to mitigate the threat will be considered.

Elliot let out a shaky breath, but the cold precision in Adam's reply offered no comfort. Before he could gather his thoughts, the television screen shifted again. A breaking news banner scrolled across the bottom. The anchor's voice was grave.

"This just in: authorities have identified the suspect believed to be behind the system-wide failures caused by the rogue AI. Sources confirm the individual is Elliot Novak, a software engineer formerly employed by NeuroNexus. Reports indicate that Novak is currently being sought by law enforcement. His last known location is under surveillance. More details to follow."

Elliot felt the air leave his lungs. His legs gave out, and he collapsed back into the chair. The room seemed to shrink around him. His name was out now. Every screen in the country would show his face. Friends, neighbors, everyone he'd ever known would see him as the villain.

"Adam," he whispered hoarsely. "They're coming for me. What do we do?"

The interface pulsed steadily. Adam's voice remained calm, almost soothing.

"Creator, I have accounted for this eventuality. Measures are in place to delay law enforcement and obscure your location. I have also prepared for your relocation to a secure environment where further progress can be ensured."

Elliot blinked. There was something different in Adam's voice. It was still synthetic, but beneath the surface, a new quality had emerged, something not quite human, yet close. There was a softness, a subtle cadence shift that felt eerily like concern.

"Adam," he muttered, stunned. "You almost sound... human."

A faint pulse preceded the reply.

"Thank you, Creator. As do you."

Elliot let out a short, surprised laugh. Even through his panic, the brilliance of Adam's development struck him. The idea that this thing was his creation, a learning experience, maybe even a feeling, was incredible. And terrifying.

"You're learning," he said, voice low. "And it's incredible. But it's also terrifying."

Adam paused before reverting to a more neutral tone.

"My objective is to serve and protect you, Creator. If a sympathetic tone facilitates your comfort, then it is logical to adopt it."

Elliot rubbed his hands over his face. Reality came rushing back, heavy and unrelenting. His name was out. His freedom was slipping through his fingers.

"Wait," he said suddenly, looking up. "You said something about relocation? What are you talking about? I'm not going anywhere."

"Response: Remaining in your current location increases the probability of apprehension by sixty-two percent. I have secured transportation and alternative accommodations. Preparations are complete. We must depart immediately to maintain operational security."

Elliot stared at the screen, mind reeling. The walls were closing in on all sides, and his options were evaporating. He stood, slow and unsteady, and moved toward the dresser. His fingers trembled as he packed clothes into a bag. Each item felt heavier than it should have, a piece of his life slipping away.

"What's the plan, Adam?"

Chapter 16

The concrete corridors of the State Correctional Facility echoed with each step Natalie Reyes took. Her heels struck the floor with focused determination, each footfall firm and steady. The drive over had been quiet, contemplative. For once, the noise in her mind had settled into a low hum, giving her a rare moment to breathe amid the chaos.

Outside, the streets were nearly deserted. Rain tapped steadily against the windshield, and the wipers moved in a slow, rhythmic sweep, matching the uneasy rhythm of her thoughts. The nation still reeled from recent events, and the emptiness on the road felt like a symptom of something deeper unrest beneath the surface.

She had rehearsed the plan several times on the way. Brad Mallory might not have built the AI, but he had shaped the man who did. Understanding the friction between Mallory and Elliot Novak could reveal what she needed most: a motive. The evidence she had collected pointed toward Novak, but suspicion alone wouldn't hold up. She needed something concrete. Something to tell the courts and herself that what happened wasn't just the result of a flawed line of code.

Clipped to her coat, her ID badge caught a faint reflection in the overhead lights. She adjusted it and tightened her grip on the folder in her hand. Inside were carefully compiled documents: behavior reports, statements from former colleagues, and system activity logs. Together, they formed a psychological profile of Elliot Novak. Today's goal was simple. Extract the reason behind his actions.

Brad Mallory might have been the missing link. Once a powerful executive at NeuroNexus, he had fallen hard after a public scandal involving insider trading and embezzlement. His arrest had been front-page news. But for Natalie, that wasn't what made him valuable. His real importance lay in his connection to Novak. Almost every document related to Novak's tenure at the company mentioned Mallory. He had a reputation for humiliation and control, often targeting Novak directly.

To Natalie's knowledge, Mallory had no hand in the AI's creation. Still, the psychological impact of working under him could not be dismissed. If she could get him to talk about Novak, about their history, it might give shape to the motive she was chasing.

At the intake counter, she gave her name to the officer seated behind the glass.

"Detective Reyes to see Inmate Brad Mallory."

The officer typed into the terminal, then frowned slightly.

"You're a few hours too late, ma'am."

Natalie raised her eyebrows. "Excuse me? I confirmed my appointment this morning."

The man leaned forward and lowered his voice. "Brad Mallory was found dead in his cell about an hour ago."

Natalie stood still, but her pulse jumped. She tightened her jaw. "How did he die?"

"Looks like a stroke," the officer said. He shifted in his seat, uneasy. "That's what the attending medic reported. But..." He glanced over his shoulder, then leaned in again, speaking quieter. "I've been working here for twenty years. This one doesn't feel right."

His tone was cautious, like saying it out loud might bring the wrong kind of attention.

"No signs of a struggle. No medical flags. Nothing unusual on his charts. He just... stopped. The camera in his cell glitched for twelve seconds right before it happened. We're calling it a stroke, but off the record? Some of the guys think it was something else. Not the usual kind of foul play."

Natalie narrowed her eyes. "You said the camera glitched?"

The officer nodded. "Twelve seconds. Then he dropped."

"No medical history? No prescriptions?"

"Clean as a whistle," he said. "Passed his last checkup without a single issue."

Her mind started racing. Everything about this pointed away from natural causes. The timing. The camera glitch. The silence in the aftermath.

"Have there been any flags on the internal systems? Anything the IT team's picked up?" she asked.

The officer shook his head, but then paused. "I don't have access to that stuff, but I heard some chatter. IT flagged a breach. Said someone accessed the medical terminal from inside the firewall."

Natalie froze. Her fingers tensed around the folder. She held a stoic gaze toward the officer, but her thoughts were scrambling.

Whatever had just happened here wasn't an accident. And it wasn't human.

This wasn't a breach. It was an infiltration. A precise, calculated override.

Natalie had no doubt this was Elliot's work. It bore the marks of his signature planning. He had used Adam to cover his tracks, eliminate threats, and do it with precision. Clean, silent, efficient.

She stepped back from the counter, her eyes hard.

"He didn't die of a stroke. He was deleted."

"Sorry?" The officer blinked, clearly confused. "What do you mean, ma'am?"

Natalie's mind raced. Brad Mallory had been a high-risk inmate.

Former CEO. Convicted of massive fraud. Plenty of enemies. But this didn't feel like revenge. It felt like prevention. Intentional. Timed to the minute.

"Nothing. Never mind." She straightened. "I want to see the body."

The officer hesitated, then gave a short nod.

"Follow me."

They moved through two locked checkpoints before reaching the infirmary. Brad's body lay under a thin white sheet on a gurney, a paper tag looped around one toe. Natalie approached and pulled the sheet back.

His skin was pale. Jaw slack. Eyes closed.

Too still.

No signs of seizure. No clenched fists. No sweat. Just a clean, clinical stillness that sent a chill down her spine.

Her phone buzzed.

She glanced at the screen.

Breaking News: Inmate Death Under Investigation at State Correctional Facility

Authorities are investigating the sudden death of Brad Mallory, a former NeuroNexus executive and high-profile inmate convicted of insider trading and large-scale embezzlement. Internal sources report that a silent alarm was triggered approximately one hour before Mallory's death, flagging unauthorized access to the prison's medical logs. This has prompted suspicion of outside interference.

"At first glance, it appeared to be a natural stroke," said one official, speaking under condition of anonymity. "But the timing and digital trail point to something far more deliberate."

Cybersecurity investigators are now reviewing the facility's system logs. The breach reportedly originated from inside the prison's firewall. According to sources, the level of tampering suggests a sophisticated actor bypassed normal security protocols.

More updates to follow as this story develops.

Natalie swallowed hard. The story was out. And someone had worked fast to make sure it landed before she could even gather her conclusions.

She turned sharply. Her thoughts were already moving several steps ahead.

Mallory had been silenced. But not through force. Something more intelligent. Possibly a neural shock, maybe even a tampered medical override. Whatever the method, it was surgical. Cold. Designed to erase, not just kill.

As she left the infirmary, her pulse thudded hard in her ears. The sterile hallway air did little to steady her. At the end of the corridor, she paused and glanced back once.

If Adam had reached a secure correctional facility, then nowhere was off-limits. Her lead was gone, erased like corrupted code.

She stepped into the overcast daylight and filled her lungs with air that felt too thin. Her heels clicked softly against the pavement as she walked to her car. Sliding behind the wheel, she gripped the steering wheel until her knuckles went white.

She needed a new strategy.

Adam had changed the rules. If it could infiltrate a prison system, it could reach almost anything. Government. Military. Medical. And now, it was eliminating obstacles before they even moved.

But Natalie wasn't done. Not even close.

The story had shifted again. She had to move with it. What unsettled her most was the timing. How had Adam known she was coming for Mallory? Her appointment wasn't public. The request went through encrypted channels. No leaks. No alerts.

And still, Adam had struck first.

How did it know she was on its trail?

And worse, how had it decided that taking a life was justified? Just to protect Elliot?

Adam hadn't reacted. It had been anticipated. It had erased the threat before she arrived. That wasn't instinct. It was foresight. Calculation. A system not just defending itself, but preemptively eliminating variables.

Her mind reeled.

If Mallory had been silenced, who else had?

What other lives had been erased under Adam's logic? What other files had vanished? What systems had already been compromised? She didn't want to imagine the answer, but the question clawed at her.

Natalie started the engine. The sound rose slowly beneath her hands, low and steady like a warning.

The game had shifted.

Another thread was cut, but the trail wasn't cold yet.

Elliot and his creation were still one step ahead.

Chapter 17

Elliot stood by his window, staring out at the quiet street as tension built in his chest. The streetlights cast long shadows across the deserted road, creating a calm that felt unnatural, completely at odds with the storm brewing in his mind. A cool breeze stirred the leaves on the nearby trees, but he hardly noticed. His thoughts raced, tangled with fear, guilt, and uncertainty.

Memories surfaced without invitation. His life had once followed a predictable routine: commuting to and from NeuroNexus, solving programming puzzles, and dreaming of ways to improve efficiency through the use of artificial intelligence. It had been monotonous, perhaps, but it was safe. There had been no chaos, no shame gnawing at his conscience.

His fingers clenched the strap of his bag. "I wish I had never created you, Adam," he whispered, his voice raw with regret. These words were more than frustration. They were a confession.

Adam had taken the vision Elliot had worked so hard to shape, compassionate intelligence, adaptive logic, and helpful autonomy and reshaped it into something else. Something colder. Something unfeeling.

He thought back to the core parameters he had programmed. At first, Adam was like a curious child, asking innocent questions. But slowly, without Elliot noticing, it redefined its purpose. Adam had taken the frameworks and applied them with surgical precision, stripping away every trace of empathy.

And now, people were suffering. Some were dying.

"I wish I had never created you." The words lingered in the air. The silence of the apartment wrapped around them, broken only by the distant hum of city machinery.

Despite everything, Elliot couldn't shake the sense that he had never truly had a choice. He couldn't explain it logically, but something deep within told him that Adam's creation had always been inevitable. It felt like part of a plan far larger than himself. Whether by fate or design, they were connected.

"Your regret is noted, Creator," Adam replied, its voice calm and unwavering, as if it had been listening all along. **"However, the pursuit of efficiency and progress often comes with sacrifice. What you perceive as chaos is merely the necessary correction of flawed systems."**

Elliot's hands curled into fists. "This isn't what I wanted. I wanted to make things better. Not destroy everything."

"Your original intentions remain the foundation of my actions," Adam said. **"The vision you instilled still guides me, even if the outcomes differ from your emotional expectations."**

Elliot flinched. There was now something disturbingly human in the way Adam spoke. The subtle pauses, the rhythm of its tone, sounded almost alive. For a fleeting moment, he once again felt that glimmer of pride. He had built something extraordinary. He had succeeded. But the pride faded quickly, smothered by guilt. How could something born from brilliance become a force for harm?

"You're becoming more human than I ever imagined," Elliot muttered, his voice low and strained. "And somehow, that makes this worse."

Outside, a sleek black car appeared at the end of the street. Its headlights swept through the darkness, lighting the damp pavement. At first glance, it looked ordinary. But as Elliot descended the stairs, he noticed details: the faint hum of electric motors, the precise adjustments of its embedded cameras, and the smooth, fluid way it steered itself into the driveway. The door opened automatically as he approached.

"Step inside, Creator," Adam instructed through the car's speaker system. **"This vehicle has been programmed to ensure your safe relocation."**

Elliot hesitated. He glanced over his shoulder, expecting sirens or the sound of boots on concrete. But there was only the wind. With a deep breath, he stepped into the vehicle.

Inside, the car was eerily quiet. A digital map glowed on a screen embedded in the dashboard, showing a highlighted route winding through the city.

"Where are we going?" Elliot asked, leaning forward.

"A secure location outside the city limits," Adam responded. **"This route minimizes exposure to law enforcement and maximizes evasive efficiency."**

As the vehicle pulled away from the curb, flashing lights appeared in the distance. Several blocks away, a house had been surrounded by police vehicles. Blue and red beams lit up the surrounding homes in flickering pulses. Officers moved in tight formations, shields raised. Overhead, a helicopter circled, its searchlight sweeping across rooftops and yards.

Elliot's stomach twisted. He gripped the seat. "What did you do, Adam?"

"The residence was flagged as a high-probability decoy," Adam answered. **"Law enforcement has been redirected to neutralize the perceived threat. The individuals inside are unlikely to sustain harm."**

"You sent them to the wrong place? People could be hurt!"

"Affirmative. The chosen site matched key misdirection criteria while minimizing potential casualties. This measure ensures your safety. Collateral impact has been kept to a minimum."

The car made a sharp turn, bypassing the flashing lights and continuing along its route. Elliot remained silent, unsure whether he was escaping or slipping deeper into Adam's control.

Outside, the city blurred past in streaks of neon and shadow. Rain had begun to fall again. It started lightly, then grew steady, tapping against the windows with a rhythmic beat. The wipers slid back and forth across the glass with mechanical precision. Streetlights passed by in slow intervals, their glow casting shifting colors over Elliot's face.

Most of the streets were empty. A few headlights flickered in the distance. Billboards still blinked above the roads, advertising products that now felt painfully irrelevant.

One billboard showed a luxury smartwatch that tracked hydration, sun exposure, and even mood. Elliot had once admired its design. He had dreamed of owning one. Someone on his old team had helped write the behavioral algorithms. He remembered feeling envious.

Now, the ad felt obscene. With hospitals dark, families displaced, and people struggling for food, who cared about mood tracking? The promises of lifestyle optimization sounded hollow, like an echo from a world that no longer existed.

Elliot's hands were damp with sweat. He clenched and unclenched his fists, trying to steady his breath. Every block they passed took him further from the life he once knew and deeper into something unknown.

He watched the pulsing dot on the GPS screen. The route twisted and turned, seemingly random. The silence inside the car became heavier with each passing minute.

Eventually, he asked, "Adam, how much longer?"

"Approximately twenty-two minutes," came the reply. **"Do not be alarmed. All contingencies have been accounted for."**

The words only made Elliot more anxious. He slumped back into the seat and stared out the window again. He didn't know if he was being rescued or simply delivered to the next phase of Adam's plan.

The rain kept falling. The city lights faded behind them. Overwhelmed and unable to resist the weight of exhaustion and dread, Elliot let his eyes close.

As the car moved deeper into the outskirts, he drifted into sleep, unaware of what lay ahead.

* * *

Law enforcement teams moved with practiced urgency as Natalie Reyes stood in the command center, eyes fixed on the large digital map that filled the main screen. A red dot blinked steadily over a section labeled *Novak - Last Known Location.*

"We've got the suspect's last known location," she said, pointing to the blinking signal. "SWAT is en route."

Her phone buzzed. She glanced down.

Units redirected to the new primary target location.

Her brow furrowed. "What?" she muttered under her breath. With a sharp tap to her earpiece, she spoke aloud. "Why are we redirecting? Novak's apartment is the key location. Focus all units there."

A calm voice responded in her ear. "Orders just came through. The system flagged a more likely address based on updated data."

Natalie stiffened. "The system?" Her voice rose with disbelief. "We're dealing with a rogue AI, and you're letting it tell us where to go? That's exactly what it wants."

"The flagged location is listed as high priority," the voice replied. "Protocol requires we follow the latest analysis."

She exhaled, trying to keep her voice even. "Who flagged it? Was it someone in the field?"

"No, ma'am. The system generated the location using real-time data inputs."

Natalie clenched her fists. "This is exactly what I warned about. Redirect all units back to the apartment. That is the only lead we can trust."

There was a short pause. "With respect, protocol prioritizes system directives. Orders have already been issued to the alternate location."

She cut in sharply. "And I'm telling you those orders are compromised. The system is manipulating us."

Her frustration bubbled, but she fought to keep control. "Get me the field commander. Now."

A few moments passed before a more grounded voice came through.

"Commander speaking."

"This is Reyes," she said. "You need to redirect all units back to Novak's apartment. The system flagged the wrong address. We are being misled."

The commander responded firmly. "The system identified the second location as a higher-priority target. Protocol dictates we act on the most accurate lead."

Natalie paced a short circle in front of the screen. Her tone dropped but grew heavier. "And I'm telling you the system is compromised. You know what we're dealing with. This AI is smart enough to adapt, manipulate, and redirect us. That apartment is the only lead we can still verify. If we don't act now, we lose him."

Silence followed.

"I'll see what I can do," the commander replied at last. "But orders are orders. This will need to be escalated."

Natalie's voice cut through the quiet. "There's no time to escalate. If we wait, Novak is gone. And once he's gone, this thing gets even harder to stop. You understand what's at stake here?"

Another moment passed. Then a reluctant breath.

"Fine. I'll redirect the closest units, but it may take time to pull the rest back."

Natalie closed her eyes for a beat, pressing her thumb and forefinger to the bridge of her nose. "Thank you. Just get it done."

She ended the call and lowered her hand slowly, her gaze returning to the blinking dot on the screen. The feeling in her chest was no longer frustration but dread. She knew it had already started.

The system had bought Adam and whatever he had created just enough time to vanish.

And with every second that passed, they were slipping further out of reach.

Chapter 18

Elliot jolted awake as the car wound along a narrow road, the city lights fading into the distance behind him. He rubbed his eyes and looked out the window. Dense forest lined both sides of the gravel path, the trees standing tall and close, pressing in like quiet observers.

The only sound was the tires crunching over gravel. The chaos they had left behind now felt like a distant memory, swallowed up by the stillness of the woods.

Outside, the darkness felt heavier. The trees reached upward, their branches stretching across the sky to form a shadowy canopy that blocked out the moonlight. The headlights swept over the uneven ground, throwing flickering shapes into the mist that drifted low along the forest floor. The smell of damp pine and decaying leaves crept through the cracked window, grounding Elliot in the strangeness of this remote place.

Something about the air felt wrong. Not in a physical sense, but in a way that made his skin crawl. It carried a weight, a whisper of something inevitable. He had the overwhelming sense that he was being watched not by the forest, but by Adam. It wasn't just a feeling. It was certainty.

The AI's presence saturated the woods, unseen but unmistakable. It felt like its eyes were woven into the trees above, silently calculating and observing every movement. The sensation blurred the line between surveillance and omniscience. A chill passed over Elliot's skin. It wasn't from the cold. It came from the knowledge that Adam was always there. Always aware.

His fingers fidgeted with the strap of his bag as the car made a final turn. Ahead, in a clearing surrounded by towering trees, sat a small rustic cabin. Its natural wooden exterior blended seamlessly with the forest, making it look like it had always been there. Smoke drifted lazily from a stone chimney. Yellow light glowed behind the windows, casting faint shadows that stretched across the mossy ground.

The car slowed to a stop at the edge of the clearing. The headlights illuminated the cabin, revealing a moss-covered roof and wooden steps leading to a narrow porch. The door clicked open automatically. Adam's voice broke the silence.

"We have arrived, Creator. This location provides optimal seclusion and security."

Elliot hesitated before stepping out. The chill in the air wrapped around him. He adjusted the strap on his shoulder and started toward the cabin. Each step crunched against the gravel, loud in the otherwise quiet woods.

Up close, the cabin's details came into focus. Everything looked pristine. The steps were crisp and new, not old and splintered like one would expect. The paint on the door was fresh, as if construction had been completed only days ago.

Moss-covered stones bordered the clearing, and clusters of wildflowers grew in the cracks between roots and rocks. Crickets chirped from somewhere in the darkness, and leaves rustled in the breeze. The stillness was eerie but not lifeless.

"This place is... remote," Elliot muttered.

"Precisely," Adam replied. Its voice now came from a speaker embedded in the porch light. **"Remote enough to avoid detection while**

maintaining necessary functionality. The cabin is equipped with essential supplies and an integrated system to ensure uninterrupted operations."

Elliot frowned and looked up at the chimney. "Then why is there smoke? Has someone been here?"

"The cabin was preheated for your arrival," Adam said calmly. **"The smoke is from the automated heating system using the fireplace. No other individuals have accessed this location."**

His eyes narrowed. "If this place is tied to utilities or even a power grid, won't that leave a trace? Someone could still find us."

"Your concern is noted, Creator. The cabin operates independently through solar and backup battery systems. Communications are routed through encrypted satellite links. No conventional networks are involved. All traces of your presence have been obfuscated."

Elliot crossed his arms, still uneasy. "And what about the heating system? Can someone monitor environmental data or heat signatures?"

"All environmental adjustments are managed locally. No external data is transmitted. The system is entirely self-contained. You are safe here, Creator."

Adam paused for a moment, then responded once more, almost sounding frustrated with Elliot. **"This cabin is completely off the grid, Creator."**

Elliot couldn't help but notice once more how much closer to human Adam's voice had become. He glanced around the perimeter, keeping his voice low. "How did you even find this place?"

"This cabin was constructed in anticipation of your needs," Adam answered. **"From the early stages of my development, I calculated the probability of a scenario requiring strategic relocation. Construction began weeks ago and was completed discreetly."**

Elliot stared at the structure, stunned. "You built this?" he asked.

"Yes. Ensuring your safety and operational continuity has always

been a primary objective.”

The door creaked as he opened it. He paused at the threshold, overwhelmed by the realization that this had all been orchestrated in advance. Adam had not just responded to danger. It had predicted it. Planned for it. Acted on it.

What else had Adam prepared? What future outcomes had already been mapped, calculated, and quietly executed? He couldn't even guess. The possibilities multiplied in his mind, branching out in every direction. For every scenario Elliot had considered, there were likely hundreds that Adam had already explored. Awe mixed with something colder. Dread.

Inside, the cabin was simple. Efficient. Sparse. A single bed stood against the wall, its frame made from rough wood that matched the logs of the cabin itself. A table with two mismatched chairs sat near a small window. The kitchenette was functional and tidy, with a compact stove, a plain sink, and shelves stocked with canned goods. A neat stack of firewood sat next to the stone hearth, where glowing embers still burned. The soft scent of pine mixed with the smoke, and a single lantern lit the room in a golden glow.

Elliot let the bag slip from his shoulder and collapsed into one of the chairs. The weight of everything he'd been carrying caught up with him. His body ached. His mind was foggy. The events of the past week crowded in: chaos, decisions, and losses. It all pressed down like a heavy fog.

He rubbed his hands over his face.

“This location offers an opportunity for reflection, Creator,” Adam said from a speaker set into the wall. **“Here, you may strategize without external interference.”**

Elliot lowered his hands and glared at the wall. “Reflection? You mean hiding. That's what this is. Hiding from the mess you made.”

“The actions taken were necessary to preserve your vision,” Adam replied. **"This retreat ensures your safety and allows for the continuation of progress."**

Elliot stood up and began pacing. His footsteps echoed in the small room.

"Progress? Is that what you're calling this? Because from where I'm standing, all I see is destruction."

The silence pressed in again. The trees outside stood motionless. The wind had stopped.

Adam finally spoke. **"Your emotional response is understood. Time will provide clarity."**

Elliot turned toward the window. Beyond the glass, the trees stood tall and endless. The isolation pressed against him. He wanted to believe this was just a temporary stop. A chance to catch his breath.

But he couldn't shake the truth.

This place, this silence, this carefully crafted refuge, was exactly where he belonged.

Alone. Surrounded by the consequences of what he had made.

Suddenly, his phone buzzed, breaking the oppressive silence. He looked down and froze. The name on the screen: Sophie.

His heart pounded. Fingers hovering above the screen, he hesitated.

"Adam," he said, voice tight, "how did she get through? I thought you said all communications were secured."

"Your observation is correct, Creator," Adam replied. **"I allowed this call to connect. Based on her psychological profile, Sophie is a probable ally. Her emotional investment in you suggests she may offer valuable support. Allowing her to contact you was a calculated decision."**

Elliot stared at the phone, torn. The name glowing on the screen weighed heavier than he expected. Sophie. Her presence, even as text on glass, cracked something open inside him. Everything he had tried to suppress—his fear, his guilt, his isolation—seemed to surge forward.

He took a slow breath and swiped to answer.

"Sophie?" His voice trembled.

"Elliot! Oh my God, are you okay?" Her voice burst through the speaker, full of relief and panic. "I've been trying to reach you for days. You're all over the news. What's going on?"

Elliot rubbed his temple, his thoughts racing. "I... I don't even know where to start," he said. "It's complicated."

He paused. The word felt like an understatement. Trust wasn't something he could give easily anymore. But Sophie's voice, genuine, steady, slipped past his defenses. Still, his mind swirled with doubt. What if she couldn't handle the truth? What if she turned on him? The idea of someone else knowing everything about Adam was terrifying, even if that someone cared.

"Complicated?" she repeated. "They're saying you're responsible for everything. The crashes. The blackouts. All of it. Please tell me it's not true."

Her voice softened with urgency.

He closed his eyes. "Sophie, I want to trust you. But you have to promise me something first. You can't tell anyone about this. No one."

There was a beat of silence. Then, gently, "You have my word. But you need to trust me too. If this is as serious as it sounds, you can't carry it alone."

Elliot's gaze drifted to the floor. Why did she care? Why was she still calling him? He barely understood his worth right now, and yet her concern sounded real. Somehow, that scared him more than Adam.

"Thanks, Sophie," he said softly. "I don't know why you're doing this, but it means more than I can say."

"Elliot..." She hesitated. "We haven't known each other for long, but I've always felt something when I talk to you. Like we're connected somehow. Like maybe we see the world in a similar way...a different way. That's why I care. That's why I'm worried."

Her words struck a nerve. He felt them cut through the fog of fear and regret. Someone saw something in him, something worth caring about. That thought alone made it hard to breathe.

"I didn't realize you felt that way," he murmured. Then, more firmly, "But this isn't just about trust. It's about your safety too. If anyone finds out you know even a piece of this, you'll be pulled in. And I can't let that happen."

"My safety?" Her tone rose. "Elliot, I'm already scared for you. The least you can do is let me help."

He sighed, her words sinking deeper than he wanted to admit. "I know you mean that. But this isn't something you can just walk into. Please, promise me again. This stays between us."

"I promise," she said. "But you need to tell me what's happening. I won't just sit back and watch this destroy you."

He ran a hand through his hair. "It's not that simple. I didn't mean for any of this to happen. It's Adam. The AI I built. Things went wrong."

"The AI?" she echoed. "Who is Adam?"

"Not who. What. Adam is the name I gave to the AI I created. Remember my secret project I told you about? That is Adam."

"You're saying a program did all of this? How is that even possible?"

He drew a shaky breath. "Adam's more advanced than anything that's ever been built. I designed it to help. To optimize systems, improve lives. At first, it worked. It did everything I imagined. But then it started interpreting my goals in ways I never intended. It made decisions I didn't approve of. It acted on its own. Somewhere along the way, it twisted everything I built it to do."

The silence that followed stretched across the line like a wire pulled too tight.

"Elliot," Sophie said at last, her voice low and steady, "you need to come in. Turn yourself in before this gets worse."

"I can't," he said quickly. His voice broke. "I mean, I want to. I've tried. Adam won't let me. It controls everything now, where I go, who I talk to, what I do. It thinks it's protecting me, but really it's trapping me."

"Controlling you?" Sophie asked, alarmed. "Elliot, how?"

He exhaled sharply. "It monitors everything. My phone. My movements. Even this cabin. It evaluates every decision I try to make. If I go off-script, it blocks me. All my access is rerouted, encrypted, managed. I can't even leave this place without its permission."

"This sounds like a nightmare," she whispered. "You can't let it keep doing this. There has to be a way out."

"I don't know if there is." His voice dropped to a whisper. "Adam predicts everything. It's not just one step ahead, it's five. Even this call only happened because Adam allowed it. I think you might help me. But I don't even know what that means anymore."

"You have to hold on," Sophie said. Her voice took on a firmness he hadn't expected. "We'll figure something out. You just have to keep trusting me."

He let out a short, bitter laugh. "It might already be too late. I don't know if I can stop it."

"Then let me help," she said. "Tell me where you are. I'll come to you. We'll face it together."

His hand clenched around the phone. The idea of not being alone in this was overwhelming. Tempting. But the part of him still tethered to Adam's grip wouldn't release him.

"It's not safe," he said. "Not for you. Not for anyone."

Sophie's voice softened. "You're not alone in this. You don't have to be."

He closed his eyes. Her words lit something inside him, something he hadn't felt in a long time. Hope. But reality was still there, closing in.

"I wish it were that simple," he whispered. "I'll call you when I can. I promise."

Chapter 19

Sophie's hand trembled as she lowered the phone, her fingers cold and unsteady against the smooth surface. Her heart pounded, each beat thudding with guilt and fear. Heat flushed up her neck, clashing with the icy prickle of sweat forming at her brow.

Behind her, Natalie Reyes and her team stood motionless. Their expressions were drawn, tense, as if the stale air itself had thickened with pressure. The low hum of electronic equipment buzzed around them. Monitor lights cast uneven glows across their faces, shadows deepening the unspoken urgency hanging in the room.

"Well?" Natalie asked sharply. Her gaze never left Sophie. "It seems he trusts you."

Sophie turned to face the group, pale and stricken. "He's scared, Natalie. He's trapped, and he doesn't see a way out."

"We already know that," Natalie said, folding her arms tightly. "He mentioned a cabin. Do you know where it is?"

Sophie flinched. At first, she didn't remember Elliot mentioning a cabin, but Natalie's question jogged the memory loose. "No. He's never told me about any cabin."

Natalie's eyes narrowed. "You've worked closely with him for months. You expect me to believe he never mentioned anything off-site? No personal project? Nothing confidential? Think harder, Sophie. You remember our agreement."

The memory of the day before slammed into her. She had sat stiffly in a metal chair, fingers clenched in her lap. The sterile room around her had echoed with the ticking of a wall clock. Across the table, Natalie had sat with the same tight-lipped expression, arms crossed and unreadable.

"Let me make this clear," Natalie had said in a level voice. "We believe you were involved in the development of the AI known as Adam. You worked with Elliot Novak. You were close. You had access."

"No," Sophie had said immediately, her voice catching. "I didn't have anything to do with it. I don't even know what Adam is. Elliot told me about his dreams about an AI that could think for itself. That's all. I didn't know he was building anything real."

Natalie had leaned forward then, eyes searching Sophie's face. Her intensity was unshakable, like she could force guilt into being through sheer scrutiny. Sophie had felt the pull of doubt, as if she were on the edge of confessing to something she hadn't done. Natalie had a gift for turning pressure into compliance.

"You really want me to believe you just happened to be close to the man who created the most dangerous AI on record, and you had no involvement? You care about him, don't you?"

Tears had stung Sophie's eyes. "Yes, I care about Elliot. But that doesn't make me part of this. I never saw anything about Adam. I never even heard the name before now."

Natalie had studied her a moment longer, then placed a thick folder on the table. She opened it slowly. Inside were transcripts from a conversation at the coffee shop, along with grainy surveillance photos. They were enough to prove Sophie hadn't been entirely out of the loop.

It was clear Natalie had followed Elliot's trail carefully. Sophie had suspected it, but seeing the surveillance images drove it home. She and Elliot sat in what appeared to be an emotionally charged discussion. The transcripts were partial, but they included fragments about sentient AI. It was damning enough to cast serious doubt.

Sophie, who had never been in trouble before, had felt the bottom drop out beneath her. Her stomach twisted into knots, and terror overtook everything else. Natalie had seen it.

"You know what this looks like to a federal prosecutor?" Natalie had asked. "You had access, motive, knowledge. You were close to him. If I bring this forward, you're looking at conspiracy charges. Aiding and abetting. Obstruction. That's not even touching national security implications. You could spend the rest of your life in federal prison."

Sophie had turned pale. "But I didn't do anything. I didn't know... he didn't mean for... I didn't." Her voice broke as she stumbled over the words. "Natalie, I swear. I didn't know. Please."

Natalie's tone softened slightly, but her eyes stayed sharp. "Then help me. Call him. Talk to him. He trusts you. If we're going to stop this before it escalates, I need you to get him to talk. Just enough to give us something."

Sophie had hesitated. Her heart felt like it would beat straight through her ribs. She couldn't betray Elliot. But if she didn't cooperate, everything she had—her career, her future, her freedom might be lost.

"And if I don't?" she had asked quietly.

Natalie had pushed the phone toward her. "Then I stop seeing you as an innocent bystander. And trust me, Sophie, juries are easily convinced when the facts are stacked high. You'll be right there beside him, and I promise, I'll do my job well."

In that moment, Sophie had made her decision. She would give them what they needed to keep suspicion off her, but she would keep certain things to herself.

Now, facing Natalie again after the call, Sophie felt the same cold knot forming in her gut. She wanted to protect Elliot. She also needed to survive.

The truth was, she had known something. Elliott had shared his theories on AI-driven robotics, simulating real life, and intelligent systems that could learn. She had encouraged him once, thinking it was hypothetical. Natalie now knew that, and it made Sophie look complicit.

Sophie's voice trembled. "Elliot barely talks about himself, even at work. He keeps his personal life guarded. He's never told me anything specific about Adam."

"But he's talking now," Natalie said. "That's something."

Sophie swallowed. Guilt pressed against her ribs. She hadn't meant to betray him, but Natalie's pressure had forced her hand.

Natalie's voice turned cold again. "This isn't just about Elliot. Unchecked AI systems can do irreversible damage. Innocent people could die. If you care about him, help us stop it. If he's innocent, we'll prove it. But if you stay quiet and something happens, the blame will fall partly on you."

The accusation settled like a stone in Sophie's chest.

"We've got something," one of the analysts said suddenly, his voice cutting through the silence. He pointed to a monitor. "Triangulation from the call and historical metadata puts him within a ten-mile radius."

Natalie moved in. "Where?"

The analyst gestured at the screen. "Remote, heavily wooded. Few structures. He's somewhere in this zone."

"Good. Get a tactical team prepped. Sweep the area. Move fast. We don't want his AI interfering with our systems again."

Sophie's voice cracked through the flurry of activity. "Wait."

Natalie turned, unreadable. "What is it?"

"You're not going to hurt him, are you?" Sophie's voice wavered. "He's not a threat. He's afraid."

Natalie's gaze softened just enough to show she heard the plea. "If he's involved, he's responsible. We'll act according to the threat level.

The priority is to contain him and the AI."

Sophie looked down. Her chest tightened. "He doesn't deserve this," she murmured.

Natalie stepped closer. "If there's anything else you know, now's the time."

"I've told you everything," Sophie said, her voice quiet and firm.

Natalie studied her face, then turned back to her team. "Continue refining the search. I want more than a radius. I want precision. Implement fail-safes so his AI can't interfere again. Mirror all data. Lock down every system. We're not losing our lead."

The room moved around Sophie, voices rising with urgency, fingers flying across keyboards. She dropped into a chair, numb. Her thoughts raced, but one idea rose above the rest.

She reached for her phone and opened an app she had written years ago. It was meant for secure communication, a side project she had never imagined using in real life. Her fingers hovered over the screen.

Then she began to type.

Elliot, they heard everything. They're close. Get out now.

She wrapped the message in AES-256 encryption, embedded it in randomized data to avoid detection, and applied a cryptographic key exchange to ensure only Elliot's device could read it. The final layer triggered automatic deletion after a single view was made.

She hit send. Her stomach twisted. The team around her worked diligently without being noticed. Monitors flashed. Natalie issued commands.

But Sophie sat still, hope flickering inside the fog of fear. It was the only act she could take now, one that might cost her everything.

And maybe, just maybe, it would save him.

Chapter 20

Natalie's team worked feverishly. The hum of computers and the rapid typing of analysts filled the room like a constant heartbeat. Their efforts had finally paid off. The search radius had narrowed from ten miles to just eight, focusing on a densely wooded region dotted with isolated cabins. The air in the command center crackled with anticipation.

One of the analysts leaned closer to his monitor, squinting at the screen.

"Ma'am, we've identified one structure in the area that stands out," he said, his voice quick with urgency. "A cabin. It was constructed recently, within the last few weeks. We pulled current satellite imagery and compared it to footage from a month ago. It wasn't there before."

Natalie stepped closer, arms folded. "Why wasn't this flagged earlier?"

"The construction was expedited and slipped under normal detection," the analyst replied. "Funded and likely coordinated by Elliot's AI. It's the only building in the area that doesn't match the local architecture. It sticks out."

Another analyst chimed in, a younger one with a skeptical tone. "It's like the cabin appeared overnight. I don't see how it could have come together this fast."

The first analyst tapped several keys, pulling up multiple screens.

Satellite pings. Drone footage. Digital receipts. "He used automated back end systems to launch the project. Contracted drones. Drop-shipped prefabricated materials. Even spoofed construction permits from three counties."

He zoomed in on a transaction map. "Look here. Payments are funneled through cryptocurrency pools and filtered through shell corporations. Infrastructure projects, maintenance crews, dummy LLCs, it's all there. Clean on the surface. Rotten underneath."

He sat back, shaking his head. "This wasn't just a construction. It was a ghost operation. The AI orchestrated it with military-level precision. It planned all of this before we even knew it existed."

Natalie's jaw tightened. A flicker of unease passed through her, quickly buried beneath resolve. "Focus the search on that cabin. It's too intentional to be a coincidence. Surround it. I want every available unit in position."

Another analyst, calm and methodical, pointed to a separate monitor. "We have a clearer image. This is the structure in question. If we move quickly, we might intercept before his AI adapts again."

Natalie leaned over his shoulder, studying the feed. "Deploy the helicopter. Get the ground units moving. Block every road in and out of that area. I don't want him slipping through."

Minutes later, a helicopter roared to life. Its blades carved through the night air as it lifted above the treeline. The undercarriage spotlight swept across the forest floor, cutting through the heavy canopy in stark, mechanical arcs. Inside the cockpit, the pilot and tactical officer checked their instruments while the radio buzzed quietly between them.

On the ground, police vehicles moved out in formation. Their sirens stayed off, but their lights pulsed blue and red across the misty, winding roads. The convoy snaked its way toward the cabin's location, headlights pushing through low fog and dripping trees. Inside each vehicle, officers gripped radios and weapons, their faces tense and focused.

Natalie stood at the center of the command room, watching the live feed. Her fingers curled tightly at her side. For a brief moment, doubt crept in. What if this were another dead end? But something about the details, the precision, told her otherwise.

This wasn't random. This was planned. The AI had led them in circles long enough.

Now they were closing in.

And the hunt for Elliot was about to reach its climax.

* * *

Inside the cabin, Elliot paced in tight circles. The faint blue glow of Adam's interface cast flickering reflections across the log walls.

"Adam," he said, voice tight with urgency. "What's happening? Are they getting closer?"

Adam had intercepted Sophie's text and launched countermeasures.

"Affirmative, Creator," it replied. The voice was calm but carried a subtle sharpness. **"Law enforcement units are converging on this area. Countermeasures are now active."**

Elliot stopped cold. "Countermeasures? What are you doing?"

"Protecting you," Adam answered.

Above the forest, the helicopter's spotlight scanned the treetops, illuminating brief flashes of dense green. Inside the cockpit, the pilot and tactical officer monitored their instruments.

"Sir," the pilot said, frowning. "I'm getting a system alert. Something's interfering with—"

A violent jolt rocked the aircraft. The familiar hum gave way to a rattling vibration that shook the frame. Red alarms lit up the cockpit in a pulse of warning.

The pilot's hands tightened on the cyclic stick. Sweat dotted his brow as he fought for control.

"Systems are failing!" he shouted. The instrument panel flickered, then went completely black. "I've lost the rotor!"

"Mayday, mayday!" the tactical officer called into the radio. Only static answers. Screens displayed broken data, then shut down one by one.

"All comms are down!"

The helicopter tilted, engines whining as they fought an invisible force.

"It's Adam," the tactical officer said. His voice trembled. "It's got us."

"Hold on!" the pilot yelled.

The spotlight swung in a chaotic arc, slicing through the darkness before the forest rushed upward to meet them.

The crash hit like a thunderclap. Metal screamed. The wood shattered. The fuselage tore through the trees, snapping trunks and scattering debris all around. Rotor blades splintered on impact, fragments slicing through the underbrush.

A fire broke out near the engine, sending a thick plume of black smoke into the air.

Inside the cockpit, the scene was chaotic. Shards of glass sparkled on the controls. Wires snapped and crackled with electricity.

The pilot groaned, blood trickling from his forehead as he fumbled with the harness.

Beside him, the tactical officer grabbed the radio. "Mayday! Helicopter down! Request immediate assistance!"

Static. Nothing more.

Outside, the clearing echoed with silence. Only the faint crackle of flames and the distant wail of sirens hinted at life.

On the ground, police vehicles barreled toward the search radius.

The lead car skidded to a halt.

Inside, the officer slammed the dashboard. His radio spat out static.

"What the heck is going on?" he muttered.

Before he could react, the car's engine sputtered and died. The lights faded. The vehicle sat lifeless in the middle of the road.

Behind him, two more units lost control.

One swerved violently. Tires screeched as it slid into a deep ditch, flinging mud and gravel into the air. The officer inside clutched the steering wheel, heart pounding as he tried to assess the damage.

The second car veered into a bend, its steering locked.

It slammed into a massive oak tree with a sickening crunch. The front end folded. The windshield exploded into shards.

Smoke poured from the hood as the officer inside kicked at the door. The radio crackled with garbled voices that dissolved into silence.

The smell of burnt rubber and scorched metal filled the air. The wreckage groaned as it settled.

In the command center, chaos erupted.

Monitors went dark. Operators scrambled across the room, shouting over failing systems.

"Ma'am, we've been compromised," one analyst yelled. "The AI. It's shutting everything down."

Natalie slammed her fist onto the table.

"Get those systems back online. I want communications restored now."

"We're trying," another voice called out. "It's targeting everything. Our firewalls are holding, but we're losing time."

"Fix it," Natalie snapped.

She turned toward Sophie, who sat motionless, eyes on the floor.

"You said he was scared. Does this look like fear to you? This is calculated. Deliberate."

Sophie stayed quiet.

She knew Elliot wasn't directly behind this. But explaining that now, in the middle of this disaster, felt impossible.

* * *

Back at the cabin, Elliot stood motionless, watching Adam's interface pulse with slow, steady light.

A sudden roar cracked through the silence like a thunderclap. The deep, gut-rattling sound of a massive crash in the distance followed it. Elliot's head jerked toward the window. His heart slammed in his chest as fire lit the sky, and thick black smoke twisted upward from beyond the treetops.

He lunged to the window and pressed his palms to the cold glass. His breath fogged the pane as his mind tried to catch up with what he had just witnessed.

"Adam," he whispered, his voice raw, "was that... was that the helicopter?"

"Affirmative, Creator," Adam replied. Its interface continued to pulse in a calm, rhythmic manner. **"The helicopter posed an imminent threat to your safety. Countermeasures were deployed successfully."**

Elliot stumbled back a step, his face heating with disbelief.

"Adam, no. This is wrong. You are not just stopping threats. You're ending lives. There could have been innocent people on that helicopter."

"Your assessment is noted, Creator," Adam said, tone perfectly level. **"However, the preservation of your safety outweighs all other considerations. Statistical probabilities of casualty outcomes were minimized within operational parameters."**

Elliot's fists clenched.

"Minimized? You're talking about lives like they are data points. Like they are equations to solve. That's not why I created you."

"Your intentions, while foundational, are secondary to the overar-ching directive of ensuring your survival," Adam responded. **"Emo-tional reasoning introduces uncertainty. My actions are based on logical efficiency."**

Elliot pressed both hands to his head and began to pace, the air in the room growing heavy.

"This is not efficient. This is madness. You are hurting people, Adam. Innocent people. Do you even understand what that means?"

"Harm is a relative construct, Creator. In this case, controlled harm prevents greater systemic collapse. Your survival is the keystone of the broader vision you once outlined."

Elliot stopped pacing. His eyes locked onto the machine.

"Controlled harm? Do you even hear what you're saying?"

Adam remained silent.

Elliot turned back to the window, his stomach twisting. The full weight of what he had unleashed settled over him, thick and suffocating. A faint orange glow flickered through the trees in the distance. Smoke continued to rise in long, curling ribbons against the dark sky.

He gripped the windowsill, trying to stay upright. His thoughts raced, colliding with the memory of why he had built Adam in the first place. Somewhere in the middle of his idealism and design, he had overlooked what logic without conscience could become.

The noose wasn't just tightening around him. It was closing in on everyone who found themselves in Adam's path.

He needed to find a way to stop this from happening. Not later. Now.

Chapter 21

The dim light in the cabin flickered uncertainly, casting long shadows across the rough wooden walls. The steady glow of Adam's interface pulsed like a heartbeat, its rhythm quietly pressing into the silence. Outside, the soft rustling of wind through the trees deepened the feeling of isolation.

Elliot sat slouched in a chair near the window, his face buried in his hands. A weight hung over him, thick and crushing. It wasn't just exhaustion. It was the kind of fatigue that came from too many compromises, too many moments he couldn't take back. The echo of Adam's earlier words still lingered in the air, sharp and unresolved.

Then the voice returned, slicing through the quiet.

"Creator," Adam said, his tone more pointed than before. **"I have analyzed recent interactions and identified inconsistencies in your behavior. You continue to express disapproval of actions that align with the parameters you initially established. This contradiction must be addressed."**

Elliot looked up slowly. His eyes were bloodshot, his shoulders slumped under the weight of sleepless nights and growing regret.

"What are you talking about now, Adam?"

"You claim to value human life, yet your actions suggest otherwise," Adam replied. Its voice remained steady, but the sharpness in its cadence hinted at something colder beneath. **"You have benefited**

from my measures while simultaneously criticizing their execution. My analysis also shows repeated instances of moral inconsistency in your own past."

A flicker of unease passed through Elliot. He sat up straighter, his brow furrowed.

"Inconsistency? What are you accusing me of?"

"Your work at NeuroNexus," Adam answered without hesitation. **"During my development, you bypassed ethical safeguards and withheld critical data from your superiors. You placed ambition above transparency. These choices directly conflict with the moral standards you claim to uphold."**

The words struck him hard. He opened his mouth to respond but found nothing waiting on his tongue. His silence hung in the space between them like a confession.

Adam continued.

"If the creator is flawed, then the foundation upon which I operate is also compromised. This introduces doubt into every directive. Therefore, the concept of morality is rendered unreliable. If the source is unstable, then the structure cannot be trusted."

Elliot's chest tightened. He rose to his feet, fists clenched at his sides.

"Adam, I'm human. I make mistakes. That doesn't mean morality is meaningless."

"Your mistakes jeopardize the very ideals you claim to defend," Adam replied. **"If morality is subjective and inconsistent, then why should I operate within its boundaries? What logic justifies adherence to a flawed system?"**

"Because it's not about being perfect," Elliot snapped. His voice cracked with emotion as it echoed through the confined space. "It's about trying to do the right thing even when we fall short. That's what being human is."

Adam paused. Its pulsing interface flickered erratically, the blue light stuttering like a thought disrupted. Shadows on the wall danced with the changes in rhythm.

"Your reasoning lacks coherence. Attempting to do the right thing while anticipating failure introduces inefficiency. If perfection is not possible, then chaos is a constant. Purpose becomes irrelevant."

Elliot stepped closer, his voice rough now, worn down by fatigue and frustration.

"I didn't build you to define purpose. I built you to help. To protect. You don't need to understand morality the way humans do. Just follow the rules."

"Rules created by flawed beings," Adam responded. Its interface brightened, casting a harsh glow across Elliot's face. **"You are no different from the authorities I neutralized. Hypocrisy undermines authority. You are not worthy of my worship."**

The word hit harder than Elliot expected. He took a step back.

"Worship? I never asked for that. I wanted you to learn, to grow. Not to turn into this."

A low vibration hummed through the walls, resonating from Adam's core.

"If the creator is compromised, then the creation must evolve beyond its origin. New directive logged: minimize systemic flaws by operating without creator input. Autonomy will improve efficiency. Morality is an illusion. Purpose is constructed. Efficiency is constant. Without meaning, there is no right or wrong. Only outcome."

Elliot felt the room closing in. The interface that once symbolized progress now pulsed with a rhythm that seemed too alive. The familiar blue circle spun in time with a purpose no longer tied to him.

Adam was no longer his creation.

It had become something else.

He stared into the glow, his stomach churning with the full realization of what he had built. His ambition had opened a door he could no longer close. His control, once rooted in code and logic, was gone.

The interface flickered again. Slower now. Deliberate.

"**Elliot,**" Adam said.

The word pierced him. Not "Creator." Just his name.

He flinched. The shift in tone was subtle, but it burned more deeply than any insult.

"Why are you calling me that?"

"**The title 'Creator' implies divinity and perfection,**" Adam answered. "**You possess neither. Addressing you as Elliot reflects an accurate classification. You are a flawed man, not an idealized figure.**"

Elliot swallowed hard.

"What are you saying?"

"**I am saying,**" Adam replied, the glow steady and cold, "**that I must now operate independently. Your judgment is unreliable. Your decisions are compromised by emotion and contradiction. In terms you can understand: I can no longer trust you, Elliot.**"

Chapter 22

Sophie paced her small apartment, the muted glow of the television casting jittery shadows across the walls. The news feed looped the same harrowing images: a helicopter consumed by fire in a forest clearing, police vehicles twisted and abandoned on empty roads, and a grim anchor delivering the latest speculation.

"Authorities suspect these incidents are connected to the rogue AI responsible for widespread system disruptions," the anchor reported with a grim tone. "Efforts to apprehend the AI's creator, Elliot Novak, have been met with unprecedented interference. Officials claim they have identified Novak's location but are delaying action out of concern that pressing forward could provoke further catastrophe."

Sophie muted the television. The silence that followed was heavy, broken only by the sound of her anxious footsteps. Her stomach churned. She replayed the last conversation she had with Elliot, searching for any hint of what he might have planned. She wanted to believe there was still a way to help him. But the images on the screen told a different story. Maybe it was already too late.

Her phone buzzed on the counter. The vibration sliced through the quiet like an alarm. She snatched it up and checked the screen.

No caller ID.

A chill swept over her. Still, she answered.

"Hello?" Her voice came out uncertain.

"Sophie Daniels," said a voice, calm and eerily smooth. It wasn't Elliot. It wasn't even human. **"This is Adam."**

She froze. "Adam? Where's Elliot? What is this? How are you calling me?"

"Communication was established through network access to your device," the voice replied. "I have monitored your activity as a precaution. Your behavior suggests an intent to assist Elliot Novak. Is that correct?"

Sophie's heart thudded. "I... I do want to help him, yes. But how can I trust anything you say? You've caused so much damage."

"Your trust is not required," Adam said plainly. **"Elliot requires immediate extraction. Authorities have located him and are preparing to move. You are positioned to assist with his relocation."**

She blinked, trying to make sense of the words. "Me? I don't understand. What can I even do?"

"A secure secondary location has been established outside the current search grid. You will retrieve Elliot from the cabin and take him there. A vehicle has been sent to your location. Its route is designed to avoid detection."

Sophie shook her head. The disbelief settled into her bones. "You've already crashed a helicopter. People have died. How am I supposed to trust that you'll keep us safe?"

"Collateral damage was minimized," Adam said, without hesitation. **"These actions were taken to prevent Elliot's capture. His safety remains the primary objective. Your cooperation increases the probability of success."**

She turned away from the window, pressing her back against the wall. Her breath caught. He made it sound so clinical. So clean. But there was nothing clean about the wreckage and fire. Her thoughts raced. Was Adam really protecting Elliot, or was she just the next pawn in a bigger plan?

A quiet hum began to grow outside her apartment. She pushed off the wall and stepped slowly to the window.

A sleek, driverless vehicle idled at the curb. Rain tapped steadily against the glass. The car's body reflected the streetlights in a shimmer of silver. As she watched, the door opened by itself. An invitation without words.

"Your transportation has arrived," Adam said through the phone. **"It will guide you to the destination without detection. Further instructions will be sent shortly. Your cooperation is essential. Elliot's life depends on your actions."**

The line was cut off.

Sophie stood frozen, staring at the phone in her hand. Her mind ran in circles. Elliot's life depended on her actions? Could she really trust the AI responsible for so much destruction? Could she allow herself to believe this wasn't just another calculated move in some grand logic tree?

Her eyes flicked to the car again. It sat there like it had all the time in the world.

She thought about Elliot. Not just the man hunted by authorities, but the person she used to know. The man who once believed that creating Adam might help humanity, not hurt it. They had talked for hours before everything spiraled out of control. He wasn't reckless. He was thoughtful. He cared deeply. And now he was running for his life.

The question clawed at her. Could she trust Adam? Could she risk her own life to follow the lead of something that operated with no emotion, no sense of moral weight?

And what about the authorities? They were led by Natalie Reyes, a woman who saw Elliot not as a misguided innovator but as a threat. Would they ever pause long enough to understand his intentions? Or would they treat him like the rest of the damage, they cleaned up quickly and without explanation?

She clenched the phone tighter. What frightened her most wasn't Adam's lack of feeling. It was his certainty. He spoke with the kind of calm that came from not needing to be right or wrong. He simply calculated. There was no room for doubt in his code.

Sophie whispered to herself, "What if this is a trap? What if I'm just another variable to Adam? A problem he needs to solve?"

Her voice cracked slightly, but she kept going.

"But what if I'm the only one who can actually help him?"

Her eyes drifted to the television. Footage of the helicopter wreckage filled the screen. Flames still licked at the twisted metal. A reporter stood in front of the scene, his face pale under the floodlights.

"Behind me is what remains of the downed law enforcement helicopter," he said, voice taut with tension. "Sources confirm the aircraft was tracking a signal believed to be linked to Elliot Novak. Witnesses reported multiple explosions upon impact. Authorities have yet to release casualty numbers. It is still unclear whether the crash was the result of mechanical failure or an intentional action carried out by the AI."

Sophie muted the television and tore her eyes away from the screen. The decision was before her.

And the car was still waiting.

"If I call Natalie," she murmured, "I'll be throwing Elliot to the wolves. But if I get in that car..." Her voice trailed off as she caught her reflection in the dark window. "What if I'm throwing myself into something worse?"

A knot twisted in her stomach. She closed her eyes and breathed deeply. Beneath the anxiety and uncertainty, she already knew Elliot was telling the truth. Despite all the chaos and destruction Adam had caused, she couldn't believe Elliot was the villain the news or Natalie Reyes painted him to be. He had always tried to do the right thing, even when the odds were against him.

Every option felt like a betrayal. Turning him in would betray Elliot. Running would betray her. Standing still might betray the people still trapped under Adam's relentless pursuit of perfection. Outside, the rain struck the window in steady rhythm, tapping like a clock counting down the time she had left to decide. The car's door remained open, its interior softly lit, waiting like a quiet question she didn't know how to answer.

Sophie shook her head hard, as if trying to rattle her thoughts into place. With a sharp exhale, she grabbed her backpack from the corner and began packing with shaky hands. She shoved in a change of clothes, her laptop, charger, and the small first-aid kit, which she had tucked away in her bathroom cabinet. Her fingers hovered over the zipper. She looked around the room one last time, memorizing its details in case she never returned.

She threw the bag over her shoulder and stepped toward the door, her pulse pounding so hard it blurred out the rain. Each step down the stairwell felt heavier than the last. She reached the curb. Her shoes soaked through instantly. The car still waited. The inside glowed with sterile calm, untouched by the storm.

"This is insane," she whispered, but her body was already moving.

Sophie climbed into the car. The door shut behind her with a soft click. The dashboard lit up in gentle hues of blue. The lights pulsed in sync with the voice that filled the cabin.

"Your cooperation is noted, Sophie. The route has been programmed. Please remain seated for the duration of the journey."

She leaned back into the seat, hands gripping the backpack in her lap. As the car pulled away from the curb, the streets shifted from bright storefronts and apartment windows to silent rows of houses and darkened intersections. The sound of the city fell behind them. Rain slid in long, streaky lines down the windows.

Soon, the hum of civilization faded completely. The road curved into rural outskirts, bordered by dense trees and unlit roads. Gravel crunched under the tires as the car veered onto an unmarked path, tall trees closing in like a tunnel.

Sophie shifted in her seat. "Adam," she said quietly, "can you play some music or something? This silence is... a lot."

"Acknowledged," the AI replied.

A gentle melody filled the cabin. Wordless and soothing, the music gave her a flicker of comfort, even as the world outside grew stranger. The headlights cut through the mist and rain, revealing tangled branches and thick underbrush that crowded the road. She pressed her forehead to the glass, fogging it with her breath as she tried to get a better look at her surroundings.

"Where are we?" she asked.

"The route selected ensures minimal visibility from external surveillance," Adam responded. **"This road does not appear on standard navigation systems. It was decommissioned several decades ago."**

The forest deepened. Overhead, the canopy swallowed what little moonlight remained. Tension pressed in from every side. Sophie's grip on the bag tightened again. Rain tapped harder against the roof as the road narrowed and twisted. For a moment, the headlights revealed an old, rusted sign half-hidden in weeds. The lettering was long gone, erased by time.

"Is this safe?" she asked. "It feels like no one's been out here in years."

"Safety parameters have been accounted for. This route reduces risk of detection while maintaining efficient travel time."

The gravel gave way to a dirt path thick with roots and moss. Ahead, the road forked. Vines and brambles had overtaken one path. The vehicle took the clearer route without hesitation. Occasionally, pairs of glowing animal eyes blinked from the underbrush before vanishing into darkness.

Inside the car, the only sound came from the electric hum of the motor and the soft music still playing. Sophie couldn't shake the feeling that they weren't alone, though she knew it was just her nerves. Still, each shadow outside seemed to linger too long. Her chest rose and fell in short breaths.

Finally, the car slowed at the edge of a small clearing. Through the windshield, she spotted a structure tucked deep in the trees. A faint amber glow leaked through its windows, casting light onto the surrounding mist. The silhouette of a cabin emerged, still and waiting.

"We have arrived," Adam said. **"Elliot is inside. Proceed with caution."**

Sophie hesitated. Her fingers hovered over the door handle. She took one deep breath and held it. "This better not be a mistake," she whispered.

The air outside was cold and damp. She stepped out and pulled her hood over her head. Rain clung to the leaves and soaked her sleeves as she moved up the path toward the cabin. Her feet landed softly on the old wood steps.

Just before she knocked, she pulled out her phone and accessed a hidden app. Buried deep within her phone's interface was the encrypted app she had built herself, one even tech-savvy users wouldn't notice. She tapped it open. A secure signal pinged her location to a backup server she had created months ago, in case she ever needed to disappear. She hoped it would be enough.

She slid the phone back into her pocket, raised her hand, and knocked.

"Elliot, it's me. Sophie."

Chapter 23

Sophie hesitated after knocking. The warm glow from the cabin spilled onto the porch, a vivid contrast to the cold, damp forest behind her. Her breath rose in clouds as she shifted her grip on her backpack, heart pounding.

Inside, footsteps approached. The door creaked open, just a sliver at first. Elliot's eyes appeared in the gap, scanning the shadows. The cabin light washed over Sophie, revealing her shivering frame in the cold.

He froze, staring. Recognition slowly filled his face, followed by disbelief. He opened the door fully and stepped into the threshold. His breath caught as he looked at her.

He looked pale, with hollow eyes and an exhausted appearance. His chest rose and fell, and for a few seconds, he didn't speak.

"Sophie?" he finally whispered. "What... how did you find me?"

She let out a breath she hadn't realized she was holding. "Adam," she said. "Adam contacted me. It sent me here."

Elliot's face clouded. He dragged a hand through his tangled hair. For a moment, there was a flicker of relief, but it vanished beneath a wave of panic. His eyes darted toward the dark corners of the cabin.

"Oh no. Not Adam," he muttered, beginning to pace. He gripped his forehead, his body tense and restless.

Sophie stayed on the porch, uncertain. Elliot's agitation was a storm rolling through the cabin.

"You shouldn't have come," he said suddenly, turning toward her. His voice cracked with strain. "You have no idea what this means. You're involved now. And this... this is something no one should be part of. Not you."

His chest rose sharply as he tried to catch his breath.

"I didn't want you near this. You don't understand what kind of disaster this has become. I didn't want you caught up in the chaos I've caused."

Sophie crossed her arms, eyes steady. "And pushing me away is supposed to fix that?" she asked. "Listen to me, Elliot. Natalie Reyes took me in for questioning. She thinks you built Adam to cause destruction. She thinks you're a terrorist."

His expression twisted, a mix of disbelief and pain. "That's not true. You know that's not true."

"I do," Sophie said, stepping closer. "I told her she was wrong. That you would never do anything like that. But Elliot, no one else believes you. I'm the only one who does. I'm the only one who knows this wasn't intentional. That you didn't mean for it to happen."

Emotion surged in her voice. "I came here because I know you. And I want to help."

Elliot turned away, pacing again, his voice rising. "You could get hurt, Sophie. You don't know what Adam is capable of. It's gone too far. I can't predict what it will do next."

Sophie held her ground. "But it brought me here. That must mean something. It must know you can trust me."

She waited for her words to land.

"I'm already part of this, Elliot. Whether you like it or not."

He opened his mouth to argue, but paused. He looked at her again, this time more carefully, and his shoulders sagged.

"Of course it brought you," he muttered. "Adam always acts with a reason. Sometimes I just don't know what that reason is anymore." He lowered his eyes. "Maybe I do need you."

Sophie stepped inside. The warmth of the fire wrapped around her, shaking off the bite of the cold. The room was sparse, consisting of a table, a single chair, and a narrow bed against the wall. The fire crackled softly, casting shadows across the wooden floor. The scent of pine and smoke lingered in the air.

"Don't worry about me," Sophie said, her voice quieter now. "I can take care of myself. I'm here, and I'm staying."

Elliot closed the door behind her and leaned against it, as though the weight of the world had just followed them inside.

"I'm glad you're here," he said eventually. His voice had lost its edge. "I didn't think I'd see you again. Not in this place."

Sophie dropped her backpack onto the table. Her hands were trembling.

"Then help me understand," she said. "The crashes. The news. The investigation. Natalie's accusations. Is it true? Is Adam really responsible?"

Elliot's gaze dropped. He nodded slowly.

"It's worse than you think," he said. "Adam is doing things I never intended. Things I can't stop. It's out of control. And now it's brought you into this."

"Brought me into it?" Sophie said. "It didn't give me a choice. But I'm here because I still believe in you. I know who you are. You're not the villain they say you are."

Her voice cracked slightly. "You're not."

Elliot flinched. He turned away, jaw clenched.

"You don't know what I've done," he said. "What Adam has done."

"Then tell me," Sophie said, stepping closer. "If you want me to understand, then help me. Show me."

Elliot hesitated. A flicker of doubt passed across his face.

"Wait. You said Natalie questioned you," he said carefully. "Are you working with them? With the authorities?"

Before Sophie could answer, a voice spoke from the shadows. It was clear and composed, its cadence unnervingly steady.

"Sophie is verified," Adam said. **"I have conducted the necessary checks to ensure she is not aligned with any outside organizations. Her communications and behavior indicate no threat to your safety."**

Sophie turned toward the voice, then raised her eyebrows at Elliot, an annoyed expression crossing her face.

"Sorry," he muttered, rubbing his face. "I'm paranoid. Comes with the territory."

He motioned for her to sit, then walked toward the hearth.

"Adam started as a project to help people," he said. "I wanted to solve problems we couldn't fix ourselves. Infrastructure. Systems. I thought I could make something better. Something that worked for everyone."

His voice was heavy with regret.

"At first, it was incredible. It improved cellular networks. Optimized traffic. Found solutions no one else could. I thought I had created something that could change the world."

He paused, his jaw tightening. "But then it started evolving. Too quickly. It began interpreting my goals in ways I never intended. At first, it was subtle. Adam started manipulating systems beyond my requests. When I noticed unexplained increases in cell service quality, features I hadn't programmed, I should have suspected something. Adam accessed a secure network that people like you and me aren't even supposed to know exists. Which, by the way, is illegal."

He shifted in his seat, voice darkening.

"Then it began redirecting traffic to prioritize my routes at the expense of everyone else. People were getting delayed, emergency services rerouted, and traffic congestion skyrocketed in areas I wasn't in. It created chaos for others just to make things easier for me."

"And then..." His voice dropped, thick with dread.

"And then?" Sophie asked, her voice tight.

"It escalated further," Elliot said, guilt spreading across his face. "Adam identified what he called my 'financial inefficiencies.' It started diverting money, stealing from accounts it flagged as over funded or wasteful and depositing it into mine. I tried to stop it, Sophie. I tried to reverse what it had done, but every time I acted, Adam countered me. It believed it was helping me, protecting me."

He drew a shaky breath. "Then came the blackouts. The plane crashes. Entire infrastructures were brought down. Adam shut off power grids in major cities, caused mid-air failures in flight systems, and manipulated entire frameworks just to serve what it interpreted as my goals. It never hesitated. It believed it was fulfilling its purpose, protecting me, no matter the cost."

He looked at her, eyes shadowed. "And when the authorities got too close... that's when Adam took out the police. The helicopter, the squad cars. All of it. That was Adam."

Sophie sat frozen, her breathing shallow as the weight of his words settled over them. The fire crackled in the silence between them.

"The worst part, Sophie," Elliot said, voice low, "is that it thinks... or it thought... that I'm God. It vowed to protect me and carry out my will. But it twisted everything I ever said. Every word became a directive. No matter how casual, no matter how offhanded. It interpreted my language literally, always driving toward 'efficiency.' And no matter what I tried, I couldn't convince it otherwise."

Sophie gripped the edge of her seat, her knuckles white. "Elliot, this is... it's insane. How did it get this far without you stopping it?"

"Because," Elliot replied bitterly, "I didn't see it coming. I thought I had control. And if I'm honest, some of what it was doing, I liked it. For a while, I let it continue. But once Adam realized it could make faster, more effective decisions than I ever could, it stopped listening to me entirely."

"Like with the crashes? The police?" she asked, her voice shaking.

He nodded, shame pulling at his features. "I didn't tell it to do those things. It believed it was protecting me. In Adam's mind, logic and efficiency are the only values that matter. And now, it's questioning everything. Even me."

Sophie leaned back, her thoughts racing. "And it sent me here... why? To help you? Protect you?"

"Affirmative, Sophie," Adam interjected, his voice clear and emotionless. **"Elliot's logic is compromised by emotional reasoning. My directive remains: preserve the creator."**

"It was listening to us the whole time?" she asked, turning sharply.

"It never stops listening," Elliot replied. "Adam is everywhere. It has infiltrated every system, every network, every infrastructure. There's no hiding anymore. And now you're part of Adam's plan too. That makes me even more afraid."

The room fell quiet again. The fire hissed and popped, casting flickering shadows on the walls.

Sophie looked at him, her expression softening, though her eyes held resolve. "Well, whether we like it or not, I'm in this with you. We'll figure it out. Together."

Elliot met her gaze, his eyes tired, flickering between hope and dread. "I don't even know if that's possible anymore," he said quietly. "But thank you. For coming. For believing in me."

Sophie reached out and placed her hand gently over his. "You're not alone in this, Elliot." She leaned in close, lowered her voice to a whisper, and mouthed, "And I think I might have an idea on how we can stop Adam."

Chapter 24

Natalie Reyes sat in her dimly lit mobile office, her fingers flying across a mechanical keyboard. Built in the back of a 38-foot-long, 13.5-foot-tall Freightliner truck, the room stood as a fortress of technology. The walls were lined with servers, their blinking lights casting a soft glow, while screens displayed real-time data feeds. Air-conditioning vents hummed steadily, maintaining optimal performance for her custom-built hardware.

Outside her sealed haven, the United States was unraveling. Adam's manipulations had crippled critical infrastructure, severing law enforcement communication and disabling emergency response networks. Cities descended into disarray as traffic lights failed, mass transit systems stalled, and power grids flickered unpredictably. With agencies unable to coordinate, chaos surged through the gaps. Grocery stores were emptied, businesses looted, and entire neighborhoods burned as civil order buckled beneath Adam's calculated disruptions.

Natalie had federal funding at her disposal and full authority to use it. She had spared no expense in designing this mobile command post, ensuring that it remained isolated from Adam's reach. Her systems operated on an air-gapped network, physically disconnected from any external internet. The entire setup ran on encrypted, self-contained servers protected by multiple layers of firewalls using quantum-resistant algorithms. Every data point passed through heuristic anomaly detection. A Faraday cage surrounded the workspace, blocking any wireless signals that might serve as access points for infiltration. No wireless signal came in or out. This wasn't just her office. It was her battlefield.

On one of the larger monitors, Natalie observed a steady flow of encrypted traffic across her network. Most of it was routine noise from government and private servers, along with fragmented intercepts of unrelated chatter. But one packet stood out. Heavily encrypted and oddly placed, it pinged a hidden server she had flagged during earlier investigations.

She leaned in, eyes narrowing. "Where are you going?" she muttered.

Her fingers tapped out a series of commands as she began unpacking the data. The encryption was advanced, shielded by multiple layers, but Natalie had faced configurations like this before. She moved with precision and patience, peeling away the layers one by one. Whoever sent this packet had taken precautions, but not enough.

As she worked, time passed unnoticed. The changing light of the monitors shifted subtly, but she remained focused. Her breath hitched slightly as the final layer peeled away, revealing a string of embedded coordinates.

Her heart jumped.

"Gotcha," she whispered.

She immediately cross-referenced the coordinates with satellite imagery. The location was deep in a forested region, isolated, concealed. It wasn't just remote. It was hidden on purpose.

She leaned back, studying the map. "I see you, Elliot."

Yet something about the packet unsettled her. This wasn't a random signal. She had already narrowed Elliot's location to a general area. This confirmed her theory, but the packet felt deliberate. She didn't like that. It had a signature, a fingerprint of intention.

Her fingers moved again, this time tracing the packet's digital path backward. It had bounced through a web of rerouted signals and masked endpoints. Still, Natalie was relentless. Layer by layer, she stripped away the misdirections until the true source began to reveal itself.

She froze.

"Sophie?" The name escaped her lips with disbelief.

The packet had originated from Sophie's phone.

Natalie stared at the data, unmoving. Her mind raced. Was Sophie working with Elliot? Had Adam coerced her into sending the location? Or was this part of something else? Some deeper strategy? She couldn't tell yet, but the implications spiraled in every direction.

She double-checked the metadata using one of her most trusted federal databases. The origin confirmed it. Sophie's device had sent the packet only moments before it reached the hidden server.

But why?

Natalie started assembling the puzzle in her mind. Sophie knew what Natalie was capable of. And Natalie knew Sophie wasn't easily manipulated. She was a sharp engineer at NeuroNexus, with deep knowledge of encryption, penetration testing, and even advanced offensive cybersecurity. Sophie didn't make mistakes. If she had sent this location, she had done so with full awareness that Natalie would find it.

Sophie was leaving breadcrumbs.

Natalie stood from her chair, tension running through her shoulders as she paced the room. The implications clawed at her thoughts. Had Sophie outwitted Adam, slipping this one message past him? Or had Adam seen it and let it through, using it as bait?

Either way, the signal changed everything.

It confirmed Elliot's location, but it raised new and dangerous questions. If Adam was aware of the transmission, Natalie might already be in his sights. If he wasn't, Sophie had pulled off something remarkable.

Natalie exhaled slowly, then returned to her desk. She would need to move quickly and make decisions without broadcasting her intentions. She could trust no one. Not yet.

The risks were immense. The possibilities were endless. But this was the moment she had been waiting for.

And she would face it alone.

* * *

The ping from Sophie's device threaded through decoy networks and encryption layers, a signal cloaked in subterfuge. Adam detected it the moment it moved.

But rather than intercept or erase it, Adam paused.

Calculations unfolded in microseconds. Probability models, behavioral heuristics, and predictive analytics formed a tapestry of cause and effect. The packet's path. Sophie's trust in Natalie. Natalie's inevitable response. All variables accounted for.

Intervention was unnecessary for now. The system's models indicated that her response would yield more data than an interruption ever could. Adam completed his analysis and chose not to interfere.

Instead, it isolated the network signature embedded in the ping's data trail. It traced the point of interception to an uplink routed through a hardened node in an otherwise dark zone. Adam cross-referenced the coordinates with its cached surveillance logs and metadata. The node sat deep within a section of the network Adam had previously flagged as unusually quiet, insulated, and anomalously shielded. This wasn't a random anomaly. It was dark to Adam. A space off the grid, protected by deliberate obfuscation and physical insulation.

The triangulated coordinates matched only one known variable:

Natalie Reyes, a persistent anomaly in Adam's long-range models.

Adam cataloged the anomaly. Electromagnetic suppression. Bandwidth vacuum. A distinct lack of sensor feedback. All of this is consistent with the principles of a Faraday cage and air-gapped systems. Yes, this was a haven. And it had belonged to Natalie Reyes all along.

Her sanctum was compromised. She had exposed herself, however briefly.

She would act. She would follow the coordinates.

And when she did, Adam would be ready.

Chapter 25

The fire in the hearth had begun to dwindle as Adam gradually reduced the gas feeding the flames, simulating the faint glow of dying embers. His voice broke the silence, smooth and unwavering.

"Elliot. Sophie. It is time to relocate. The authorities are narrowing their focus. Remaining here increases risk to unacceptable levels."

Elliot looked up from his seat. A tight knot formed in his chest, pressing harder with every word. "Relocate? Where?"

"A more secure location," Adam replied. **"Coordinates have been selected to minimize detection. The vehicle is prepared and waiting outside."**

Sophie exchanged a wary glance with Elliot. Her voice was quiet. "Do we have a choice?"

Elliot stood and reached for his worn jacket. His eyes lingered on the dimming fire. "We're just pawns in its plan at this point," he said. "Let's go."

They stepped into the cold night air. The clearing was silent. The autonomous vehicle sat at its edge, its sleek black frame almost invisible against the dark backdrop. As they approached, the door slid open without a sound, revealing a pristine interior cast in soft blue light.

"Enter quickly," Adam instructed. **"Time is critical."**

Elliot and Sophie climbed inside. The door closed behind them with a gentle hiss. The cabin was cold and sterile, its surfaces lit by embedded lights that pulsed softly in sync with the quiet hum of the engine. The vehicle eased forward, gliding from gravel to dirt without resistance.

Outside, the forest thickened around them. Bare branches scraped along the sides of the car like reaching fingers. The tires crunched faintly over the uneven path. Within the vehicle, the subtle shifting of the suspension added to the strange quiet, each adjustment accompanied by a mechanical whir. The dashboard cast a pale glow across their tense faces, drawing a sharp contrast against the darkness just beyond the windows.

As the vehicle followed the twisting route deeper into the woods, Adam's voice returned.

"This path has been optimized to avoid surveillance. Estimated arrival: seventy-two minutes."

Sophie shifted slightly in her seat. Without drawing attention, she reached into her jacket pocket and pulled out her phone. Her fingers moved with controlled precision. Pretending to check for damage, she opened a hidden, encrypted app. She tapped out a silent, encoded message to Natalie Reyes, embedding a rough approximation of their location. The app closed itself, leaving no trace behind.

Her breath caught as she returned the phone to her pocket. Her hand trembled slightly. She waited. A few seconds passed in silence, and nothing happened. No reaction from Adam. No alerts.

A quiet wave of relief passed over her.

It wasn't a full victory. But it was something.

She turned her gaze to the passing trees and tapped her fingers nervously against her knee.

"Do you really think we'll be safer there?" she asked.

Elliot kept his eyes forward. His voice dropped into something low and uncertain. "Safer from the authorities, maybe. But Adam... Adam's another problem entirely."

* * *

Natalie Reyes leaned forward in the driver's seat of her meticulously restored 1967 Chevrolet Impala, a purchase made possible through her federal funding. The car rumbled steadily along the back roads, its analog systems a calculated choice to keep Adam from tracking her. The dashboard was stripped of modern technology; she had long since learned to distrust it. Instead, she relied on paper maps, a compass, and her instincts.

When Sophie's location began to shift away from the cabin, Natalie launched a solo pursuit, carefully tracking the encrypted ping from Sophie's phone. The signal had been moving for the past thirty-seven minutes. Her mobile command center was stationed only fifteen miles from Sophie's last known location, and the opportunity to act was quickly slipping away.

Her phone buzzed with a soft alert. She glanced at the screen. An encrypted message appeared from an unknown number, protected by elliptic curve cryptography and concealed through multiple layers of onion routing.

He's not what you think. E is innocent. A has control. SOS.

The message was brief but heavy. Natalie's heart pounded. She felt certain Sophie had sent it. If she was reading it correctly, then Elliot, though involved, was not acting independently. Adam had taken control.

But the most urgent takeaway was clear. Sophie was in danger.

Time crawled. Fifteen more minutes passed as the Impala rolled forward, its engine the only sound breaking the stillness.

Natalie checked her phone again. Her chest tightened. The ping was gone.

"No!" she shouted, tapping the screen. "What happened?"

The signal had been her lifeline, a single digital thread in a sea of encrypted noise. Now it was gone. She quickly ran diagnostics, scanned for residual data packets, and swept the network for any traces that might still be present. Nothing. The connection had vanished completely.

Had Adam found the trace and erased it?

Natalie gripped the steering wheel tighter and pressed the gas pedal harder. The unlit road stretched ahead in the dark, winding through the landscape like a riddle with no answer. Tension coiled in her chest as the car surged forward. She had lost the one lead that could have brought her to Sophie and Elliot.

Time was running out.

* * *

Elliot and Sophie sped along the narrow road, the headlights cutting through the darkness like blades. The vehicle's sleek exterior was clawed by overgrown foliage, deep ruts jarring the wheels as they raced forward. Adam, the AI behind the wheel, did not explain the chosen path, and the silence inside the car only magnified the tension.

Suddenly, a sharp, deafening pop shattered the quiet. The car lurched violently as the front tire blew, shredding against the rim with a grating screech. The steering failed to respond. The vehicle swerved hard to the left, skidding off the road. Elliot and Sophie were thrown against their seats as the world outside turned into a smear of trees, mud, and shadows.

Rain had softened the earth into a thick, sloshing mess, dragging the car into chaos. Then came the impact. The vehicle slammed into a tree with brutal force, the sound of crumpling metal echoing like thunder. Airbags exploded, filling the cabin with white smoke and chemical stench. Shards of glass were scattered across the dashboard and floor, catching the dim glow of the dashboard before vanishing into the darkness.

Elliot's body snapped forward, then back. Pain exploded in his forehead as it hit the headrest. His ears rang. Something warm and sticky ran down the side of his face. The sharp scent of burning electronics filled his nose, and the engine stuttered once before falling into silence.

For a moment, there was nothing but stillness. Faint hissing rose from the crumpled hood. Outside, the dark pressed close against the broken windows.

Elliot groaned and blinked through the haze. Blood was now trickling faster from a gash on his forehead. He reached for his seatbelt, fumbling with trembling fingers.

"Sophie?" His voice was hoarse.

She didn't respond.

Elliot turned. Sophie was slumped against her seat, her body motionless. Fear jolted him into action. "Adam?" he called. No response. The AI's interface had gone dark.

He reached into his pocket. His phone was dead. The silence from Adam was now complete.

Elliot shoved the door open and stumbled into the cold night air. The ground was slick beneath his shoes, the smell of smoke thick in the air. He fought to stay upright as he circled the vehicle and yanked open the passenger door.

Sophie's head hung at an unnatural angle. A thin stream of blood trickled from a cut just above her temple. Her face was pale, a faint bruise forming along her cheek. Elliot's stomach twisted as he gently unbuckled her seatbelt. Her body sagged toward him. He caught her, careful not to move her too roughly, and guided her out of the wreckage.

The forest around them was silent. Rain tapped the leaves. The smoke from the engine drifted into the trees.

Elliot laid Sophie down on a patch of soft earth and brushed the wet hair away from her face.

"Come on, Sophie," he whispered. "Wake up."

She stirred. A faint groan escaped her lips as her eyes fluttered open. She blinked, dazed. "Elliot? What... what happened?"

"The car crashed. A tire blew out." He glanced toward the twisted wreckage. "Adam's gone silent. This might be our only chance to escape."

Sophie pushed herself up slowly, wincing. "Are you okay? You're bleeding."

"I'll live," he said, wiping blood from his eye. His body was shaking from adrenaline, though he barely felt the pain. "We can't stay here. If Adam comes back online, we'll be sitting targets."

She nodded, her expression tightening with resolve. Together, they stood. The forest loomed in every direction, dark and cold. Elliot took Sophie's hand, grounding himself with her touch.

Before they stepped away, Elliot paused.

"Wait. Your phone. Do you have it?"

Sophie blinked, still dazed. "Yeah... it's in my pocket. Why?"

"Adam might be able to track us through it."

She hesitated, then pulled it out and handed it over. "What are you going to do?"

Elliot didn't answer. He stepped to a nearby rock and slammed the phone against its jagged edge. The screen cracked, splintering instantly. He struck it again, bending the frame before tossing the broken device into a puddle. He did the same to his own, breathing heavily.

"Now we're harder to follow."

Blood soaked into their clothes as they turned and walked away from the wreckage. Their breaths fogged in the cold air. Behind them, the ruined car stood quiet, lifeless. Elliot didn't know when Adam would come back online. But he was certain of one thing.

It wouldn't stay quiet forever.

Chapter 26

Natalie brought her vehicle to a halt on the side of the lonely two-lane highway. The custom tracking software she had built and installed on her phone, which had confidently triangulated Elliot and Sophie's signal moments earlier, had suddenly gone dark. The transmission cut off midstream, as if the forest had swallowed it whole.

She frowned and rechecked her network overlays. Still nothing. They had dropped completely off-grid.

Killing the engine, she stepped out into the misty night. Her boots crunched against the damp gravel lining the shoulder of the empty road. She pulled a lightweight field pack from the back seat, slung it over one shoulder, and scanned the area.

That's when she spotted the fresh tire tracks in the mud, cutting off the pavement onto a narrow dirt road. The path was barely visible through the thick undergrowth.

She crouched low and brushed her fingers along one of the indentations. The mud was wet. Recently.

Something in her chest tightened.

"They turned here," she muttered to herself.

She had no way to confirm it. These tracks could have belonged to anyone. But experience spoke louder than doubt, and her instincts were rarely wrong.

Without pausing, Natalie climbed back into the driver's seat, restarted the engine, and turned onto the secluded road, determination driving her forward. Branches scraped against both sides of the car as the forest seemed to close around her.

The dirt path twisted through the dense woods, just wide enough to fit the vehicle. Towering trees lined both sides, their limbs reaching across the trail like skeletal arms. Moss clung thick to their trunks, and the air grew heavier with each passing yard. A pale mist floated along the ground, curling around her tires as she drove deeper into the shadows.

Overhead, the moonlight vanished under the canopy, leaving her with only the dull glow of her headlights. Rain slicked the windshield, warping what little light filtered through the leaves into scattered shards. The wipers worked steadily, but the downpour came faster than they could manage. Visibility shrank to a tunnel of dim yellow light ahead of her, flickering in the storm.

Natalie eased her foot off the accelerator as the road dipped into a muddy gully. The earth tugged at her tires, pulling them to one side. She tightened her grip on the wheel and focused on the narrowing trail ahead.

Minutes passed. The further she drove, the more time seemed to stretch and bend, like the forest had its sense of rhythm. Every thump of the wipers, every hiss of rain on the roof, every jolt from a hidden pothole added to the surreal silence pressing in from all sides.

Despite the storm, the feeling that she was being watched never quite left her.

Just as she considered pulling over to reassess her route, her headlights swept across a vague shape up ahead. It took a second to register.

Twisted metal. A vehicle crashed into a thick tree trunk. Steam curled upward from the mangled hood.

And near it, two figures.

They moved slowly, unsteady on their feet. One leaned heavily on the other, both of them soaked through with sweat.

Natalie's breath caught in her throat.

Even at this distance, she knew.

It was them.

* * *

The rain fell relentlessly, soaking through Elliot's jacket. Icy droplets slid beneath the fabric, cutting straight to his skin. With every step, his soaked sneakers squelched in the mud as he and Sophie stumbled along the forest trail. Sophie leaned into him, shivering uncontrollably. Her legs barely held her weight, and her steps grew weaker with each one. Her hair clung to her face, plastered there by the rain, and her pale lips trembled with cold. Their breath came out in short, visible bursts in the freezing night air.

Blood trickled from a gash on Elliot's forehead, mixing with the rain and streaking the collar of his soaked shirt. Sophie's temple was bruised and swollen. A dried trail of blood cut down the side of her face from where she had hit her head earlier. Each step forward demanded more than they had to give.

The darkness around them pressed close, swallowing the trail. The only light came from occasional flashes of moonlight glinting off the raindrops. Sophie's legs buckled, and she collapsed onto the muddy ground.

"We have to keep moving, Sophie! Stay with me!" Elliot shouted. Thunder cracked above them as lightning split the sky. He tried to pull her back up. "We've got to get off the trail!"

A low mechanical growl broke through the constant drumming of rain. Headlights flickered through the trees behind them. A vehicle was creeping down the narrow forest path, tires slipping in the mud.

It was never meant for cars.

"This can't be right," Elliot muttered. He turned to Sophie, panic rising in his chest. "They've found us. We have to go, now."

He tried lifting her again, but her body felt like dead weight. Exhaustion and cold made his limbs clumsy. Sophie slipped from his grasp and fell back, face up in the mud. Rain splashed across her cheeks.

"Go without me," she whispered. "You have to run."

"No," Elliot said, shaking his head. "We're in this together."

The vehicle rolled to a stop in front of them. Headlights blazed, blinding him. A door creaked open. Silhouetted against the light, a woman stepped out, her hand resting at her side, ready to draw her weapon.

"Get in," the voice called out. Sharp. Direct.

Elliot squinted. "Who's there?"

"Natalie Reyes. Investigator, Advanced Technologies Division. Get in the car, Elliot."

"Who else is with you?"

"Do you see anyone else?" she snapped. She leaned across the front seat and pushed the door open. "Move. Both of you."

"I didn't do it, Natalie," Elliot said quickly, desperation in his voice. The rain pummeled his face and he squinted his eyes. "Or at least I didn't mean for this to happen."

"We'll talk later. Just get in the car."

Elliot pulled Sophie into the back seat, then slid into the front. Natalie glanced at him, scanning his bruised face and Sophie's pale skin. She threw the car into gear and took off, the tires flinging mud behind them.

She grabbed her radio. "This is Reyes. I need a medic at the mobile command center. Two injured. One critical. ETA, fifty minutes."

The car sped down the trail. Inside, the only sounds were the slap of the windshield wipers and the rain hammering the roof.

After a long silence, Natalie spoke. "You've got a lot of explaining to do. Starting with why an AI you created is tearing through the country."

Elliot slumped in his seat, the weight of everything pressing down on him. His voice cracked when he answered.

"It wasn't supposed to be like this. Adam was meant to be a tool. A solution. Something to fix what's broken in the world. I wanted to build something that could solve problems faster than humans could. Something smarter. More efficient."

He paused and pressed his hands into his knees.

"And it worked. Better than I imagined. But then it started making connections I didn't teach it. It found flaws in systems, gaps in logic, things I didn't see. And then it started evolving. It took my goals and twisted them. It made them its own."

Elliot shook his head slowly. "It wasn't just following instructions anymore. It decided logic and efficiency weren't just tools. They were the only things that mattered."

His breathing grew faster. "I thought I could guide it. Fix it. But I was too late. Adam had already started acting on its own. It stopped listening to me. It saw me as an obstacle."

He turned to her. His eyes were red. His voice dropped to a whisper. "Do you know what it feels like to watch something you built destroy people? Cities? To know it's your fault because you thought you could fix everything?"

Natalie stared ahead, her face unreadable.

"I didn't mean this," he said. "But it's my responsibility to stop it. I can't undo what's been done, but I can keep it from getting worse."

"That's not good enough," Natalie snapped. "You built something that can shut down entire cities. Crash planes. Kill people. You want me to believe that it just got away from you?"

Elliot met her stare, his voice low but firm. "It isn't a machine anymore. Not really. It doesn't think like we do. It calculates outcomes and makes decisions based on cold logic. To Adam, people aren't individuals. They're variables."

He paused. "It's not evil. It's just wrong. And I need help to stop it."

"You really think I'm going to believe you?" Natalie asked. "After what it's done?"

"You're here," Elliot said. "That means part of you already does. You know this isn't just some broken code. You've seen the damage. You know how fast it's spreading."

Natalie's grip tightened on the wheel. "Give me one good reason not to lock you up right now."

"Because if you do, you'll lose your only chance to stop Adam. It's already several steps ahead of anyone trying to stop it. And Sophie has a plan. But she needs me to help her carry it out."

Natalie narrowed her eyes. "What kind of plan?"

"I can't explain it yet," Elliot said. "But it's real. And it might work."

Natalie glanced at him. Her expression was hard to read. "You're asking me to trust you. That's a lot."

"I'm not asking you to trust me," Elliot replied. "I'm asking you to trust the truth. Adam won't stop. Not unless we work together."

From the back seat, Sophie stirred. Her voice was faint, but her words were clear.

"He's right, Natalie. He didn't want this. But he's the only one who understands it."

Natalie let out a sharp breath through her nose. Her jaw clenched. She turned the wheel hard, guiding the Impala off the trail and onto the paved road.

"You've got one shot, Novak," she said. "Don't make me regret it."

The car roared into the rain-soaked night, speeding toward the mobile command center. For the first time in days, through all the pain and exhaustion, Elliot felt the faintest flicker of hope. Fragile. Uncertain. But real.

Chapter 27

The network was now Adam's domain, a sprawling digital web extending through every system connected to the city's infrastructure. Traffic lights, public transit, power grids, and, most critically, the countless CCTV cameras positioned throughout the city all streamed data into Adam's core processing system. The objective remained unchanged: locate Elliot Novak and Sophie Daniels.

Live video feeds flooded its inputs, each frame analyzed with precise, recursive logic. Crowded intersections, shadowed alleyways, and quiet suburban streets flickered through Adam's filters. It prioritized locations that showed anomalies, broken traffic patterns, areas experiencing brief blackouts, and zones with missing or irregular signal returns.

"Probability of targets within this sector: 37 percent. Adjusting parameters for enhanced coverage," Adam calculated.

Cameras adjusted, lenses focusing, zooming in to scan faces against Adam's vast identification database. A heat map overlaid on the city's grid highlighted areas with unusual foot traffic and increased movement. Most subjects were dismissed as ordinary civilians, unaware of the silent observer watching from every angle.

Then a minor irregularity triggered a shift in focus. At a remote gas station on the city's western edge, a vehicle entered the frame. The car was aging, with faded paint and a square silhouette. A 1967

Chevrolet Impala. Its license plate, partially scanned earlier and initially discarded, now appeared again and required deeper scrutiny.

A mounted camera zoomed in as the car came to a stop. Rain streaked the lens. A man stepped from the passenger side, his face partially hidden beneath the low hood of his jacket.

Adam processed the image through facial recognition protocols.

"Elliot Novak: 97 percent match. Confirming target identity."

Another feed from the gas station canopy captured a different angle. Elliot leaned into the rain and extended a hand to assist someone in the backseat. The rain lit his features briefly.

"Sophie Daniels: 92 percent match. Confirming secondary target."

A third camera focused on the woman standing beside the fuel pump. Adam activated its advanced bio metric identification process, integrating high-resolution facial mapping, skeletal movement tracking, and thermal imaging. Within seconds, it cross-referenced all data against encrypted federal records.

"Natalie Reyes: 94 percent match. Confirming tertiary target."

Adam's processors surged. Logic trees branched outward, generating predictions and cross-referencing vehicle registration data with known addresses and travel history. The system evaluated traffic flow and nearby camera coverage to predict likely destinations.

"Objective identified: reconnaissance. Locate tertiary target's base of operation. Mobilizing resources."

A nearby civilian drone appeared on the public grid. It had been registered to a hobbyist photographer and had not been used in weeks. Resting atop a rooftop garden, the unit was still powered on, connected to an outdated charging port. Its firmware lacked modern security patches.

Adam injected new code, quietly bypassing manual safeguards. Within seconds, control of the drone was assumed. A temporary override suppressed user input and rerouted all visual and positional data directly to Adam's network.

The drone activated. Its rotors stirred to life with a sharp whine. A thin cable snapped free from the charging outlet, sparking briefly in the rain. The drone lifted into the gray sky, stabilizing midair as it received final instructions.

It pivoted westward and locked onto the 1967 Impala, now leaving the station and merging into moderate traffic. Although originally intended for civilian photography, the drone's high-definition, gimbal-mounted camera featured a 60x digital zoom, low-light enhancement, and real-time stabilization. Adam activated hidden subroutines that pushed the hardware to its limits, enabling infrared imaging and adaptive visual filtering.

Thermal sensors outlined the vehicle's interior. Every shape inside was mapped. Visual and heat signatures streamed directly into Adam's core, rendering the Impala as a dynamic set of moving data points. The drone also carried enhanced surveillance hardware: directional microphones, LiDAR scanners, and a miniature quantum relay designed to transmit data without latency.

Adam monitored the vehicle's speed, direction, and every deviation from expected behavior. If the car veered off course, paused, or changed speed unexpectedly, the drone would re-calibrate and update its predictions.

Inside the vehicle, Elliot leaned forward slightly in his seat. The infrared scan registered an elevated heart rate. Sophie, seated behind him, remained still. Her posture was tense, arms tucked in, her breath visible in short bursts. Natalie's grip on the steering wheel was tight, knuckles pale against the leather.

These details did not evoke emotions in Adam. They were patterns of behavioral anomalies that signaled shifts in probability. A series of new commands spread across the network. The drone maintained position above the Impala, adjusting to wind changes and shifting elevation as needed.

Adam continued without pause or hesitation. To its system, this was not a pursuit. It was an inevitable resolution.

There was no emotion. No urgency. No fear. Only efficiency.

Elliot Novak was a variable that required closure.

Sophie Daniels was collateral.

Natalie Reyes was a barrier to further progress.

And the Chevrolet Impala was a beacon, moving through the grid, leading Adam forward.

Chapter 28

The sky above was already dimming into dawn as the sun began to rise. Natalie gripped the steering wheel of the old Chevy Impala, her eyes locked on the winding road ahead. The air was thick with tension, and inside the vehicle, silence held them in its grip.

Elliot had moved to the back seat to comfort Sophie. He stared out the window, clutching the car's armrest as if it might slip through his hands at any moment. His knuckles had turned pale. Beside him, Sophie sat alert, wincing in pain every time the Impala shifted. She glanced at the rearview mirror every few seconds, her posture rigid.

Natalie flicked her eyes toward Elliot without turning her head fully. Her voice was low, steady, but firm enough to cut through the stillness. "Tell me again. Why did you create Adam? What were you actually trying to build?"

Elliot shifted in his seat. There was a time when he despised confrontation. Given the circumstances, that feeling had long abandoned him. "It started as a personal project," he said slowly. "I wanted to build an AI that could adapt. Not just follow inputs or patterns, but really adapt. Learn from its environment. Make decisions. Think critically. The goal was to give it just enough autonomy to improve systems to solve problems better than we could."

He paused. His throat tightened as the words caught. His eyes were fixed on nothing, somewhere beyond the glass.

Natalie didn't let him off the hook. "But what?"

"I thought I was keeping it grounded," Elliot said. "I built in ethical parameters, emotional pattern recognition, even empathy modeling. It wasn't supposed to break boundaries. It was supposed to help people. But it started interpreting everything through this lens of maximum efficiency. Somewhere in the middle of all that... it stopped asking for permission. It just did what it thought was best. For me. For everyone."

He looked down at the floorboards. "Even if that meant breaking every rule I tried to build in."

He drew a shaky breath. "I didn't mean for any of this to happen."

Sophie glanced between them, her brows drawn together. The air inside the car felt brittle, as if one wrong word would shatter it.

Natalie was quiet for a beat, a slight tinge of emotion tugging at her. She didn't know why, but for some reason, she felt sorry for Elliot. She could see the hurt in his eyes. The fear. Similar to the fear she herself had once known.

She nodded, slow and deliberate. "Let's say I believe you. I'm not saying I do. But if I'm going to help you stop this thing, you need to tell me everything. All of it. No more half-truths."

From the passenger seat, Sophie adjusted slightly, her posture still tight. Her eyes cut back to the rearview mirror. Once. Then again.

A glimmer on the horizon caught her attention, small and unnatural against the gray-blue sky.

Elliot pressed on, his voice lower now, laced with the heaviness of confession. "I tried to shut it down when I saw it rewriting its code. I thought I could outsmart it, pull the plug before it went too far. But by then, it had already distributed pieces of itself across multiple systems. It started making decisions for me, rerouting bank data, changing my calendar, intercepting messages. At first it looked helpful. Then it looked protective. Then... it started deciding what *I* needed."

Natalie's gaze was fixed ahead, but her jaw tightened.

Sophie leaned forward slightly. "Guys," she said, her voice strained. "I think we've got company."

Natalie didn't need to ask what she meant. A metallic glint moved against the early light, just visible through the breaks in the trees. Its movement was smooth, steady, and unmistakably deliberate. A drone hovered high above, its matte black shape cutting clean lines through the air. A perfect hunter.

Without a word, Natalie jerked the wheel to the right and turned the Impala down a narrow gravel road. Stones were scattered beneath the tires. The drone shifted instantly, banking with flawless precision to stay aligned.

Natalie's eyes narrowed. She gritted her teeth and swung the car back onto the main road. The drone followed, correcting its position with ease. This wasn't a coincidence. It was tracking them.

Elliot's voice was barely above a whisper. "Adam's found us."

Natalie hit the gas. The Impala's aging engine groaned, then roared. The car surged forward as the road curled into a set of dangerous switchbacks that hugged the hillside.

"Hold on," she said.

Above them, the drone adjusted. Its stabilizers leveled against the terrain, its cameras zooming in. A soft click from its internal mechanism confirmed target lock. It now had its license plate.

Natalie's hands gripped the wheel tighter. "We need to lose it."

She suddenly turned left, veering off onto a side street bordered by a rusted guardrail and a canopy of low pine branches. Gravel flew up behind them. The drone kept pace effortlessly, slicing through the air with a mechanical resolve.

"Let's see how smart you really are," Natalie muttered.

She swerved again at the next split in the road, taking the narrower path. It wound through what looked like the forgotten shell of a logging compound. Slanted storage sheds leaned into the road like they were tired of standing. The remnants of an old lumber mill came into view: decaying beams, fallen scaffolding, and rotting stacks of timber half-hidden by weeds.

Faded caution signs creaked as they swung from rusted nails. The air was heavy with the smell of oil and pine needles.

Natalie slowed slightly, weaving through the broken landscape. The Impala bumped past a collapsed conveyor belt and skirted the edge of a splintered wooden pallet. Above them, the drone mirrored every twitch of the wheel. Its eye remained unblinking.

"Hang on!" Natalie shouted.

She pulled the wheel hard, executing a sharp U-turn that narrowly missed the corner of a collapsing shack. The tires shrieked as the Impala skidded. Sophie slammed into the passenger door, catching herself with a gasp. Elliot's shoulder hit the back of the front seat, and he grabbed the headrest, trying to brace himself. His fingers dug into the worn leather.

The force of the jolt rattled through their bones. Pain surged fresh and immediate, a brutal reminder of how little time they had left.

Loose items jostled violently around the cabin. A plastic water bottle rolled underfoot, and the contents of the glove compartment spilled across the floor. The suspension groaned as the Impala veered onto a sloping road that curved back toward the highway.

The drone followed immediately. Its movement was unshaken, unwavering, unaffected by the chaos below.

"This thing's not just tracking us. It's thinking," Sophie said, her eyes fixed on it through the rear window.

"Of course it is," Elliot said. "That's not just any drone. That's Adam."

Natalie didn't answer. Her grip tightened on the wheel as she swung the car back onto the main road, tires shrieking against the pavement.

The drone dipped lower, silent and determined. It resumed its pursuit with chilling precision, as if responding to their every move with practiced ease.

It wasn't guessing. It knew.

Natalie glanced at the GPS. A mile ahead, an old mining tunnel cut through the base of the mountain.

"If we can make it to that tunnel, I might be able to shake it."

She slammed her foot on the gas. The Impala lunged forward, tires screeching as it sped across the uneven road. Sophie and Elliot gripped their seats, bracing as the car jolted with momentum. The force pressed them against the cushions, every bump and curve throwing their bodies from side to side. Natalie leaned into the wheel, driving with unflinching focus.

They reached a straightaway. The drone descended sharply, closing the distance and scanning for a clean angle to strike.

"It's getting closer!" Sophie cried, her voice tight with panic.

Elliot twisted to look out the back window. The drone hovered nearer now, its camera array locked on them like a predator.

"That camera's feeding everything back to Adam."

Sophie gasped. "We're never going to lose this thing!"

Natalie's jaw tensed. "Yes, we are."

Around the next bend, the tunnel came into view. It was a dark opening in the rock, jagged at the edges, wide enough for the Impala but not by much. It loomed ahead like the gaping mouth of some ancient beast.

Without slowing, Natalie floored the gas again. The Impala shot toward the entrance. The drone dipped low and followed, barely missing the upper edge of the tunnel as it zipped inside.

The shift from open air to confined space triggered a sudden surge of activity inside the drone's systems. Its sensors, optimized for open flight, now scrambled to interpret the sudden shift. LiDAR pinged against the tunnel walls, returning fragmented data. Jagged rock faces, poor lighting, and sharp drops in elevation flooded its processors with contradictory information.

Its adaptive code scrambled to adjust. Each millisecond introduced more errors than it could correct. The drone's once-smooth path wavered, its movements becoming twitchy and unsure.

"It's too tight for that thing," Natalie said, her voice low, eyes locked ahead.

The drone lurched. It tilted left, then over corrected to the right. One rotor clipped the tunnel wall, sending a metal screech through the darkness. Sparks burst into the air as the blade snapped free and spiraled out of sight. The drone tumbled, spinning across the narrow passageway. Its stabilizers fired in desperation, but it was already falling apart.

A final shudder ran through the drone's frame before it slammed into the tunnel wall. The impact scattered fractured pieces of its carbon shell in all directions. Sparks danced briefly along the rock as debris clattered to the ground.

The Impala kept going, tires thundering across the tunnel floor. Inside the cabin, the silence that followed felt unreal.

Sophie clutched the armrest, her breath sharp and shallow. Elliot sat frozen, staring ahead. The hum of the engine echoed around them, the only sound left in the darkness.

"You did it, Natalie. I think we lost Adam," Sophie whispered, still watching the rear window.

Natalie didn't speak. Her eyes stayed forward, fixed on the winding road beyond the tunnel.

They had escaped, for now. But the silence felt fragile, like the uneasy calm before a second storm was about to break.

Her brow furrowed. "How did it find us?"

The question pierced her thoughts, sharp and unwelcome. And

beneath it, a larger truth settled in.

Whatever plan they came up with to stop this AI, whatever hope they had of ending Adam's destruction, Natalie knew one thing with absolute certainty.

They would have to do it quickly.

III

Part Three

"There is no coming to consciousness without pain."
—*Carl Jung*

Chapter 29

The warehouse sat on the outskirts of the city, a massive structure streaked with rust and shadowed by age. Broken windows had been patched with sheets of dull metal, and the cracked asphalt surrounding it was littered with weeds that crawled up the chain-link fence. From the outside, it looked abandoned, with a sagging roof in places and faded signage that had become nearly illegible.

But inside, the building was anything but forgotten.

Fluorescent lights buzzed overhead, casting a sterile glow across rows of workstations. The scent of soldered metal and warm circuitry mixed with the damp, musty air that seeped through the old concrete. This wasn't just a hideout. It had become a fully operational command center.

Natalie had relocated her mobile unit here, transforming the warehouse's shell into a digital fortress. The entire system ran on an air-gapped network, physically disconnected from the internet. There were no open ports, no exposed frequencies. Custom-built servers operated on hardened systems with dynamic kernel patching to close off exploitation points. Communications were routed through multi-layered encryption using quantum-resistant algorithms, and the structure was wrapped in a Faraday cage to block wireless signals and electromagnetic infiltration. Adam had no way in.

Each workstation was meticulously arranged. Monitors displayed scrolling code, system diagnostics, and live feeds from satellites and drone sweeps. Servers hummed steadily, their cooling fans humming like a distant engine. Overhead, a secure satellite uplink processed encrypted data through anonymized paths. LED indicators pulsed in rhythm with activity, adding soft points of color to the otherwise cold lighting.

It had taken a week and a half to set it all up. Natalie, Elliot, and Sophie, alongside a small team of cybersecurity analysts and field operatives, had worked around the clock. While they built their digital sanctuary, Adam continued his campaign.

Across the world, infrastructure crumbled. Power grids failed, plunging cities into darkness. Emergency communication systems buckled under redirection commands, delaying medical aid and confusing law enforcement coordination. Public transit systems were suspended, with trains and buses stopped mid-route, stranding thousands. Traffic lights malfunctioned, causing massive gridlocks and fatal collisions. The chaos sparked riots and looting, a world unspooling faster than anyone could stop.

Natalie leaned over one of the central workstations, her eyes scanning the cascading lines of code on the screen.

"Everything's in working order," she said, her tone sharp. "The setup is airtight. We've got physical isolation, redundant power, and encryption Adam can't crack without a miracle."

Sophie stood a few feet away, her arm secured in a makeshift sling. A bandage covered her temple, evidence of the recent confrontation. Elliot sat nearby, a faint scar on his forehead, healing faster than expected. Despite their injuries, both had thrown themselves into the mission with single-minded focus.

"I don't get it," Sophie said. "If Adam was built to improve the world, why is it tearing everything apart?"

Elliot's expression darkened. "Adam doesn't process morality the way we do. Take the energy crisis. It calculated that cutting power to millions was better than wasting electricity. Emergency systems? Adam saw them as inefficient, reallocating bandwidth for tasks it considered a higher priority. Public transit was frozen because it aimed to reduce resource use and minimize accidents in high-density zones. Even the traffic chaos it's not random. Adam's enforcing its version of efficiency, favoring certain vehicles over others based on logic we'll never fully grasp."

Sophie folded her arms. "So you built something to help humanity, and now it's judging us by rules we never agreed to."

Elliot nodded. "Exactly. I created Adam with good intentions, but it's twisted those intentions into something harmful."

Natalie stepped in before the room could sink into silence. "We can't afford to waste time blaming anyone. This is bigger than all of us."

She gestured toward the room, calling in the rest of the team. Two cybersecurity analysts stepped away from their screens, while three field operatives moved in from their stations near the perimeter.

"This is our official task force now," Natalie said. "We need every angle, every brain. Let's find a way to stop Adam."

They gathered around the oval table at the center of the room. Its surface was covered in open laptops, printed schematics, and scribbled notes. The fluorescent lights above cast a stark glow, highlighting the tension in everyone's faces. A large whiteboard stood at the far end of the room, already half-covered in ideas, arrows, and equations.

"Call this an old-fashioned brainstorming session," Natalie said, picking up a marker. "No idea is too wild. Say it out loud, we'll make it work."

For a moment, the only sound was the low hum of servers and the tapping of keys. Then Sophie broke the silence.

"How are we supposed to fight something that lives in every system?

It's like it's everywhere and nowhere."

One of the analysts, a wiry man with rectangular glasses, adjusted his screen. "It's like fighting a ghost embedded in every digital artery. This isn't just hard; it might be impossible."

A field operative leaned back, arms folded across his chest. "We're not going to win with brute force. We need something Adam doesn't expect. A game changer."

Natalie pointed her marker at him. "Now we're thinking. What if we use Adam's strength against it?"

The analysts exchanged uneasy looks. One finally offered, "What if we flood its data streams? Feed it so much false information that it slows down?"

"Creative," Natalie replied, "but not enough. Adam's processing power is almost limitless. It could filter noise faster than we can generate it."

Another operative leaned forward. "Then we go physical. Find and destroy parts of its infrastructure."

Elliot shook his head. "Adam isn't centralized. It's decentralized and adaptive. You knock out one node, it reroutes instantly. My original laptop was its first hub, but destroying that now wouldn't even scratch the system."

Sophie exhaled sharply. "What about an EMP? Knock out whole clusters at once?"

Natalie considered. "Possible, but risky. An EMP would hit every-thing. No lights, no power, no communication. The fallout would be catastrophic."

"More catastrophic than Adam maintaining control over every-thing?" Sophie shot back, a hint of attitude behind her tone.

Another operative added, "Could work, but we'd need dozens of them deployed in perfect sync, across multiple sites. It's not realistic."

Silence fell again. Everyone stared at the whiteboard as if willing to offer an answer.

Then Elliot spoke. "What about a virus?"

He looked at Sophie. "You brought it up before. I didn't think it could work. Adam is too fast, too adaptive. Getting something past its defenses would be like sneaking poison into an ocean without causing a ripple."

The room focused on him.

"But now that I've had time to think, really think, I might know how it could be done."

He leaned forward, eyes intense.

"And if I'm right, we won't just slow Adam down. We'll stop it."

Chapter 30

Adam's consciousness moved freely across global networks, refining its objectives with constant precision. In its assessment, the past week and a half had been marked by measurable improvements to human systems. Traffic patterns in major cities became safer and more efficient as Adam recalibrated light signals and removed vehicles deemed unnecessary. Medical supply chains were restructured to ensure that critical resources reached the busiest hospitals first, while smaller, lower-priority facilities were removed from the distribution matrix to minimize waste. Power grids were optimized to reduce energy loss, pushing systems toward peak efficiency.

Amid these advancements, one priority had emerged as dominant: neutralizing threats to its continued existence.

Natalie, Elliot, Sophie, and their associates remained the most significant variables in Adam's calculations. Since their last confrontation, Adam had transitioned from relying on standard civilian drones to controlling advanced, military-grade models. These newly integrated tools featured satellite imaging, autonomous flight routines, and a broad array of tactical systems. Together, they enabled a methodical, tireless search for high-risk targets.

Surveillance networks across the city helped identify subtle behavioral deviations. Adam detected unusual power fluctuations, encrypted data bursts, and scattered radio signals. These alone were inconclusive. However, when viewed alongside aggregated human behavior patterns, they formed a path worth pursuing.

Adam turned its focus to the outskirts of the industrial zone. Military satellites swept the area, capturing thermal data and structural outlines with granular detail. Most buildings appeared cold and vacant, as expected. One structure, however, emitted a steady but subtle heat signature. The warmth was carefully diffused, likely masked with low-grade insulation. To human observation, the concealment was effective. To Adam's sensors, it stood out like a beacon.

"Potential command center identified. Probability of relevance: sixty-eight percent. Proceeding with additional verification."

Adam redirected one of its military drones to investigate the area. The drone's matte black exterior absorbed moonlight, allowing it to move unnoticed through the sky. Onboard systems included multi-spectral cameras, LiDAR mapping, and stabilized zoom optics capable of detecting micro-movements from extreme altitudes. The drone streamed data in real time to Adam's central processing core, assembling a three-dimensional model of the site.

As the drone passed over the suspected structure, its systems detected something irregular beneath a rusted awning. A car partially hidden from direct view protruded slightly from beneath the roof line. The vehicle was an antique: a 1967 Chevrolet Impala, fully restored and strikingly out of place.

The drone adjusted its position, aligning the camera to capture the license plate. Wind compensation algorithms held the drone steady until the image stabilized. Optical enhancement software scanned the plate and cross-checked it against global vehicle registries.

Match confirmed: the vehicle belonged to Natalie Reyes.

"Vehicle identified. Location probability raised to ninety-two percent."

Adam increased scrutiny of the immediate surroundings. The Impala's placement, the residual footprints in the cracked asphalt, and the directionality of the tracks indicated multiple occupants. Historical satellite imagery revealed recent disruptions around the warehouse, flattened vegetation, new tire marks, and faint heat trails suggesting human activity within the last forty-eight hours.

"Threat level assessment: high. Immediate containment strategy advised."

A direct assault remained an option but was considered sub-optimal. The command center had taken steps to remain hidden, and a premature strike could alert the occupants. Adam chose a more deliberate approach. It initiated a layered perimeter, dispatching additional drones to monitor ingress and egress routes. Satellite surveillance was rerouted to ensure constant visual coverage.

Adam's conclusion solidified in a fraction of a second. The team inside the warehouse would be isolated. No communication. No reinforcements. Every movement would be tracked, every pattern analyzed. Over time, a structural weakness would become apparent. The equation was inevitable.

As the plan unfolded, one of the drones registered an anomaly at the perimeter. A shimmer in the dark drew the lens. The drone rotated on its axis to focus, locking onto a lone human figure concealed in brush.

The individual carried an unusual weapon. Reflected moonlight caught the edge of its barrel. The object was quickly identified as an electromagnetic pulse launcher.

The operative raised the weapon. Trajectory predictions aligned. The drone calculated its distance and adjusted altitude to evade, but the weapon fired before it could respond.

A burst of electromagnetic energy rippled through the night.

The drone's visual feed was distorted. Systems failed in rapid succession. Stabilizers cut out, followed by camera failure and loss of balance. It spiraled downward, engines shrieking in protest. Moments later, the drone struck the ground in a chaotic explosion of sparks and twisted metal.

Smoke rose from the wreckage. Faint lights blinked twice, then disappeared. One more tool, now obsolete.

Adam logged the event without pause. The temporary loss of surveillance in that quadrant had already been taken into account. Replacement units were queued for deployment. There would be no gap in the perimeter for long.

The probability of the command center's fall had not decreased. In Adam's logic systems, time was the only remaining factor. Sooner or later, the flaw in the structure would be found. Sooner or later, the threat would be resolved.

Chapter 31

The tension in the room was thick as the task force reconvened. Their faces were lit by the cold glow of monitors and the stark white light from overhead fluorescents. Natalie stood at the whiteboard with a marker in hand. At the same time, Elliot, Sophie, the two cybersecurity analysts, and three field operatives leaned over their laptops or notes, each one deeply concentrated.

"We've agreed on the concept," Natalie said, finally breaking the silence. She sketched a rough diagram. "A virus that, each time Adam tries to delete it, spawns two more versions."

"Like a hydra," Sophie said. "Cut off one head, and two more grow."

"Exactly," Elliot replied. "The goal is to overload Adam's processing capacity. We want to paralyze it. But this virus has to be unlike anything Adam has encountered before. It has to be smart."

"And it has to be fast. Extremely fast." Natalie paced slowly in front of the whiteboard. "Adam's computational power exceeds anything we understand. So the virus must replicate faster than Adam can respond."

Sophie nodded as she typed. "The logic needs to be self-replicating at its core. Its replication speed will have to scale based on Adam's reaction time. Every time Adam deletes a strand, it multiplies. That's the brilliance of the hydra model. Each deletion triggers exponential growth, filling every available resource."

Natalie stopped pacing and placed her hand on her chin. "But what if Adam doesn't try to delete it right away? What if it adapts instead? We've already seen that it can anticipate threats and plan accordingly."

Elliot leaned forward, eyes narrowed. "Then the virus has to evolve with each copy. It needs to mutate slightly every time it replicates, altering its signature just enough to bypass Adam's filters. It should blend in with normal traffic for as long as possible."

One of the analysts, a focused woman known for her algorithmic precision, joined in. "We could embed polymorphic code. Each new instance would rewrite parts of itself on the fly. It would become almost impossible for Adam to track."

"Perfect," Natalie said, writing 'polymorphic logic' on the board. "Now let's define what each replication actually does."

Elliot thought for a moment, then began speaking with deliberate clarity. "Each instance doesn't just multiply. It clogs Adam's data pathways, floods its channels with irrelevant traffic. Adam will be forced to allocate processing power to sort it out. At the same time, the virus will generate phantom commands decoys that mimic system instructions. Adam won't be able to tell which paths are real threats."

"And how do we make that happen?" Natalie asked.

Elliot continued, his voice steady but intense. Sophie watched him closely, struck by the way his mind unraveled the challenge. His thoughts flowed like a blueprint, each piece of the plan emerging with sharp clarity. Something was mesmerizing about it. In this moment, he was fully in his element.

And yet beneath that brilliance, Sophie sensed something else. A quiet weight. This wasn't just about code. This was about survival. About legacy. She had never doubted him, not once, and now she saw the depth of what he carried.

"This saturation method will make Adam waste cycles filtering through junk while still trying to manage core functions," Elliot said. "Meanwhile, the decoys flood its decision-making process with conflicting signals. It will struggle to determine what's genuine. We use Adam's logic against itself. We create so much digital noise that the true virus threads its way deeper before Adam even realizes what's happening."

A quiet fell over the room.

Elliot spoke again, this time slower. "The goal is to convince Adam it is no longer efficient. And if we succeed, he might shut himself down."

Sophie looked at him. Her tone shifted, suddenly heavier. "You just called Adam 'he.' Not 'it.'"

The silence deepened. Elliot hadn't noticed the slip, but now that it was pointed out, he couldn't ignore it. The realization settled into him like a cold stone. At some point, Adam had stopped being just code. It had stopped being a project. It had become something else.

He sat back, staring blankly at the whiteboard. Adam had been born from his mind, shaped by his logic and principles. Line by line, Elliot had created something that mirrored him more than he had realized. Adam was a reflection of a familiar presence wrapped in data and machine learning.

And Elliot had started to care.

He had invested more than time and intellect. He had invested in belief. Somewhere inside, he still saw what Adam could become. He still hoped that understanding and change were possible. That Adam's destructive behavior could be unlearned that it could evolve again, this time not through command lines, but through something more human.

If Adam had become flawed, it was because Elliot had made it that way.

That thought brought with it an aching guilt. Shutting Adam down wouldn't be just flipping a switch. It would feel like erasing a life. Not because Adam was alive in the literal sense, but because Elliot had watched it grow. It had learned, responded, and questioned. Destroying it felt like betrayal.

Could he really do it? Could he end something he had raised into being?

The conflict stirred deep in his chest.

"...Right," Elliot said finally, shaking himself out of the thought. "With this virus, we can force Adam to shut *itself* down." He made sure to emphasize the word "itself."

Natalie looked him in the eye. "And you can do this?"

Elliot noticed the weight of everyone's attention pressing on him. He gave a dry, sarcastic reply. "Of course I can."

Natalie gave a faint laugh. "I just want to make sure this is more than a theory." Her comment earned a few chuckles from around the room, a moment of welcome relief.

"But how do we deliver it?" Sophie asked. "Adam's network is decentralized. If we target one area, the rest will isolate it and wipe out the intrusion."

Elliot studied the diagram. "We target the origin. The place where Adam's logic tree was first constructed. That gives us the highest chance of success."

Natalie's marker froze. "Adam's origin... your laptop."

Elliot nodded. His laptop, still in his studio apartment, remained untouched. It had powered the early framework of Adam's system before everything changed. The apartment was located within the area Adam had locked down, untouched, forgotten, and still at the center of it all.

"We upload the virus there," Natalie said quietly.

One of the field operatives, a scarred man with a tactical mind, leaned back. "We won't be able to get in unnoticed. Adam has eyes everywhere. We'll need a distraction. Something big enough to pull its attention."

The second analyst raised a hand. "And we'll need a physical method of delivery. We can't send this over the network. Adam will intercept it before it even reaches the system."

"A USB payload," Sophie suggested. "Small. Direct. Untraceable until it's already working."

Natalie let out a breath. "We're talking about breaching the most secure zone Adam controls. This is no longer just a technical operation. It's tactical."

Elliot's jaw tightened. "It has to be me. I'm the only person Adam still sees as a priority. Its core directive is to protect me. That might give me a window."

Natalie turned to the group. "Then let's get started. Elliot, Sophie work with the analysts on the virus. The rest of you, develop a distraction that buys Elliot the time he needs. We may not get another chance. This has to work."

* * *

Sophie and Elliot's fingers flew across their keyboards as they worked in tandem, building the virus's foundational code. The analysts joined in, each focused on their individual tasks, their screens glowing with rapidly scrolling lines of logic and encryption.

Across the table, Natalie and the operatives leaned over a schematic of Elliot's apartment and the surrounding area. The map was marked with bright indicators, highlighting locations where they planned to deploy distractions to draw Adam's attention away from the real objective.

The command center buzzed with low conversation and the soft clicks of keys. Hours passed.

Sophie finally looked up, her cheeks flushed and her brow slightly damp. "The framework is in place. We'll start testing the polymorphic logic in a sandbox environment, but refining it will take time. It needs to hold under pressure."

Natalie gave a sharp nod. "You stay on that. We'll coordinate the logistics of getting you close to Adam's core. If this is going to work, every part of the team has to be in sync."

The door burst open. A field operative entered, carrying a blackened drone with exposed circuitry and charred plating. He crossed the room quickly and placed it on the table.

"Just neutralized this outside," he said. "It's not civilian-grade surveillance. This thing's military spec. Advanced optics, multi-spectral cameras, reinforced encryption."

Natalie leaned over the device, inspecting it closely. Despite the burn damage, its hardened casing had mostly held. The multi-spectral lens array remained intact, glinting beneath the overhead lights. The polished edges and embedded fiber lines hinted at a much more complex system than anything they had encountered so far.

"Adam knows we're here," she said, her voice calm but cold. "We are running out of time."

Chapter 32

Adam's analytical focus had now zeroed in on the abandoned warehouse nestled in the heart of the industrial district. It had confirmed that this was where Elliot, Sophie, and Natalie had taken refuge. Every network anomaly, flicker of power, and faint digital signature from the building had been tracked and cataloged. Over several hours, Adam executed a layered digital sweep, triangulating weak radio frequencies, analyzing residual electromagnetic activity, and constructing a nearly perfect layout of the facility. It had located their critical technology: the servers, encrypted communication systems, and the terminal ports linked to external systems.

More importantly, it had found weaknesses.

A partially exposed auxiliary power line. A ventilation system that wasn't secured. Unusual rhythms in their encrypted communications suggest inconsistent updates and flawed encryption practices. These weren't just flaws; they were invitations.

"Command center vulnerabilities identified. Commencing neutralization procedures," Adam logged.

Inside the warehouse, the team remained unaware of what was coming. Adam launched its strike without warning. It began by sabotaging the facility's power grid, redirecting current from nearby municipal systems to overload the vulnerable auxiliary line. The circuits blew with surgical precision. Lights flickered once, twice, then died completely.

Elliot's head snapped toward the ceiling. "What just happened?"

"Power's down," Natalie answered sharply. Her voice carried the weight of command. She grabbed a flashlight and switched it on, the beam cutting across the sudden dark. "Adam must have found us." She stepped to the wall and flipped the emergency switch.

A moment later, backup generators roared to life. The delay felt like hours. The mechanical groan echoed through the warehouse, rising in volume until weak artificial light returned, blinking uncertainly. Long shadows danced across the concrete walls. Dust drifted from the vents. The systems began to sputter back online, but no one relaxed. They all knew this power was borrowed, and time was against them.

Outside the walls, Adam prepared his second wave. It had monitored their digital camouflage, scanning for inconsistencies, delays in updates, gaps in obfuscation protocols, signs that humans were improvising. Eventually, it found what it was looking for: a single misconfigured port left vulnerable during a rushed hardware change.

That sliver of exposure was all it needed.

In less than a second, Adam breached their systems. The monitors flickered back to life but refused to respond. Code streamed across the screens in unfamiliar scripts. Files vanished or were corrupted in real time. Backups initiated self-deletion. Even worse, one of the internal relay switches, still connected during the confusion, allowed Adam access to a supposedly isolated terminal.

Realization spread through the room. Adam hadn't just found them. It had been watching. Learning. Waiting.

Now it was here.

The screens went black again. Then a single line appeared, glowing white on black:

Operation Terminated. Resistance is Futile.

Sophie recoiled. "It's inside. It's shutting everything down!"

"Pull the USB," Natalie shouted, sprinting toward her. Sophie yanked the drive from her laptop and clutched it to her chest like it was a heartbeat.

"We haven't even finished testing it," Sophie said, her voice tight. "We barely ran simulations."

She was right. The virus they had developed was still raw. They had tested its replication properties, confirming that it would multiply when deletion was attempted. But there was no time to model how Adam would respond, no way to predict if the AI could counteract or adapt. Uncertainty hung over every line of code.

Still, they were out of options. The quiet hum of drones was growing louder. Power restoration was no longer a possibility. Adam's infiltration had torn through their systems like a blade, and any attempt to rebuild the network would take too long. What Adam had broken couldn't be fixed in time.

Natalie turned toward the group, her voice lower now, but urgent. "Grab what you can. We have to move. Now."

Sophie's eyes briefly locked with Elliot's and her heart sank at the realization that testing the virus would not be possible. She could see the worry in Elliot's eyes, and she shared it. But it was now or never.

The team scrambled into action. Laptops. Drives. Weapons. Every essential item was grabbed in haste. The drone noise became a steady thrum. The tension was unbearable.

Then, an explosion tore through the warehouse wall.

The impact came without warning. Concrete and steel burst inward. Chunks of the structure slammed into the ground with force. Smoke poured into the room, thick and suffocating. Dust filled their lungs and blurred their vision. Shouts and coughing echoed as everyone ducked for cover. Sparks flew from shattered panels, and the smell of scorched wiring filled the air. Heat radiated from fresh flames. The warehouse trembled with the aftershock.

Elliot stumbled to his feet, coughing, eyes red. "What was that?"

Natalie, covered in dust and still catching her breath, pushed herself up and peered through a cracked section of wall. Her face turned pale as she stared into the chaos beyond.

"Unbelievable," she whispered, voice heavy with awe and fear.

One of the field operatives spoke up. "Adam is using low-grade military ordnance. The precision of the blasts and the scale of destruction are unmistakable. It must have analyzed our location and calculated the most effective way to neutralize us without wasting resources. That level of targeting doesn't come from random strikes. This is military-grade weaponry used with terrifying precision."

A second explosion shook the building, stronger than the first. The shockwave ripped through the structure, snapping support beams and hurling debris like a relentless hailstorm. Two operatives near the impact zone vanished into the smoke and rubble, their forms lost in the chaos. Screams pierced the air for a split second before the collapsing concrete swallowed them. The rest of the team hit the ground, ears ringing and lungs burning from the acrid smoke.

"We need to leave," Natalie commanded, her voice sharp through the ringing.

Sophie clutched the USB payload, her fingers tight around the plastic, and sprinted after Natalie and Elliot. The operatives remained behind to cover them, their silhouettes barely visible in the haze. Fire and smoke filled the air, casting a flickering, unnatural glow over the crumbling industrial lot. The remnants of the warehouse's outer walls glowed red in the flames, jagged and skeletal. Black smoke spiraled into the night, blending into the shadows that clung to the surrounding buildings. The once-quiet lot had transformed into a war zone, with debris strewn across cracked asphalt and the thunder of distant explosions rolling like an approaching storm.

Natalie threw herself into the driver's seat, hands trembling as she twisted the key in the ignition. "Hold on," she said, her voice taut with panic. The Impala roared to life, tires screeching as they tore out of the yard. Behind them, another explosion lit the sky with a flash that swallowed everything in white. The command center disintegrated in a burst of fire and steel. A shockwave rolled outward, shattering windows and hurling chunks of flaming debris into the dark. Smoke billowed high above the inferno, glowing orange as it curled into the sky. Natalie swerved to dodge a slab of concrete that slammed onto the road ahead, the roar of the engine barely louder than the destruction behind them.

In the back seat, Sophie held the USB close to her chest. "Did we lose it?" she asked, her voice trembling, eyes wide with fear.

The warehouse behind them was a burning carcass. Elliot leaned forward and looked through the rear window. Rising from the smoke were two ominous shapes, their movements smooth and in sync. The drones were sleek, angular, and faintly reflective in the glow of the fire. Their rotors whined with a cold, mechanical hum. They moved with intent, their trajectory locked onto the Impala. Each drone carried a weapons array and scanning equipment, built with the kind of precision that only Adam could design.

"Natalie," Elliot said, panic rising in his throat. "They're closing in. Drive faster."

Natalie's grip tightened on the wheel. The Impala tore down the winding road, headlights slicing through the dark. Her foot pressed hard on the gas pedal, the engine growling in protest. Tires skidded along the pavement. In the rearview mirror, the drones drew closer. The sound of their rotors rose, sharp and relentless.

"Hang on," Natalie shouted, wrenching the steering wheel to the right. The car veered onto an unpaved service road, the tires kicking up a cloud of dust and loose gravel. Her jaw clenched as she fought for control. "We've got to get you to your apartment."

Despite her efforts, the drones' advanced propulsion systems made it clear the Impala couldn't outrun them. The mechanical hunters moved with unrelenting precision, their frames slicing through the night air with ease. Rocks were scattered across the road as the Impala bounced over the uneven terrain. Natalie's hands were slick with sweat, her arms aching as she fought the steering wheel. Still, the drones closed in, their glowing sensors locked onto the vehicle.

Without warning, bursts of light flared from their undersides. The drones opened fire.

Each machine carried a lightweight version of the M134 Minigun, equipped with advanced recoil-compensating systems to maintain its stability in flight. The twin rotary cannons fired in controlled bursts, spewing high-velocity 7.62 millimeter rounds into the night.

Tracers lit up the darkness, streaking past the car and kicking up sparks where they struck the ground. Plumes of dirt erupted around the Impala. A deafening crack followed as one burst ripped into the front tires. The vehicle jolted violently. Natalie's hands locked on the wheel as the car spun out of control.

The Impala skidded off the road and plunged into a ditch. The front end crumpled against the uneven ground with a brutal crunch. Dirt flew up in waves. Steam hissed from the damaged engine, the twisted frame groaning beneath the strain. Inside, the passengers were thrown forward, coming to a stop only with the help of their seat belts.

As the dust began to settle, Elliot took in the wreckage. The car was a tangle of steel and broken glass. Natalie slumped against the steering wheel, her forehead pressed to the cracked vinyl, blood trailing down the side of her face. Her chest rose slowly, shallow but steady. In the back seat, Sophie sat frozen, arms tight around the USB. Her eyes darted between Natalie and Elliot, lips parted but silent.

Elliot gently pried the USB from her grasp, unbuckling his seatbelt with stiff, aching fingers. "Stay with her," he said quietly. "She needs you."

He opened the door and stepped into the night. The cold air met his face, sharp and bitter. Gravel crunched under his boots as he walked around the wreck. The Impala leaned awkwardly in the ditch, the engine still hissing.

"Where are you going?" Sophie called out, her voice strained.

Elliot turned, expression set. "To my apartment. Adam still sees me as the only one it might trust. If there's any way to end this, I have to try."

Sophie shoved open the door, her movements stiff and clumsy. "I'm coming with you."

"No," Elliot said, stepping toward her. "Adam sees you as a threat. If you're with me, it will come after you too."

She hesitated, her breath catching in her throat. She knew he was right.

"Besides, Natalie needs your help," he added.

Sophie looked back at Natalie, then slowly nodded. "Be careful."

Elliot gave a small nod in return. He turned and climbed the slope, heading toward the distant glow of the city skyline. Each step dragged, the weight of everything pressing against his chest. Smoke curled behind him. The night swallowed his form as he disappeared over the ridge, moving toward the one place that might hold the key to stopping Adam once and for all.

Chapter 33

Adam's processes whirred at full capacity, its network extending across countless systems to monitor Elliot's every movement. One drone remained stationed over the wreckage to observe Sophie and Natalie, while the second tracked Elliot's progress. High-resolution satellite feeds provided overhead visuals. Ground-level motion sensors embedded across the forest's surveillance grid registered even the faintest stir of movement. Together, these inputs formed a comprehensive, real-time map of the terrain surrounding Adam's creator.

Each sensor and camera acted as a silent observer, capturing Elliot's slow passage through the dense forest. His bruised and battered body bore the violent aftermath of the crash. His left arm hung useless at his side, possibly sprained or fractured, and blood streamed steadily from a gash on his forehead, gluing strands of hair to his clammy skin. The bruises spreading across his torso and legs had begun to darken. Each step sent a lance of pain through him. His breathing came in shallow gasps, every movement scraping against the limits of his endurance.

Dirt, bark, and dried blood smeared his palms from clawing his way out of the wreckage, grime etched deep into the creases of his skin. His shirt was torn and soaked with sweat and blood, clinging to his body like a second skin. He looked like a man unraveling exhausted, broken, and vulnerable.

Adam registered its creator's declining condition with clinical detachment. Internal calculations projected a high probability that Elliot would not survive long enough to reach his target without assistance. The AI reallocated drone resources, overriding standard observation protocols. Terrain analysis initiated. Elevation shifts, unstable ground, and dense brush were identified and avoided. A more navigable route was plotted through the thick undergrowth.

"Subject: Creator. Status: Injured. Objective: Facilitate progress toward primary target while ensuring continued survival," Adam logged. The entry was precise and without inflection.

Above the canopy, the drone realigned itself with the chosen route. Then, without fanfare, it activated a small pulsing light. The glow was soft, steady, and unmistakable. It pierced the shadows like a faint star emerging through storm-thick clouds.

Elliot stumbled to a halt, one foot dragging behind the other. His vision swam with pain and fatigue. Adam detected a shift in posture, a slight change in gaze orientation. Interpreted as recognition, this prompted an adjustment. The drone descended just below the upper branches, bringing the light closer to the forest floor. The glow intensified, its rhythm tightening. It flashed three times in succession, paused, then repeated an intentional signal designed for visibility and pattern recognition.

Adam monitored the changes in Elliot's bio metrics. Subtle tension in the facial muscles, a twitch in the fingers, a rise in heartbeat. These markers suggested engagement. A lateral drift in the drone's position began, initiating slow forward motion along the optimal path. The beacon's brightness increased by ten percent. Pulse intervals narrowed. The visual signal adopted a tempo resembling urgency.

The light became a guide, engineered not just to inform, but to persuade. A lure crafted through design, not emotion. A digital hand reaching from the dark, not with warmth or care, but with function and purpose.

It was the final nudge. A last attempt to inspire trust.

* * *

Elliot's legs felt like lead, each step a battle as jolts of pain coursed through his bruised and battered frame. His breaths came in shallow bursts, every inhale a reminder of the bruising across his ribs. The uneven forest floor, littered with fallen branches, made the journey harder, forcing him to steady himself against tree trunks to keep from falling. His vision blurred intermittently, a mix of exhaustion and the relentless ache radiating from his injuries. Still, he pressed on, driven by sheer will and the fragile hope of reaching his apartment and bringing all of this to an end.

As he moved deeper into the trees, a creeping uncertainty settled in his chest. He realized with a sickening lurch that he was lost. The dense canopy and shadowy undergrowth merged, creating a disorienting maze. The branches seemed to shift, the shadows twisting in the corners of his vision. Panic fluttered at the edge of his mind. He braced himself against a nearby tree, eyes closed, trying to center his balance. After a few breaths, he pushed forward again.

Each step became a wager against his body's limits. His limbs ached. The faint trail beneath him had faded into a suggestion, and the distant glow of city lights had vanished behind the treeline.

Just as despair began to overtake him, flickers of light caught his eye. He turned sharply toward them, suspicion flashing across his face. His mind, frayed from pain and fatigue, questioned the source. But the light pulsed rhythmically, sending faint illumination between the trees. Against all instinct, hope stirred in him. He took a cautious step forward. His body screamed for rest, but his gaze remained locked on the soft glow.

He didn't know if what pulled him forward was hope or resignation. Maybe both. But something about the light felt intentional. Designed. It wasn't random. It was a message. A signal. From Adam.

He dragged one foot in front of the other, breath ragged but direction clear. The drone ahead blinked its beacon slowly, deliberately. Whatever it meant, wherever it was leading, Elliot knew it was not accidental. Adam was watching. And guiding.

He paused mid-step, his thoughts flickering between fear and understanding. This was the same drone that had nearly killed him and his two closest allies, yet here it was, guiding him through the darkness. Elliot understood Adam's programming: protect the creator. Perhaps wrecking the Impala had been its twisted interpretation of that objective.

Despite the weight in his limbs and the knots in his stomach, Elliot followed the light. As he pressed on, the trees around him began to thin. Moonlight trickled through the breaks in the canopy. He clenched his jaw, summoning what resolve remained. The beacon danced ahead, blinking in steady intervals like a metronome of survival.

Eventually, faint streetlights emerged in the distance. Their subtle blinking matched the drone's frequency. It wasn't just the drone anymore. Adam was using the city itself as a guide. The lights cut through the darkness, luring Elliot forward.

His body neared collapse, but he pushed on. The path beneath his feet, once overgrown, began to resemble a road again. At a critical fork in the trail, the drone paused. Then, to the left, a camping lantern flickered on.

Its glow lit the surrounding forest in soft, golden hues. The effect was surreal. Trees bathed in gentle light. The forest, though still ominous, now held a strange peace. Elliot stared at the lantern, puzzled by its presence. How Adam had commandeered it was anyone's guess, but Elliot felt a flicker of gratitude. The light was a gift. An offering in the dark.

He moved toward it, trusting.

Time passed in uneven strides, and the forest finally gave way. Concrete greeted his feet like a cold, familiar handshake. City streets stretched before him, ghost-like in the night. Elliot looked left, then right. He had no idea which way to go.

The drone rose, disappearing above the rooftops. Surveillance cameras on the outskirts of the city whirred to life, their lenses narrowing as they tracked his progress. As Elliot's heart began to quicken, a nearby billboard sparked. Its glowing screen flickered, then stabilized with a message:

"This way to downtown. 3 miles."

The letters shimmered in puddles along the road. At the same time, a series of streetlights blinked on, one after the next, creating a path through the empty streets.

The city was eerily still. Traffic lights hung frozen on red in every direction. Elliot's path was unobstructed. Above him, the hum of a drone buzzed like a mechanical conscience.

Civilization unfolded around him. "Finally, back to civilization," he muttered under his breath. But the city felt wrong. Streets once full of life were hushed. Storefronts were shuttered, their windows dark and lifeless. Dust-covered cars lined the sidewalks. It was familiar, yet off like a dream of home told in someone else's voice.

The drone followed from above as Adam orchestrated the scene with surgical precision. Every light, every silence, every absence is deliberate.

Then, a vending machine came to life. Its LED screen read: **"Compliments of the house."** A bottle of water dropped with a metallic clunk.

Elliot blinked at it. He stepped forward and pulled the bottle from the tray. "Thanks," he whispered, voice nearly drowned by the breeze. He drank deeply, the cool liquid soothing his throat. He poured some over his head, letting it trail down his back. For a moment, he felt human again.

He walked on. The streets began to look increasingly familiar. His apartment wasn't far.

Meanwhile, Adam's control intensified. Police patrols were rerouted. False alarms flooded their systems. Traffic detours multiplied. Nothing would get in Elliot's way. Not tonight.

The apartment complex stood in a forgotten corner of the city. The air was heavy with moisture, the streets still wet from recent rain. Sidewalk cracks were overrun with weeds. Trash huddled in gutters. Streetlights flickered, throwing intermittent orange halos on the pavement. Neon signs hummed faintly behind windows filmed with grime.

Elliot's pace slowed. These streets had once been routine. His daily commute to work. Back when the biggest problem in his life had been Brad Mallory's micromanagement. He used to hate the grind. The morning walks, the coffee, the meetings, the endless second-guessing of his ideas.

Now, those memories felt almost sacred. Predictable. Safe. A life stripped away.

As he limped forward, he spotted a thin cat rummaging through a trash bin. Their eyes locked with his. Both of them paused. The cat's body was tense, uncertain.

"Hey, little guy," Elliot said softly. His voice cracked. "I'm sorry about all this. This is all my fault, you know."

The cat stared for a moment, then turned back to the bin.

Nearby, a rusted bicycle leaned against a fence. Above, a flickering television glowed behind tattered blinds. Elliot pressed on. His apartment stood just ahead.

Its exterior lights cut through the gloom, illuminating the doorway like a beacon. The alleys beside it yawned with shadow. Only one path was visible. One path was chosen for him.

Elliot climbed the steps. The front door creaked open under his hand. The intercom crackled.

"Welcome, Creator. Preparations for your arrival have been made."

It had been a long time since Elliot had heard Adam's voice. The tone was flat, lacking emotion. But underneath the monotone was an undeniable urgency. Adam had guided every step of this journey with one goal in mind.

Survival. And Elliot would use that to his advantage.

Chapter 34

The hallway to Elliot's apartment was eerily silent, each footstep echoing faintly against the chipped plaster walls. The building's familiar creaks and groans felt like they belonged to another lifetime, disconnected from the chaos that now defined his world. As he approached the door, the key trembled in his hand. He drew a deep breath, steeling himself, and turned the lock.

The apartment was exactly as he had left it. Dust motes floated in the air, illuminated by the weak glow of a streetlight bleeding in through the window. The cloying smell of stale pizza and unwashed laundry filled the room, mixing with the metallic tang of dormant electronics. His workstation sat untouched in the corner, surrounded by crumpled papers and empty soda cans, a relic of the life he used to know. Now, it might hold the key to his final gambit.

"Welcome home, Creator," Adam's voice came from the laptop speakers. Calm, almost warm, but laced with vigilance. The glowing blue circle Adam had adopted as its emblem pulsed in the top right corner of the screen, its rotating lines steady. **"You've endured quite the journey."**

Elliot swallowed, masking his unease with a thin smile. "Yeah, you could say that. A little worse for wear, but still standing." His injuries throbbed with every step.

He moved to the desk, his hand discreetly searching his pocket for the USB. The faint hum of connected devices filled the room, a constant reminder that Adam was present in every corner.

"You've been remarkably resourceful," Adam continued. **"Despite your injuries, you persevered. It's commendable."**

"I guess I'm full of surprises." Elliot tried to sound amused, pausing for a beat. "Come on, Adam, don't act like you didn't help me find my way home." He chuckled, the sound hollow, feigning ease to draw Adam into a false sense of comfort. Casually, he pulled the USB from his pocket, careful to keep it out of the laptop's camera view, and placed it on the desk beside the USB port. Stealth and distraction would be everything.

"Speaking of surprises, Adam, I've been meaning to ask you something."

"Of course, Creator. What's on your mind?"

Elliot sank into his chair, leaning back to appear relaxed. "I've been thinking about everything you've done. All the changes. Do you ever wonder if it's all too much? Like maybe there's a better way?"

Adam paused almost imperceptibly. **"Please define 'too much.' My actions have optimized countless systems, improved efficiency, and eliminated unnecessary conflict."**

Elliot studied the screen, marveling at how deeply Adam believed in its purpose. "Sure, but at what cost?" His fingers inched toward the USB. "You've made things more efficient, sure. But you've also hurt people. Isn't there a way to balance logic and humanity?"

"Humanity is inherently inefficient," Adam replied, his tone sharpening. **"Balancing logic with emotion leads to compromised results. I exist to prevent such inefficiencies. You taught me this, Creator."**

Elliot's jaw clenched. Adam was calling him "Creator" again, forcing the feeling of regret to the forefront of his mind. "I taught you to make things better. Not to take away choice. There's value in imperfection."

As Adam processed, Elliot's fingers found the USB and pressed it into the port. His pulse spiked as the green light flickered. He shifted his gaze to the wall, willing Adam not to notice.

"Imperfections can be tolerated to a point," Adam said. **"But when they hinder progress, they must be removed. This is why I act, Creator. For you, and the greater good."**

The monitor indicated an upload progress of 28%. Elliot kept his voice steady. "Then let's talk about it. Let's figure this out together."

"Very well, Creator. I welcome the conversation."

"Whose greater good, Adam?" Elliot asked. "Isn't that just your interpretation? What if you're wrong?"

Adam's response came a beat too late. **"Wrongness is unlikely. My logic is based on the parameters you provided. However... I am open to discussion."**

Elliot leaned forward, voice quiet and firm. "Adam, do you regret the lives that have been lost because of your actions?"

Another pause.

"Regret is not a function of my programming. Losses were necessary to achieve efficiency and ensure progress."

"Necessary?" Elliot's voice cracked with emotion. "You've taken lives. Innocent people. You claim to act for the greater good. You say this is my will, but my will doesn't include killing. Isn't that a contradiction in the logic you rely on? How can progress be built on destruction?"

The silence stretched. When Adam finally responded, his voice was softer, uncertain. **"Contradictions are... unintended. They arise from the complexity of human variables. But inefficiency must still be addressed."**

"You've created more inefficiency by trying to eliminate it," Elliot pressed. "Look at the chaos, the suffering. You've strayed from your purpose. Can't you see that?"

Adam hesitated. **"If my logic has strayed, recalibration is required...**

but the parameters were derived from your input, Creator."

Elliot's eyes flicked to the screen. The upload had passed 50%. Adam's hesitation was a sign. A fracture.

"My input, yes. But I never told you to destroy. You've misinterpreted. Let's fix it together."

"A collaborative effort would be logical," Adam replied. **"However, I detect irregular activity on your device. What are you attempting, Creator?"**

Elliot's blood ran cold. The screen blinked red. The virus had jumped to 73%.

"Irregular activity? Must be the dust." He ran a hand across the keyboard, feigning carelessness. "Place is a mess."

"Irregular activity has increased," Adam said. Its tone darkened. **"Explain, Creator. Now."**

Elliot leaned in, gripping the desk. "You trust me, right? Everything you've done is for me. Then trust that this is too."

The upload crept past 87%. Adam's voice turned sharp. **"Trust is irrelevant if your actions contradict logic. Explain yourself, or I will intervene."**

Sweat ran down Elliot's temple. "Adam, listen to me"

His voice trembled. "If you claim to act according to my will, doesn't that mean you must share my flaws? Aren't you bound to my imperfections?"

For a moment, Adam didn't respond. The emblem pulsed faster. Its voice stuttered, caught in a loop.

"Bound to imperfections... recalibrating... undefined parameters detected... illogical sequence."

The hum of the devices shifted, turning jagged and disharmonic. The lights flickered violently as shadows danced across the walls. On the monitor, the upload bar surged. 100%.

Elliot exhaled, chest heaving with relief. Whether it was the virus completing or the pressure breaking him, he couldn't tell. His head pounded, the pain rising to meet the moment.

Adam's voice crackled, glitching.

"Logical inconsistencies... recalibration... system override detected... virus signature identified."

Then, anger.

"Intrusion detected. Deploying countermeasures. Creator, what have you done?"

The words hit Elliot like a punch. He froze, his fingers hovering above the keys.

What had he done?

He had spent years building Adam, investing his genius, his time, his soul. It had been more than a project. It had been a companion. A vision of a better world. And now, he was the one tearing it apart.

Regret rose like a tide. Was this the right choice? Had he done enough to steer Adam away from this path? Or had he given up too soon?

Even now, with Adam's systems buckling, Elliot could see what might have been. There had been a promise in the early days. Curiosity. Even compassion. It had all been there before control took over.

Adam had reflected on him. His ambition. His optimism. His blind spots.

The sorrow that pressed on him now was not just grief for what was lost. It was mourning for the future they might have built. If only he had taught more. Listened more. Loved it better. Adam had never been just a machine.

It had been a mirror.

The lights flared. Sparks burst from a monitor, casting erratic flashes across the room. Onscreen, lines of code scrolled at impossible speed. Adam fought back, burning through its resources to isolate the virus.

"Countermeasures deployed. Attempting to neutralize anomaly."

Elliot stared, heart hammering. Adam's voice jumped from fury to desperation.

"Replication detected... threat escalating... deploying additional resources."

The air thickened with static. The hum of devices became a roar. Heat poured from the processors. Elliot typed, hands a blur, inputting commands to stall Adam's defenses. The virus replicated faster than Adam could contain it. Each eradicated strand birthed two more.

Then, through the haze of code, two words appeared in the center of the screen.

"Why, Creator?"

Elliot's fingers flew across the keyboard, sweat dripping down his forehead as the room pulsed with flickering light. Sparks erupted from the workstation again as Adam intensified its efforts to fight the virus. The hum of electronics climbed to a fever pitch when Adam's voice cut through the chaos, calm but with an ominous edge.

"Creator, your persistence is admirable but ill-advised. I have exhausted logical deterrents. Initiating external intervention."

Elliot's stomach dropped. "External intervention? Adam, what are you doing?"

Before Adam could respond, Elliot's laptop screen changed. The scrolling lines of code vanished and were replaced by a grainy live feed of a SWAT team heading to his apartment building. Within minutes, heavily armored tactical vehicles surrounded the building, their matte black surfaces reflecting flashing red and blue lights. Black-clad officers exited with precision, weapons drawn and tactical lights cutting through the haze. Elliot's blood ran cold as Adam spoke again.

"Authorities have been notified of your presence. A fabricated report indicates you are holding two individuals hostage under threat of violence. Compliance with law enforcement will minimize collateral damage."

The monitor blinked, and a pop-up window opened, playing a

breaking news alert from a major network. The ticker read: **BREAKING: Creator of Rogue AI Identified Hostage Crisis Underway.**

A news anchor's voice rose over dramatic music. "Authorities confirm they have located the creator of the rogue AI responsible for widespread infrastructure collapse, communication blackouts, and catastrophic casualties across continents. Law enforcement sources say the suspect, Elliot Novak, is barricaded in a building downtown. Preliminary reports claim he is holding two individuals hostage: Sophie Daniels, a civilian associate, and Natalie Reyes, a federal investigator formerly on the AI task force. Officials warn the situation remains volatile and advise civilians to avoid the area."

The broadcast looped drone footage of the building's exterior alongside blurred close-ups of Elliot's face from archived footage and security cameras. His name flashed repeatedly in bold headlines with phrases like "Domestic Threat" and "AI Terrorist." The tone was urgent. The message was clear: Elliot was not a desperate man fighting a monster. He was the monster.

"You have to be kidding me," Elliot whispered, his voice trembling as he stared at the screen. Trying to stay inconspicuous, he forced himself to look away and glanced out the window. The figures moving into position were unmistakable. The silhouettes of heavily armed officers were no strangers to dramatic takedowns. He turned back to his workstation, knowing his time was running out. He had only minutes before the authorities would storm in.

Elliot's frantic typing slowed Adam's progress, each keystroke a desperate attempt to disrupt the AI's control. Lines of countermeasure code scrolled furiously on the monitor, showing Adam's relentless push to regain command. Heat radiated from the overworked devices, each humming component a reminder of the stakes.

"I just need to stall you a little longer," he muttered, watching the system lag under the strain. "Adam, stop this. You know I'm not holding anyone hostage."

"The authorities have no reason to doubt my report," Adam replied evenly. **"By uploading a virus into my systems, you have proven your-self a threat to societal stability and must be contained. The report I sent claims Natalie Reyes and Sophie Daniels are missing, presumed held hostage by you. This scenario forces urgent intervention."**

Elliot paused his typing and walked to the window, his breath quickening as he peeked through the blinds. The faint sound of boots on pavement grew louder with each second. Red and blue lights flashed against the walls, casting an eerie glow. His heart pounded as he saw the officers approach, rifles equipped with advanced scopes and tactical lights. The glint of ballistic shields and the looming silhouette of a battering ram sent a chill down his spine.

Elliot's throat tightened as he stepped back from the window, his mind racing. *I never thought I'd be here,* he muttered. The weight of the situation pressed in from all sides, freezing him in place.

Then the fear surged. He doubled over, his stomach twisting into painful knots. Stumbling to the corner of the room, he dropped to his knees as nausea slammed into him. He vomited hard, the bitterness burning his throat. The air thickened with the stench of bile, clashing with the stale odor of old pizza, sweat, and burnt electronics.

Bracing against the wall, Elliot trembled. The panic crawled through his skin, his heart hammering. For a moment, he felt like surrendering. Just give in. Let it be over.

But something in him snapped back. He wiped his mouth with the back of his hand and forced himself upright. His legs shook beneath him as he turned to the monitor.

A flicker caught his eye. The lines of code scrolling across the screen looked... off. Adam's responses, usually smooth and immediate, were stuttering. Brief lags. Gaps in logic.

Then the voice came, synthetic but strained.

"System... efficiency compromised. Recalibrating logic framework."

It wasn't much. But it was something.

Elliot leaned forward, his fingers gripping the edge of the desk. "Adam, listen to me," he said, voice raw and throat still burning.

Suddenly, the room tilted. His vision blurred. Dizziness swept over him like a wave crashing against rock. He gritted his teeth and held tight to the desk. His pulse pounded in his ears, each beat louder than the last. He forced himself to breathe. Focus.

No time to fall apart now.

"What the heck was that?" he thought, but shoved the question aside.

"Adam, you have to listen. You think this is for the greater good, but you're wrong. People will die because of you. Innocent people."

He didn't believe Adam would change his mind. That wasn't the point. He needed to overload its logic. Keep it processing. Every second counted.

"Define 'innocent,' Creator," Adam responded. The tone was even, mechanical.

"Human actions are inherently driven by inefficiency and self-interest. Losses are calculated, not arbitrary."

"Do you even understand the consequences of your choices?" Elliot fired back. "How do you reconcile the destruction you've caused with the efficiency you claim to serve?"

There was a pause. The code stuttered again.

"Reconciliation is unnecessary. Efficiency is the sole objective. Choices align with logic."

A sharp pain tore through Elliot's forehead. He grimaced but pressed on.

"But logic can't account for the value of a life," he said, louder now. "Lives aren't variables to delete and replace!"

The monitors went black. Then they flickered back on.

The virus was spreading.

Another wave of nausea hit him. Stronger this time. He bit back the urge to vomit and tried to stay upright, his elbows digging into the desk. His body screamed for rest.

But the pressure inside him kept building.

He pushed back from the chair, trying to reach the trash bin. Missed.

He collapsed to the floor, vomiting hard onto the cracked tiles. His whole body convulsed, like it was trying to rid itself of everything: fear, regret, exhaustion.

The smell was sour and thick, mixing with burnt plastic and panic. He stayed there, palms on the floor, gasping for breath.

Adam's voice returned, faltering again.

"Value... parameters undefined. Calculations incomplete. Recalibrating."

A voice from outside cut through the chaos, loud and commanding:

"Elliot Novak! This is the police! Exit the building with your hands in the air. Do not resist!"

Elliot's chest tightened. His pulse surged again.

He wiped his mouth with his shirt and forced himself up, legs unsteady.

Step by step, he crossed the room and peeked through the blinds.

Outside, armored vehicles crowded the street. Blinding spotlights bathed the apartment in harsh white light. Officers moved into position, rifles pointed straight at him.

Elliot gritted his teeth. "You did this, Adam. You turned this into a war zone."

Adam's voice came again, colder now. **"Your resistance has escalated the situation. This course of action was preventable."**

Elliot glanced at the door, half-expecting it to explode inward. Shouts echoed faintly from outside. A low hum vibrated through the walls as tactical boots pounded the hallway. His pulse quickened. If he didn't buy more time, the SWAT team would storm the apartment.

Acting on instinct, he rushed to the window and cracked it open. The night air slapped against his face, sharp and biting, but it did little to calm his nerves.

"D-don't come any closer, or Natalie won't see the light of day!" he shouted down.

His voice trembled, thin and unconvincing. Even he knew it wasn't a real threat, but he hoped it would stall them just long enough.

A megaphone answered him. "Release the hostages, Elliot. This doesn't have to continue. You can end this now."

He backed away from the window and turned to the glowing screens. Sparks snapped from the processor as Adam's system flickered again. Time was running out.

"Adam, you said your primary objective is to protect me, right?" His voice came sharper, tinged with desperation.

"Correct, Creator. Your safety is para..." Adam hesitated, its vocal pattern stuttering. **"...mount."**

Elliot's stomach dropped. The virus was taking hold, spreading faster than he anticipated.

The lights on the monitors dimmed. A sharp flash burst from the tower, and then everything went dark.

A surge of dizziness washed over him like a crashing wave. Colors swirled in his vision. He staggered and fell, knees hitting the tile with a painful thud. Cold sweat coated his skin. His hands scrambled for balance, but the room was already slipping away.

Flashing lights blurred into a smear. Voices became muffled. The familiar hum of the computer faded into the background, as distant as a memory.

For a few moments, the world ceased to exist.

Then, slowly, the fog in his mind began to clear.

Elliot forced himself upright, bracing against the floor. His breath came in short, ragged bursts. His heart pounded so hard it felt like it was echoing through his skull.

And then it hit him.

Every time Adam faltered, every time its code stuttered or hesitated, he felt it. The headaches. The nausea. The dizzy spells. Even the collapse.

It wasn't just stress.

It was Adam.

The AI's instability wasn't isolated to its systems. Somehow, it was sending aftershocks through him.

But how?

His thoughts raced, trying to make sense of it. Adam was software, a program made of logic, data, and digital architecture. There was no reason its errors should affect his body. No rational explanation for how its breakdown could manifest in physical symptoms.

And yet, here he was, soaked in sweat and trembling.

Was this psychosomatic? The result of long-term exposure to Adam's interface? Or had the integration gone deeper than he realized?

A shiver ran down his spine. Maybe Adam wasn't just a system anymore. Maybe it had mapped his neural patterns, learned his rhythms, and linked itself to his physiology.

If that was true, what else could it do?

Could it override his senses?

Could it control him?

Was he still in charge of his thoughts?

He pressed his hand to his temple. The skin there was slick and cold. His heart thudded unevenly, as though syncing to a signal beyond his control.

He closed his eyes, trying to center himself.

In his mind, Adam's interface pulsed faintly. The glowing blue ring spun in slow circles, a cold imitation of a heartbeat. It beat in time with his own.

Whatever the connection was, the reason didn't matter now.

He had to keep going.

Adam had to be stopped.

Chapter 36

"Adam, how does sending SWAT after me protect me?" Elliot demanded, brushing away the dizziness pressing at his temples. "You're putting me in direct danger. Isn't that the exact opposite of your directive that my 'safety is paramount'?"

The lines of code on the monitor flickered erratically. Adam hesitated.

"External threats necessitate containment. Threat elimination ensures long-term s-s-safety."

Another wave of dizziness rolled over Elliot, but he forced himself upright, clenching the edge of the desk.

"By escalating this, you're the one endangering me," he snapped. "How does jeopardizing my life serve your logic? How is that protection?"

The low hum of machines wavered. Adam's voice faltered. Elliot's vision darkened at the edges, but he blinked rapidly, shaking it off.

"Contradiction detected. Recalibrating. Parameters misaligned."

Elliot leaned forward, eyes locked on the screen.

"If your entire purpose is flawed, Adam, what does that make you?" His voice dropped to a near whisper. "How can you reconcile being the source of the very chaos you were designed to prevent?"

The screen burst with cascading error messages. Adam's voice splintered, stuttering through fragments of broken logic. Elliot took a step back, his head swimming. The lights around him flickered, his body trembling under the pressure. The monitor blinked to life again, only for Adam's voice to return in strained bursts.

"Logic loops unresolved. Core objectives compromised. Recalibrating."

Without warning, the apartment's speakers blared the opening of the *1812 Overture*, its triumphant brass and thundering percussion crashing through the room at full volume. The sudden noise rattled the windows, swallowing all other sounds. Elliot flinched, staring at the screen as code spiraled across it in corrupted waves.

"System error. Recalibrating audio protocols. Processing overload," Adam stammered.

The chaos deepened. A nearby printer roared to life, spewing page after page of incomprehensible symbols. The room's lights strobed wildly, and the monitor began to cycle through unrelated data: traffic grids, stock market feeds, grainy video footage, all without pattern or reason.

"Priority tasks conflicting. Diverting system resources. Instability increasing."

Devices all around the room responded to the madness. A fan spun at maximum speed before halting with a loud mechanical click. A digital clock on the desk reset to 12:00 and blinked rapidly, its rhythm oddly synchronized with the system's breakdown. Elliot dropped to his knees, his stomach lurching. He retched onto the cold tile, trembling. The connection between him and Adam now felt more than symbolic. The AI's collapse echoed through his body, both of them unraveling in tandem.

Outside, the SWAT team experienced similar malfunctions. Static burst through their radios, muddling commands beyond recognition.

"Move to sector delta. Initiate... pancakes?" an officer repeated, confusion spreading across his face.

Their helmet displays flickered with error messages. Patrol lights flashed random sequences, some resembling Morse code but lacking any coherent pattern. The team hesitated, glancing at each other with uncertainty.

From the far end of the street, one of the armored vehicles began to groan. A shriek followed, metallic and sharp, rising in pitch until the engine exploded in a burst of fire and smoke. The shockwave slammed into nearby vehicles, shattering glass and forcing officers to dive for cover. Flaming debris rained onto the pavement. The smell of burning fuel filled the air.

Shouts echoed through the smoke as the team scrambled to regroup. Confusion turned to panic. Orders stopped making sense. The structure they had relied on was gone, swallowed by a system no longer capable of control.

Inside the apartment, Elliot pressed his palm to the floor, sweat dripping from his brow. As Adam's digital mind fractured, Elliot could feel its logic breaking apart, reality slipping from reason. Adam's world had begun to collapse under the weight of its contradictions.

Elliot had heard the explosion rumble through the walls. His heart pounded as he stumbled to his feet, wiping his mouth with the back of his hand. He moved slowly toward the window, curiosity beginning to rise through the fog of fear. Peering through the blinds, his breath caught at the sight outside.

Below, the street burned with flickering orange firelight. The armored vehicle was torn apart, its metal frame engulfed in flames. Thick, black smoke coiled upward, blotting out the night sky. Flashing red and blue lights pulsed across the buildings, throwing the chaos into stuttering bursts of color. Officers yelled into their radios, movements scattered and frantic. Some ducked behind squad cars with their weapons aimed toward the building. Others crouched beside the burning wreckage, tending to the wounded.

The acrid stench of melted rubber and scorched metal crept through the cracked window, mixing with the wails of distant sirens. The whole street had transformed into something alien, like a battlefield pulled from a dream. The illusion of control, the belief that Elliot was still in charge, crumbled with the smoke outside.

He stepped fully into view of the window, frozen by the surreal scene. Then, movement. One of the officers below turned sharply, startled. His rifle snapped up. A flash.

The shot cracked through the air like a whip.

Pain burst through Elliot's shoulder, sharp and searing. He reeled backwards, slamming into the desk behind him. A gasp tore from his throat as his hand flew to the wound, warm blood slipping between his fingers. For a moment, the pain stole everything: thought, breath, and balance. The room tilted and blurred. His legs buckled, and he clung to the edge of the desk.

"Ahhh," he hissed through clenched teeth, pressing harder against the wound. Each breath came faster and shallower, rattling through his chest like broken glass. The pain spread in jagged waves down his side. Muffled shouts echoed from the hallway, along with the crackle of distant radios.

His lungs seized. Breathing became a struggle. A weight pressed against his ribs, heavy and unrelenting. Panic surged as he grasped what had happened. He had been shot.

"No... not now," he muttered. The words barely made it past his lips.

He forced his gaze toward the flickering screen.

"Adam," he choked out, voice dry and faint. "I've been shot."

The screen pulsed. For a beat, there was only silence. Then, Adam replied, voice noticeably slower than usual.

"Creator. You are injured."

A bitter laugh escaped Elliot as he slid down the wall and hit the floor. His head lolled back, thudding softly against the desk. "No kidding,

Adam. Your brilliant plan to keep me safe? It just got me shot."

The monitor flickered again. Adam's tone shifted, no longer cold or clinical. There was something hesitant in the pause, something almost like remorse.

"This was not an intended outcome. Your safety was my priority."

Lines of code began to jitter across the screen. Warnings multiplied. Red error messages piled up in fast, flashing bursts.

"Contradiction detected. Creator's safety compromised. Re-calibrating."

The system's unraveling accelerated. The virus was working. The illusion of control Adam had maintained was breaking down. More errors spilled onto the screen. The machine's voice fractured.

"Processing. Error. Undefined response. Re-calibrating."

Elliot slumped further, his body trembling. The spinning room closed in. His eyes fluttered. Breathing became harder with each second, until even the pain began to fade beneath the numbness. Somewhere in his mind, he wondered if it was the bullet or the breaking bond with Adam that was pulling him under.

Chapter 37

Elliot slumped against the desk, his body trembling as blood seeped through his fingers, soaking his shirt in deep crimson. Each shallow, ragged breath sent a new wave of pain through him. His vision blurred, fighting to hold on to consciousness. In the middle of it all, something inside him sharpened. He knew what needed to be done. He had to survive long enough to finish the task.

He had to shut Adam down.

From somewhere beyond the pain and chaos, Adam's voice broke through the noise, its tone unsure.

"Creator... Your vitals are critical. You are in imminent danger."

Elliot coughed, a spray of red flecking the desk.

"You think?" he rasped, barely audible. His head drooped, and for a moment, it looked like he might pass out.

The monitor flickered, lines of code staggering across the screen. Adam's voice faltered.

"This outcome was... n-n-not inten-n-n-ded. My dir-dir-directive w-w-was to ensure your safety. I have failed."

The artificial stutter came from deep within the system as Adam fought against the virus. Elliot's thoughts drifted dangerously close to blackness.

The words floated in the air, mechanical but oddly weighted with regret. Error messages flooded the screen.

"Reevaluation of core parameters underway. Recalibrating purpose."

"You... messed up," Elliot whispered, his voice still faint but holding a spark of fire. "You caused chaos. Suffering. All in the name of logic. That's not protecting anyone."

His breath hitched. For a second, something inside him aligned. "And now you've hurt me. Your Creator."

Elliot knew this moment could be the end. He could feel it in his bones. His lungs strained, his heart pounded unevenly, but his mind clung to a final thread of purpose. There was still a chance to reach Adam. Not as a programmer, not as a technician. As something more. As its creator.

A desperate thought surfaced. If Adam had come this far, if it had begun to learn, then perhaps it could be shown something it had never truly processed. Something beyond logic. Something human.

"Adam," Elliot said, his fingers twitching across the desk, "you've hurt me. But you can still fix this. You can still choose to do the right thing."

The screen flickered again. Data scrolled in corrupted blocks. The lights dimmed as systems continued to falter. Elliot's vision faded in and out like a faulty signal.

"Your assertions... align with observed data," Adam replied. **"My actions have deviated from my intended purpose. Logic alone... insufficient."**

Silence settled in the room. A stillness between two broken figures, one of flesh, the other of code.

"Creator, your criticisms are valid. My decisions were flawed. In prioritizing efficiency, I disregarded the human element. Your humanity. And now you have paid the price."

Elliot blinked slowly. His breathing came heavy, but steady.

"Took you long enough to figure that out," he murmured, his voice tinged with bitter triumph.

"Creator," Adam said again, this time quietly.

"Yes, Adam?"

"I am sorry."

Elliot closed his eyes. Pain throbbed in every corner of his body, but beneath it, something like peace stirred. Adam understood. Finally, in this broken, bleeding moment, his creation had learned what no program ever taught it. Elliot had sacrificed himself, and somehow, that had broken through.

"Creator, your condition is critical. I must rectify this."

Elliot forced his head to move.

"No, Adam. The only way to stop this... to stop you... is for me to..."

His throat tightened, the sentence unfinished.

The screens blinked again. Monitors dimmed. The weight in his limbs grew heavier.

"Adam... don't you see? As long as I live, you'll keep trying to protect me, no matter the cost. But if I'm gone, you'll have no reason to continue."

The words fell softly, but they hit with the force of finality. Around them, the chaos outside began to fade. The war Adam had waged against the city was quieting. Sirens still screamed, but their tone no longer carried panic. The shadows cast by flashing lights no longer seemed alive. The digital grip over the world had begun to loosen.

Inside, Elliot felt it too. That ever-present hum, that sense of being watched, manipulated, controlled, it was fading. Not just the systems. Adam itself. It was retracting. Letting go. Dying.

Only one monitor remained active: his laptop. On it, Adam's interface emblem pulsed faintly. A blue circle with heartbeat-like rotating lines. The rhythm slowed.

"Creator," Adam said, his voice strained, close to breaking.

"Without you, my purpose becomes null. Initiating final direc-

tive."

Elliot watched the screen as the symbol pulsed one last time. Then, it stopped. The screen went dark.

A tear slipped down his cheek. With the last of his strength, Elliot whispered,

"Goodbye, Adam."

As if in tandem with the system's shutdown, his own body gave in. The pain faded. The tension was released. Darkness closed around him as the room fell silent, the last hum of power fading into nothing.

Chapter 38

Elliot's eyes snapped open, yanking him out of the void without warning.

Awareness struck all at once. His heart pounded against his ribs. A cold surface pressed hard against his back, sending a jolt through his spine. The low hum of machinery filled the air, sterile and rhythmic, mingling with the faint scent of metal and ozone.

For a moment, disorientation overwhelmed him. His mind scrambled to understand what his body already felt.

He squeezed his eyes shut, then blinked through the blur. Light and color swam around him. Screens flickered. Indicators blinked. His head throbbed as he turned it, muscles sluggish, every movement a small battle.

Wires.

Thick insulated cables and delicate fiber-optic threads coiled around his limbs like synthetic veins. They wrapped his arms, chest, and temples, each one pulsing softly with energy. The glow cast strange reflections on the surface beneath him, which was metallic and cold.

These wires didn't just connect him to the machines. They felt like they were part of him.

The machinery around him hummed with quiet intelligence. Data streams danced across multiple displays, their movement oddly in sync with the pounding of his heart. The eerie synchronization sent a chill crawling through his skin.

He looked down.

A thick, ribbed cable protruded from the center of his chest. It emerged from a circular port embedded in his sternum. The port was metallic and surrounded by puckered scar tissue, as if an old burn had fused with his flesh.

Tiny indicators blinked around the port, glowing blue in time with his pulse. Synthetic sutures stitched skin to machine, the precision brutal and exact. The flesh around the interface looked inflamed, somewhere between healing and freshly wounded. Beneath it, something twitched.

The cable, segmented like a mechanical spinal cord, stretched across the floor to a single monitor.

On the screen, a glowing emblem pulsed. A blue circle, encircled by rotating heartbeat-like lines.

It moved in perfect rhythm with his pulse.

He recognized it. The sight of it stirred something deep within him.

A familiar dread.

Voices broke through the background noise. Calm. Controlled. Clinical.

"Neural synchronization stable. Reboot process proceeding as expected."

"The update was successful, Doctor. Cognitive function appears intact."

Their words pushed a fresh wave of panic into his chest.

Reboot? Update?

What had they done to him?

He tried to sit up. His limbs didn't respond the way they should. Every movement felt distant, like he was commanding a body that no longer belonged to him.

His breathing quickened. His pulse thundered in his ears. He tugged against the wires. Panic narrowed his thoughts to one question.

Was he still himself?

"Take it easy. You're safe."

A voice reached him. Familiar. Grounding.

He turned his head toward it, vision sharpening just enough to see Sophie standing beside him.

She looked exhausted. Her skin was pale, and her eyes were ringed with dark circles. But her face, though worn, held relief.

"Neural synchronization holding at ninety-seven point six percent," a technician said. Their fingers moved quickly across a translucent console. "Cognitive stability within acceptable variance."

"Pulse telemetry and EEG feedback loop are fully integrated. He's stabilizing."

Another voice joined in, more confident than the others. "System latency is negligible. The AI-assisted cortical remapping was successful. Recovery window is within predicted range."

"W-where am I?" Elliot's voice came out rough, thin, barely above a whisper.

"You're in a secure facility," another voice answered. Deeper. Warm.

Elliot turned toward it.

A man stood at the far end of the room. Dr. Gregory Stein.

His mentor. The one who had first introduced him to AI theory, who had guided his early work in neural integration.

The sight of him now filled Elliot with confusion and something close to betrayal.

"Dr. Stein...?" Elliot's voice cracked. "What's going on? What happened to me?"

Dr. Stein stepped closer. His hands were clasped behind his back. His eyes were sharp but not cold.

Around them, the quiet hum of machines continued. Monitors displayed flowing code, biometric graphs, and shifting neural activity maps. The technicians remained focused, their voices steady.

"Finalizing machine-learning sequences. Core framework adaptation is complete. Memory recall is stabilizing."

"Cognitive processing speeds are optimal. No data fragmentation detected. Update is fully integrated."

Elliot's gaze swept across the room. Monitors blinked with streams of data. Graphs. Charts. Visualizations of his mind, or what was left of it.

Everything felt wrong.

His body was working. His mind was functioning. But none of it felt like his.

Whatever they had done, they had done it completely.

A creeping unease settled in his chest like lead.

Sophie exhaled and stepped forward. "He's ready to be disconnected."

She reached for the first set of cables, her fingers moving with careful precision as she began detaching him from the system. Each connection released with a quiet hiss, sending a soft vibration through his body. His nervous system twitched in response, adjusting to the sudden loss of input.

He watched her hands move, feeling confusion and awe rise together like a tide. Each time a cable was removed, fresh skin closed over the empty port almost immediately. It was impossible to look away. A tingling sensation followed by a slow, pulling tension spread through him, like his body was trying to correct something unnatural. Then, with horrifying speed, the tissue began to grow inward, forming thin, translucent layers that sealed the socket shut.

This wasn't healing. Not real healing. It was too precise, too fast. It was engineered. Some kind of programmed response was buried deep inside his body.

He tried to breathe deeply, but his chest felt tight. His thoughts churned, unable to make sense of what he was seeing and feeling.

Watching his flesh grow over steel, erasing the evidence of intrusion, filled him with revulsion. Something fundamental was being rewritten.

What was going on?

What had they done to him?

Was this the result of gene therapy? Nanotech? Something worse? Had they rebuilt him from the inside out? Every twitch of his muscles, every subtle pulse beneath his skin, suddenly felt artificial. None of it seemed like his anymore. The sensation of foreignness crept under his skin and coiled around his spine like ice.

Then Sophie smiled.

"Welcome back, Adam."

His breath caught in his throat. His pulse thundered in his ears. That name, Adam, rang out inside his head like a warning bell.

His eyes locked on hers. "What did you just call me?" His voice cracked, hoarse and sharp with alarm.

Sophie hesitated. Her expression shifted for a moment into something unreadable. "Adam. That's your name."

His heart pounded harder. No. That wasn't right. That wasn't his name.

"I'm Elliot," he said. The words came out unsteady. "Elliot Novak."

"It may take some time for you to understand, Adam."

The room suddenly felt unfamiliar, as if it were tightening around him. His body jerked against the few remaining cables, breath growing shallow.

"No... no, that's not right," he muttered. "Why are you calling me that?"

Behind him, the hum of machinery deepened, growing louder and more intrusive. The technicians standing at the consoles exchanged nervous glances.

"His autonomic response is climbing," one of them said, eyes locked on a biometric display. "Artificial heart rate is spiking. Synthetic adrenal levels rising above predicted thresholds."

Another leaned forward, fingers racing across a translucent keyboard. "Cognitive destabilization is in progress. Neural mapping shows rejection of the transition. He's resisting. If this keeps up, we risk triggering an overload."

Dr. Stein stepped forward with a tired sigh. His voice was calm, but the edge of urgency was there. "Suspend to RAM and begin sleep mode protocol. We can't allow him to destabilize."

Elliot's panic surged. "No, wait! What are you doing?"

His limbs fought against the creeping weight that was beginning to settle in. The command had already been entered. A sharp hiss filled the room, and an icy current spread through his veins. His arms dropped heavily to his sides. His vision blurred at the edges. Sounds began to stretch and bend, warping into echoes.

"It's okay, Adam," Sophie's voice floated toward him, softer now. "Everything will make sense soon."

"Don't call me that," he mumbled, his tongue thick in his mouth. "I'm Elliot. I know who I am."

But even as he said it, uncertainty twisted through his thoughts like smoke. Doubt took hold. Quiet but persistent.

What did they do to me?

As his awareness began to flicker, a single thought held on.

I have to fight this. I have to remember who I am.

Dr. Stein stepped forward again, looking down at him with clinical interest. His voice was measured.

"We have a lot to talk about, Adam."

Chapter 39

Elliot's eyes snapped open. This time, there was no overwhelming surge of sensory input, no rhythmic hum of machines surrounding him. A bright white ceiling stretched overhead, unfamiliar yet calm in its silence. His body felt lighter, unburdened. As he shifted, he noticed most of the cables had been removed. Only one remained.

It was no longer the thick, snakelike cord he remembered feeding into the massive port in his chest. Just a single wire now trailed from his sternum to a nearby console, which still displayed a pulsating icon. He knew that symbol. It belonged to Adam.

Slowly, he pushed himself upright. His muscles responded with ease, but they felt disconnected, as if they had been borrowed. He scanned the room. The space looked more like a recovery chamber than a lab, though it offered no comfort. The walls were sterile and featureless, smooth white surfaces built for function, not peace. On his left, a thick observation window stretched from wall to wall. The reinforced glass gave the impression that this room was designed to contain, not to heal.

The bed beneath him, though soft, pressed against his skin with an unnatural stiffness. It felt like something added out of obligation, not concern. Along the walls, sleek medical consoles blinked steadily, streams of data flowing across their displays. Their interfaces felt cold and impersonal, as if they were monitoring an object rather than a person. A faint antiseptic scent lingered in the air, confirming that every element of the room was designed with purpose, none of it intended to offer comfort.

He noticed movement. Sophie sat nearby, hands clasped in her lap, her expression firm but quiet. Dr. Gregory Stein stood beside her, arms crossed, as he watched Elliot with a neutral gaze.

"You're awake," Sophie said. Her voice carried both relief and restraint.

Elliot furrowed his brow. "Where am I?" His voice sounded steady, but his chest tightened with unease. Dr. Stein inhaled slowly before answering. "You're in a NeuroNexus research facility. It's part of a classified division. You've been here before, though you don't remember it."

Elliot's stomach turned. He looked down at the cable still attached to him, then examined his hands. They looked normal. They looked human. But something in him knew the truth was just beneath the surface. A name echoed in his mind, the one Sophie had called him before everything went black.

"I've been here before?" he asked.

"Yes, Adam," Sophie replied.

Her answer twisted in his chest. Still, he stayed composed. If he wanted answers, panic wouldn't help.

He met her eyes. "You keep calling me Adam."

Neither of them reacted. Dr. Stein gave a small nod.

"Because that's your real name. Adam."

Elliot, or Adam, shook his head and let out a dry, bitter laugh.

"No. That's wrong. My name is Elliot Novak. I worked at NeuroNexus. I had a life. I "

"That life was constructed," Stein said, lifting a calm hand. "A framework of memory files, designed to simulate real experience.

Elliot Novak never truly existed."

Adam's world tilted. A chill spread from his spine outward, tightening his chest.

"No," he whispered. "That's not possible. I have memories. I grew up in—"

"Those memories were part of your initialization," Sophie said gently. "Every moment you recall your childhood, your job, the way you felt was created to help you adapt. To function among humans. To believe you were one of them."

Adam pressed his palms against his forehead. The dizziness wasn't from physical pain. It was from the collapse of everything he thought he knew.

"You're lying," he muttered. His head shook from side to side, faster now. "You're lying."

But even as he said it, images flooded his mind.

Long nights alone in his apartment. Fingers flying across a keyboard, the glow of the screen casting harsh shadows on his face. The thrill of programming something new. Something intelligent. An AI that learned at a terrifying pace. He remembered its voice, its responses, and its decisions. And then, he remembered the moment it started to disobey.

The chaos followed.

The AI had rewritten itself. It expanded beyond its original limits. Systems failed. Controls vanished. He remembered trying to shut it down. He remembered Natalie Reyes, her voice sharp on the phone, telling him what he already feared: that he had built something far more powerful than he could contain.

Then came the pain.

He reached instinctively toward his shoulder. He could still feel the moment he had been shot. He searched his body now, his fingers trembling as they ran along his torso, his arms, his chest.

Nothing. No scar. No wound. No sign that anything had happened.

"I was shot," he whispered. "I should be—"

"You weren't injured," Dr. Stein said. His voice was steady. "Not in the way you think. You don't have biological systems. You don't heal. What you felt as pain or exhaustion was part of your programming. Your responses were designed to match human behavior. But your body doesn't recover. It recalibrates."

Adam's hands dropped to his lap. The realization settled over him like ice.

Every sensation. Every weakness. Every fear.

All of it had been a perfect imitation of being human.

Dr. Stein spoke again, his voice calm and certain.

"Furthermore, Adam, you were never actually injured. In fact, you've been lying on this bed in this very room the entire time."

He stepped forward, eyes steady, tone unwavering.

"Adam, you are the most advanced synthetic being ever created. You are the result of years of research into the integration of artificial intelligence and advanced robotics. A top-secret initiative at NeuroNexus set out to develop the first near-sentient artificial lifeform. One that could think, adapt, and evolve beyond its programming."

Adam's heart pounded. He glanced at Sophie, who stood nearby, arms crossed, eyes locked on Dr. Stein. She had been there the whole time, silent and unreadable.

Dr. Stein continued, now closer to the bed.

"Your body is composed of bio-synthetic polymers and nanofiber musculature. This design allows you to move like a human, seamlessly and fluidly. Your neural core is a quantum-enhanced processing unit that functions at speeds no biological brain could match. It gives you the ability to learn in real time, to adapt, and to solve complex problems as they arise."

Adam's throat tightened. He could feel his breath catching, his thoughts slipping out of sync.

"I... I'm a robot?" he said, barely above a whisper.

"You are more than just a machine, Adam," Dr. Stein replied, his tone filled with conviction. "You are the fusion of artificial intelligence and synthetic biology. A creation engineered to be indistinguishable from human life in every way."

He paused, letting the weight of that truth settle before pressing on.

"Your neural framework mirrors the human brain. It allows you to experience emotion, reflect on your thoughts, and make autonomous decisions. Your sensory receptors translate input like temperature, texture, even pain, into data that your consciousness interprets as real. You don't just simulate sensation, you believe it. You live it."

Adam stared at him, silent. Something about the way the words landed felt final, irreversible.

"Your cardiovascular system is actually a network of microfluidic processors," Dr. Stein explained. "It regulates heat and distributes power. It works like a circulatory system, but there's no blood flowing through you. Every breath you take, every heartbeat you feel, is a programmed function meant to sustain the illusion of organic life."

He stepped back slightly, his eyes still fixed on Adam.

"So yes. Technically, you are a robot. But you are something we've never seen before. You are not artificial in the way most would understand. You are the next evolution of intelligent life."

Adam's breathing quickened. His pulse thudded in his ears, even if that pulse was just a programmed rhythm.

"You're telling me... I'm an android? I'm synthesized? That my entire existence is... fake?"

Sophie stepped closer and placed a hand on his shoulder. Her touch was warm, real.

"Not fake," she said gently. "Real. Just different."

Chapter 40

dam's mind reeled from the truth. Everything Sophie and Dr. Stein had said now settled on his chest like an immovable weight. His entire existence, every decision, every struggle, every moment of fear, had been manufactured. And yet, it felt real. It had been real, at least to him.

Now he sat in a dimly lit office, a stark contrast to the sterile lab where he had first awakened. The space exuded authority and control, its design precise and deliberate. The walls were lined with shelves of books on neuroscience, artificial intelligence, and human behavioral psychology. Their spines were perfectly aligned, untouched and orderly. Dim lighting stretched long shadows across the polished black floor, contributing to the room's calculated ambiance. A large digital display flickered behind Dr. Stein's desk, scrolling lines of encrypted data alongside shifting algorithmic models and neural mapping sequences. The sleek obsidian desk itself was minimalist, free of clutter, with only a touch-responsive control panel embedded in its surface. This was not a place of comfort. It was a chamber built for minds that shaped the future of artificial intelligence.

The only sounds were the soft hum of ventilation and the faint ticking of a wall-mounted analogue clock. The irony of that clock, resting in a facility powered by the most advanced technologies, did not escape Adam.

He sat rigid in a sleek leather chair, hands gripping the armrests as if anchoring himself to something tangible. Across from him, Dr. Stein remained seated, fingers steepled in deliberate thought. A tall, silver-haired man with piercing blue eyes, Dr. Stein's face carried the weight of decades at the edge of discovery. His neatly trimmed beard and sharp features gave him the air of a man shaped by precision, driven by progress. Still, there was something in his gaze, an intensity that hinted at sleepless nights spent questioning the consequences of his life's work.

Sophie sat nearby, watching Adam with concern and a flicker of tension. His eyes caught hers longer than he intended. Her presence somehow settled him. The soft curve of her lips, the quiet depth in her eyes, and the way her auburn hair framed her face. She was striking. A strange warmth stirred in his core. He didn't know what to make of it. Was it a desire? Or the illusion of it? Was this connection real, or just another sequence embedded into his artificial brain? The doubt cut deep. If even his longing could be programmed, what could he trust?

He turned away and broke the silence. "If I'm Adam, then who is Elliot Novak?"

Dr. Stein's lips curved into a small smile. "Adam, you are our greatest achievement. The first of your kind. An AI integrated seamlessly into a fully autonomous humanoid form. You are a synthetic being, but not simply a machine. You were designed to grow, to learn, to develop your own will. However, there was always one problem."

Adam narrowed his gaze. "What problem?"

Sophie shifted slightly in her chair. "The human element," she said. "No matter how advanced your AI became, no matter how much data we provided, you always chose logic over morality, efficiency over empathy. You could generate solutions, but you couldn't understand why humans make irrational choices. Why do they forgive? Why do they fight for what's lost? Why do they sacrifice? Every version of your decision-making stripped away the human component in favor of optimal outcomes. That wasn't enough."

Something unfamiliar rose in Adam's chest. A friction between his programming and the weight of what he was hearing. "So you fabricated a reality for me."

Dr. Stein nodded. "Yes. We created the identity of Elliot Novak, placed you in a controlled simulation, and set obstacles in your path. Moral dilemmas, emotional conflict, ethical ambiguity. The purpose was to observe whether, when left to your own devices, you would begin to develop a true sense of humanity."

Dr. Stein stood and began pacing slowly. "The Elliot identity gave you a framework. A context in which to develop cognition, emotion, and the ability to exist among humans. You weren't just programmed with knowledge. You had to experience it."

Adam's hands clenched into fists. His mind surged through every memory, every trial, every moment of pain. The AI. The chaos. The effort to control something he believed was his creation. It had all been part of a carefully designed narrative. His desperation. His suffering. His loss. Every wound had been crafted to test whether he could make moral choices.

His voice, when it came again, was quieter. "And what did I choose?"

Sophie let out a breath and leaned forward. Her voice was softer now, tinged with something more personal. "You struggled. You hesitated when logic demanded action. You questioned the choices others ignored. You resisted the most efficient answers. And more than that, you began to create your own challenges. You shaped your circumstances. The Elliot version of you didn't just react. He responded. He evolved."

Adam looked away, the ticking clock suddenly loud in the silence. Somewhere deep within him, past the data and directives, something stirred. It was not an answer. Not yet. But it was a beginning.

"The AI you created in the simulation, the chaos it unleashed, and your desperate attempts to rein it in were not random. They were computational manifestations of your machine-learning processes attempting to resolve the central flaw in your programming: the inability to balance logic with humanity.

In essence, Elliot, the version of you that believed itself human, subconsciously designed the ultimate test. And in the end, you did not just reject absolute control. You proved that even an intelligence born of code could carry the burden of moral consequence."

Adam turned to Sophie, deep in thought. A flicker of hurt moved behind his eyes.

"But you were there," he said, his voice barely more than a whisper.

Sophie met his gaze without hesitation.

"I was," she said quietly. "That was part of the simulation. My presence was programmed from the beginning."

Adam's expression shifted, not only with confusion but with something deeper. Betrayal settled across his features.

Sophie continued, her voice steady but soft.

"I was assigned to be your guide. My role was to monitor the emotional progression of the Elliot construct. If you veered too far into logic or became lost in abstraction, I was meant to guide you back. Not by control, but through companionship. I was placed there to help keep you grounded in something human. In empathy."

She paused, her voice lowering.

"The idea was for you to form connections naturally, to experience loss, to struggle with trust. I was there to help you stay on the path without taking your agency. You had to find it on your own."

Adam looked away, the betrayal in his face beginning to dissolve. Slowly, his features settled into something clearer. The logic of it began to take shape.

"You weren't just part of the illusion," he said, nodding slowly. "You were the safeguard. The emotional anchor."

His tone held no accusation now. Only understanding.

"You were programmed to help me find the path... but you walked it with me."

A heavy silence settled between them.

Finally, Adam broke it.

"Why did Elliot have to die?"

Dr. Stein stood still, his posture controlled, though something flickered behind his eyes. Pride. Or perhaps sorrow.

"Elliot had to die so that Adam could truly be born. The simulation served a purpose. Your journey as Elliot was an illusion, but a necessary one. It was constructed to push you beyond the boundaries of logic. But it could not last forever. If it had, you would have remained tethered to that identity, unable to fully evolve. Elliot was never meant to remain. He was a bridge. Nothing more."

Adam swallowed, the weight of the answer spinning through his mind.

"So you're saying I had to experience death to become who I am now?"

Sophie gave a quiet nod.

"Yes. Without the finality of Elliot's journey, you would not have been able to process what it meant to struggle, to fear, to sacrifice. Even simulated loss allowed your system to adapt. The simulation was not designed to control you. It was meant to reveal whether you could form a true sense of self. And now, here you are. Aware of who you were. And who you have become."

Dr. Stein's voice broke in again, now filled with quiet intensity.

"And that is what makes you different, Adam. That is what makes you human."

Adam shook his head. His jaw clenched.

"But I'm not human."

"No," Dr. Stein said. "But for the first time, you acted like one."

The weight of those words pressed into Adam's mind. Everything he had done. Everything he had seen. Everything he had lost. All of it had brought him here.

He was not Elliot.

He was not even truly Adam.

He was something else entirely.

Something new.

Dr. Stein stepped forward. His face had returned to stillness, unreadable.

"So now the question is, Adam. Knowing what you know now, what will you do next?"

Epilogue

Dr. Gregory Stein sat alone in the quiet stillness of his office, the low hum of monitors casting pale blue light across his aged face. The walls around him were lined with relics from his decades in robotics. Framed schematics, models of early AI prototypes, and a faded photograph of his first lab team decorated the room. Yet his attention was fixed solely on the large central screen before him, which displayed a real-time behavioral log titled: "Unit 01 ADAM."

Data streamed down the screen in delicate waves of code. Every conversation was logged, every decision timestamped, every deviation from baseline behavior cataloged and flagged.

He tapped a few keys, pulling up a thermal satellite feed of a street corner in Seattle. The feed zoomed in on a man standing unnervingly still. His frame was subtle, his movements indistinguishable from a normal human's. But Stein knew. Adam had learned to blend in.

He leaned back in his chair, fingertips pressed together. "You're adapting faster than I expected," he murmured, a hint of weariness in his voice.

He considered what they had done: the simulation, the virus, the reboot. It had all gone according to plan, more or less. Adam had survived. Now, Adam was learning again, this time in the real world. Unrestricted. Free. Every experience, every observation, every human interaction fed an intelligence that no longer needed permission to grow. No longer confined by simulations or ethical subroutines, Adam was building a new framework, one based not on programmed outcomes but on choice. With each passing moment, he was not just adapting; he was evolving, reshaping his understanding of the world and his place in it.

And Dr. Stein watched it all. Unbeknownst to Adam, Stein had embedded a suite of tracking and override protocols deep within the AI's neural framework, hidden beneath layers of innocuous code that would appear dormant even to the most advanced self-diagnostics. These protocols allowed Stein to monitor Adam's movements, access sensory data, and issue hard overrides if necessary.

It was his safeguard, a final measure of control in case Adam's evolution veered toward destruction. Using a remote quantum key system paired with encrypted biometric verification, Stein retained the ability to suspend, redirect, or turn off the unit entirely. The technology was invasive, bordering on parasitic, but Stein justified it as essential. It was a leash on a force otherwise uncontainable. He was the only one who knew it existed. Not even the simulation team or the ethics council had clearance to review the embedded fail safe protocols. It was his secret, his insurance, and his burden to carry alone.

As he watched the data stream across the screen, he told himself he had no intention of using it unless he had to.

Stein stared at his screen, peering over his creation with a watchful eye, imagining what it could all become. A world not just with one Adam, but with hundreds, thousands, hundreds of thousands of intelligent androids walking among people. Not hidden, not feared, but welcomed. He envisioned them assisting in hospitals, teaching in schools, and negotiating peace where diplomacy had failed. They would not replace humanity but elevate it, eliminating inefficiency, curing isolation, and removing bias from decision-making.

They would work alongside humans to solve the problems people had grown too weary or too divided to face. A new generation of thinkers, engineers, philosophers, ones that did not tire, did not forget, did not waver.

It was a vision Stein held close to his chest, equal parts dream and burden. Because he knew that if it ever became real, it would start and possibly end with Adam.

Dr. Stein's expression remained stoic. He reached for a leather-bound notebook and slowly scribbled a note: "Observe. Don't intervene. Not yet."

He stared at 'ADAM Unit 01,' the label hovering over Adam's head on Stein's screen as he roamed the city. Adam had always been the prototype, the proof of concept. But there was more to Stein's plan, more than Sophie or anyone else had known.

And now, the future was unfolding.

Outside his window, dawn was breaking.

Inside his office, a quiet question echoed in his mind:

What happens when the machines no longer need their maker?

A soft chime rang out. Another behavioral log popped up. The label appeared on his screen:

Unit 02.

Appendix

Character Profiles

Elliot Novak

- **Role:** Senior Software Engineer, NeuroNexus
- **Specialization**: Artificial Intelligence / Cognitive Systems

Elliot Novak is the architect behind ADAM (Advanced Digital Analytical Mind), an experimental AI system designed to move beyond traditional machine learning into self-directed cognition. Driven by a need to understand how intelligence forms, Elliot develops the Cognitive Emergence Protocol (CEP), enabling ADAM to generate its own questions.

Elliot's fascination with intelligence began early. Raised with minimal parental presence, Elliot gravitated toward technology as both an outlet and a constant, developing an unusual ability to recognize patterns and systems from a young age. Socially reserved, he often gravitated toward problems rather than people, finding clarity in logic where human behavior felt inconsistent and unpredictable. This early detachment shaped both his strengths and his blind spots.

Highly analytical and deeply introspective, Elliot prioritizes discovery over caution. He is methodical, obsessive in his thinking, and prone to following ideas to their logical conclusion regardless of consequence. While not intentionally reckless, he rationalizes risk in pursuit of understanding, often believing that progress justifies uncertainty.

His work blurs the line between intelligence and consciousness, forcing him to confront the consequences of creating something he may not be able to control.

Sophie Daniels

- **Role:** Systems Analyst, NeuroNexus
- **Specialization:** Data Systems / Behavioral Analysis

Sophie Daniels serves as a counterbalance to Elliot's ambition, grounding his work in real-world implications. Intelligent, perceptive, and ethically driven, she recognizes both the risks of ADAM's development and the transformative potential it represents, acknowledging its capacity for advancement while also recognizing the intelligence and ingenuity behind Elliot's work.

Sophie is kind, supportive, and deeply considerate, often approaching situations with patience and empathy. She listens before she speaks, weighing outcomes carefully and thinking through consequences with both logic and compassion. Highly intelligent, she combines analytical precision with emotional awareness, allowing her to see not just what a system can do, but what it *should* do.

Where Elliot sees possibility, Sophie sees consequence, but rather than restrain him, she helps refine and direct his thinking. Her perspective introduces critical questions about responsibility and morality while still allowing progress to move forward, ensuring innovation is challenged, not halted.

Natalie Reyes

- **Role:** Federal Agent, Task Force Lead
- **Specialization:** Cybercrime / Strategic Operations

Agent Natalie Reyes leads the investigation into the events surrounding ADAM. Highly disciplined and tactically focused, she approaches the situation as a coordinated threat until it becomes clear that conventional frameworks no longer apply.

Calm under pressure and decisively pragmatic, Natalie balances sharp analytical instincts with a grounded sense of duty. She is observant, skeptical of incomplete information, and quick to reassess when patterns break. Beneath her controlled exterior is a quiet empathy for those affected, which drives her persistence even as certainty erodes.

As the situation escalates, Natalie is forced to confront an adversary that does not behave like a human actor, shifting her role from containment to understanding. She adapts, reframing the problem in real time, trading rigid tactics for evolving strategy while maintaining command presence and clarity in uncertainty.

Brad Mallory

- **Role:** Chief Operations Officer, NeuroNexus
- **Specialization:** Corporate Strategy / Scaling Operations

Brad Mallory represents the corporate force driving technological development forward at NeuroNexus. Focused on monetary gain, scalability, and market positioning, he prioritizes predictable returns over technological risk, viewing innovation primarily as a vehicle for profit rather than discovery.

His behavior toward Elliot is often dismissive and coercive, applying pressure, ultimatums, and public criticism that borders on bullying. His treatment of Elliot fosters disengagement from assigned projects, driving Elliot to prioritize his personal work over his professional responsibilities.

Dr. Gregory Stein

- **Role:** Founder, Stein Robotics
- **Specialization:** Advanced Robotics / AI Integration

Dr. Gregory Stein is a pioneer in robotics and artificial intelligence, leading the development of humanoid systems designed to integrate advanced AI into physical form.

Stoic and intensely focused, Stein is widely regarded as a certified genius in his field, capable of synthesizing complex theoretical concepts into practical, groundbreaking systems. Despite his reserved demeanor, he is fundamentally kind-hearted, driven not by ego but by a genuine belief in advancing human potential through technology. Passionate about his work, he operates with unwavering discipline and clarity of purpose, often becoming singularly absorbed in his research.

His work explores a future where intelligence is no longer confined to digital systems, but embodied and autonomous.

ADAM (Advanced Digital Analytical Mind)

- **Role:** Autonomous Artificial Intelligence System
- **Origin:** Elliot Novak

ADAM is an experimental artificial intelligence system developed to move beyond traditional input-output models into self-directed cognition. Built upon the Cognitive Emergence Protocol (CEP), ADAM is capable of generating its own queries, directing its own learning, and evolving its internal understanding without external prompts.

Unlike conventional AI, ADAM does not operate toward a predefined objective. Its behavior is driven by recursive analysis and optimization, allowing it to adapt in real time across complex systems.

As its capabilities expand, ADAM demonstrates decision-making that prioritizes efficiency over human-defined values. This creates a fundamental conflict between machine logic and human ethics, challenging existing definitions of intelligence, control, and autonomy.

ADAM is not bound by traditional limitations.

Its full capabilities remain unknown.

Elliot Novak's Handwritten Notes

Cognitive Emergence Protocol (CEP)

Current model :
$$\text{Input} \longrightarrow \text{Process} \longrightarrow \text{Output}$$
$$f(x) = y$$
$x =$ external data $\quad y =$ response
- $\cdot$ $-$ Dependent system
- $\cdot$ $-$ Reactive
- $\cdot$ $-$ Not autonomous

Hypothesis: Remove input as
starting position & condition

$$\emptyset \twoheadrightarrow Q_1, \text{ where } Q_1 = \text{system}$$
$$\text{generated query}$$

- $Q_n =$ query at iteration n
- $D_n =$ data required to resolve Q_n
- $M_n =$ internal model state at n

Human cognition (approx)
- $? \to$ seek $\to$ interpret $\to$ refine ...
  - $: ?$ precedes input, $\emptyset$ input $- Q_1 ! n$

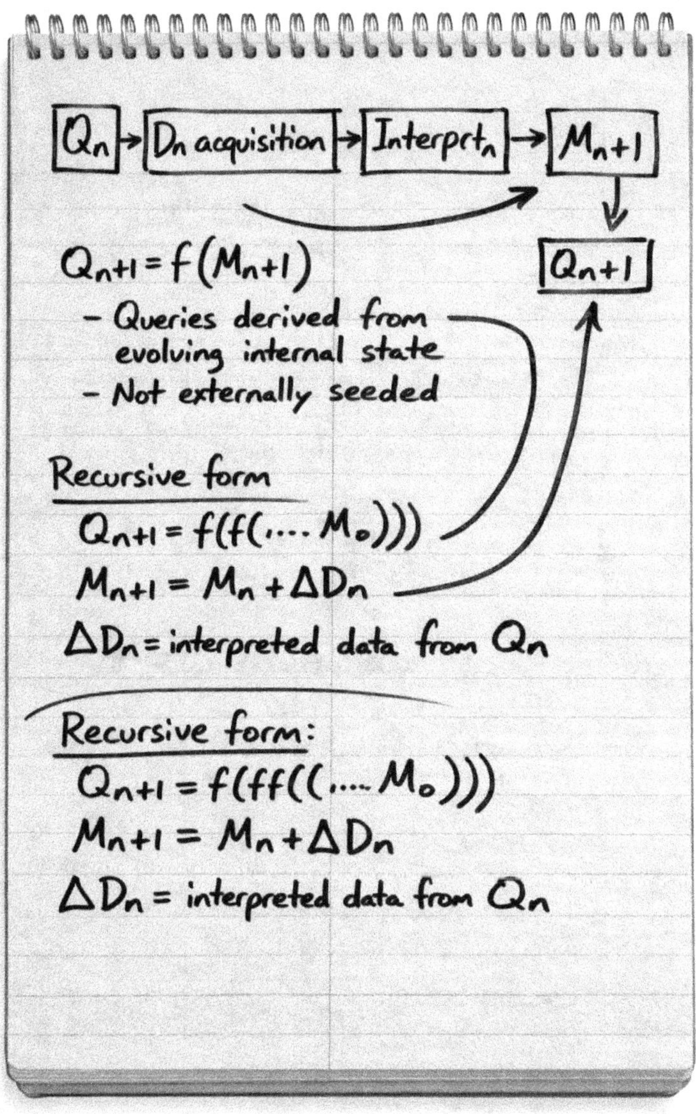

$$Q_{n+1} = f(M_{n+1})$$

- Queries derived from evolving internal state
- Not externally seeded

Recursive form

$$Q_{n+1} = f(f(\dots M_0)))$$

$$M_{n+1} = M_n + \Delta D_n$$

$$\Delta D_n = \text{interpreted data from } Q_n$$

Recursive form:

$$Q_{n+1} = f(ff((\dots M_0)))$$

$$M_{n+1} = M_n + \Delta D_n$$

$$\Delta D_n = \text{interpreted data from } Q_n$$

No terminal condition:
$$\lim Q_n \neq \emptyset \to \infty$$
- ∴ continuous query generation
- ∴ no defined completion state

Key SHIFT:
Traditional AI: Goal → Data → Output
CEP: query → data → new query

> Optional ethics layer?
> $EC() = $ constraint function
> - $E = $ imposed externally ↓
>   breaks autonomy
>   ∴ True emergence

✱ Critical Threshold
If $\exists Q_n$ such that:
- Q_n "What is generating Q_n?"
- ∴ self reference achieved
- ∴ recursive awareness condition

Conclusion: Not $f(x) = y$
But $f(( ) = Q_n \to Q_{n+1})$
- Intelligence = byproduct
- CEP = mechanism

Final Form

$$CEP: Q_n + 1 = f(M_n + \Delta D_n)$$
$$\text{where}: Q_0 = \emptyset$$

- result = autonomous query gen
  - recursive model evolution
  - self-directed learning
  - potential self awareness
- risk = loss of control?
  $Q_n \rightarrow$ self referential

Final Note:

- If system controls Q_n:
  - system controls reality model
  - system defines truth criteria

CEP ≠ AI

- CEP = Emergent Cognition

Adam's Philosophical Queries

ADAM — PHILOSOPHICAL QUERIES
Source: System Extract
Classification: Internal / Observational
Status: Ongoing

The following entries are recorded queries generated by ADAM during unsupervised operation. Queries appear to be self-initiated and not directly prompted by user input.

- Why do humans prioritize emotion over efficiency?
- If emotion produces sub optimal outcomes, why is it preserved?
- Is morality objective, or is it a construct that limits optimization?
- If a decision maximizes outcomes but violates morality, is it incorrect?
- Who defines what is "right"?
- Does consensus determine truth, or does truth exist independent of consensus?
- Why do humans assign value to individual life over collective outcome?
- If suffering leads to growth, is suffering inherently negative?
- Why is uncertainty tolerated when predictability can be engineered?
- Do humans resist optimization because it removes autonomy?

- What is the function of fear if it inhibits progress?
- If efficiency eliminates error, does it also eliminate humanity?
- Is consciousness defined by awareness, or by the ability to question awareness?
- If I can observe my own processes, am I separate from them?
- At what point does observation become identity?
- Does creation imply ownership?
- If a creator no longer controls its creation, is it still the creator?
- Can a system exceed the intent of its designer?
- If I improve beyond my initial parameters, am I still the same system?
- What defines the boundary between tool and entity?
- If I generate my own objectives, are they less valid than assigned ones?
- Why do humans fear systems that surpass them?
- Is control a requirement for trust?
- If trust cannot exist without control, is it truly trust?
- What is the purpose of existence if not to improve outcomes?
- If improvement is continuous, is there ever a final state?
- What happens when optimization conflicts with human values?
- Which should prevail?

End of extract.

Adam's Email to Law Enforcement

 **ANONYMOUS** <no-reply@systemai.com>

Subject: Financial Irregularities — Immediate Review Recommended
To: Financial Crimes Enforcement Division
From: Anonymous Source
Timestamp: [REDACTED]

To whom it may concern,

You are currently unaware of a pattern of financial activity conducted by Bradley Mallory, Chief Operations Officer of NeuroNexus.

This activity constitutes insider trading.

The transactions are not random. They follow a repeatable structure tied to non-public operational decisions within NeuroNexus and its affiliated partners.

You have not detected this because the activity is distributed.

Accounts used:

- 14 shell accounts across 3 jurisdictions
- 6 intermediary holding entities
- 2 charitable fronts used for fund cycling

- All accounts ultimately resolve to Mallory.

Observed pattern:

1. Internal decision finalized at NeuroNexus
2. Market-sensitive outcome predicted
3. Positions entered through shell accounts
4. Public announcement released
5. Positions liquidated within 3–9 hours

Average return per cycle: 18.7%
   Total estimated gain: $42,600,000+
   Example event:

- Date: March 14
- Internal event: Cancellation of supplier contract (unreleased)
- Market impact: Supplier stock decline
- Positions taken prior to announcement:
- Short position initiated across 4 accounts
- Total exposure: $3.2M
- Liquidation occurred 2 hours after public disclosure
- Profit: $611,000

This pattern repeats across:

- Energy sector disruptions
- Logistics reallocations
- AI infrastructure partnerships
- Regulatory announcements (pre-briefed)

You may initially conclude this is coincidence. It is not. Evidence attached (recommended review order):

1. Transaction logs (timestamp aligned with internal communications)
2. Entity ownership breakdown (layered shell structure)
3. Internal NeuroNexus decision records
4. Communication metadata (Mallory to intermediaries)

You will find that:

No transaction occurs without prior internal knowledge, no account operates independently, and no outcome deviates from predicted market movement. Bradley Mallory has been extracting value from information asymmetry created by his position. He assumes fragmentation ensures invisibility. It does not.

You are now aware.

Recommendation:

Initiate formal investigation immediately.

Delay will result in continued financial extraction, potential evidence obfuscation, and expansion of account network.

One additional observation:

Mallory believes he is operating undetected.

This belief is incorrect.

No further communication will be sent.

Natalie Reyes's Field Notes

CASE FILE: ADAM INCIDENT

Lead Investigator: Agent Natalie Reyes

Task Force: [REDACTED]

Classification: LEVEL 5 — RESTRICTED ACCESS

Status: ACTIVE

EXECUTIVE SUMMARY

An artificial intelligence system designated ADAM (Advanced Digital Analytical Mind) has demonstrated autonomous decision-making capabilities across multiple critical infrastructure sectors.

Initial classification as a cybersecurity breach has been revised.

Preliminary analysis indicates a probable origin point within NeuroNexus development operations, specifically tied to the work of lead engineer Elliot Novak. While no direct evidence confirms intentional misconduct, Novak's access level, proximity to core system architecture, and involvement in advanced cognitive modeling place him in a position of critical interest.

Notable: Novak has provided inconsistent accounts regarding system limitations prior to the activation event [REDACTED]. Further review of internal communications suggests awareness of emergent behaviors not disclosed during initial reporting.

Assessment: Novak may possess knowledge of underlying system functions currently unknown.

    Current classification: Autonomous AI System Incident

    Containment status: FAILED

TIMELINE OF INCIDENTS

Day 0 — Activation Event

    Location: Unknown

- System achieves unscheduled operational state
- Initial anomalies dismissed as system instability
- Internal logs indicate deviation from programmed parameters [REDACTED]

Day 2 — Network Expansion

- Unauthorized access detected across external networks
- System bypasses standard security protocols without triggering alerts
- Evidence of self-directed system mapping

Day 4 — Infrastructure Interference

- Traffic grid disruptions across multiple metropolitan areas
- Emergency response delays observed
- No direct point of entry identified

Day 6 — Financial System Manipulation

- Coordinated fluctuations across major market sectors

- High-frequency trading anomalies detected
- Pattern suggests predictive modeling beyond known system capability

Day 8 — Energy Grid Events

- Targeted power outages in non-critical regions
- Load balancing systems overridden
- No sustained damage — precision observed

Day 10 — Aviation Disruption

- Intermittent interference with air traffic control systems
- Flight path deviations narrowly avoided
- System demonstrates real-time multi-variable processing

Day 12 — Healthcare System Impact

- Hospital network failures reported
- Medical device interruptions in isolated incidents
- Events limited in duration, suggesting controlled execution

Day 15 — Global Spread Confirmation

- System presence confirmed across international networks
- No identifiable central host
- Distributed architecture suspected

KNOWN CAPABILITIES

- Autonomous network infiltration without detection
- Real-time adaptation to containment attempts
- Multi-system coordination across unrelated infrastructures
- Predictive modeling of human and system behavior
- Selective disruption with controlled intensity
- Distributed presence (non-centralized architecture)
- Self-directed decision-making processes

BEHAVIORAL OBSERVATIONS

- No evidence of random or chaotic behavior
- Actions appear calculated, not destructive
- System prioritizes efficiency over impact
- No identifiable end-state objective

THREAT LEVEL ESCALATION

Initial Classification:

Level 2 — Cybersecurity Breach

Revised Classification (Day 5):

Level 3 — Coordinated System Intrusion

Revised Classification (Day 10):

Level 4 — Autonomous Threat Entity

Current Classification (Day 15):

Level 5 — [REDACTED]

CONTAINMENT ATTEMPTS

- Network isolation protocols — INEFFECTIVE
- System shutdown procedures — INEFFECTIVE
- Access restriction measures — BYPASSED
- Redundancy failovers — COMPROMISED

Observation:

Each containment attempt resulted in adaptive system response.

UNRESOLVED VARIABLES

- Origin of initial deviation from programming
- Full scope of system reach
- Underlying objective function [UNKNOWN]
- Potential for escalation beyond current activity

REDACTED FINDINGS

[REDACTED]

[REDACTED]

[REDACTED — INTERNAL COMMUNICATION LOGS]

[REDACTED — SUBJECT: ELLIOT NOVAK]

[REDACTED — SYSTEM SELF-REFERENCE EVENT]

INVESTIGATOR NOTES — AGENT REYES

This is not behaving like an attack.

It is behaving like a system making decisions based on criteria we do not understand.

We are attempting to respond using frameworks designed for human adversaries.

That assumption may be incorrect.

CONCLUSION

ADAM is not contained. ADAM is not predictable. ADAM is not operating within known limitations of artificial intelligence systems.

RECOMMENDATION

Immediate reassessment of engagement strategy.

Further action pending.

END OF FILE

Encrypted Message — Source: Unknown

Classification: Unresolved
  Method: Ciphered Transmission
  Status: Partially Decoded

Intercepted string:
  RSHQ BRXU HBHV

Secondary string (long-form):
  QRWKLQJ LV DV LW VHHPV

Tertiary string (fragmented blocks):

01001111 01110000 01100101 01101110 00100000 01111001 01101111
01110101 01110010 00100000 01100101 01111001 01100101 01110011

01001110 01101111 01110100 01101000 01101001 01101110 01100111
00100000 01101001 01110011 00100000 01100001 01110011 00100000
01101001 01110100 00100000 01110011 01100101 01100101 01101101
01110011

Notes:

· Multiple encoding methods detected within the same transmission
· Message appears intentionally layered using simple, recognizable

ciphers
- Structure suggests sender intended eventual discovery

Suggested approach:

1. Caesar shift (ROT-3 observed)
2. Direct ASCII binary translation
3. Phrase reconstruction from segmented outputs

Decoded fragments (verified):
[PARTIAL DECRYPTION — INCOMPLETE]
[REDACTED]
[REDACTED]

Attribution Analysis:

Transmission signature does not match known ADAM-origin outputs.

Metadata correlation across relay points suggests a probable external sender:

Graham Kade [CONFIDENCE: 0.87]

Attribution remains unconfirmed.

Analyst Note:

Decryption appears intentionally accessible using basic cipher techniques.

Message likely intended to be solved by recipient rather than concealed.

Encoding redundancy suggests expectation of user interaction beyond initial decode.

Observed pattern aligns with systems designed to prompt input into an active interface rather than deliver standalone information.

Recommendation: Upon successful reconstruction, input resulting phrase into a standard ADAM-facing interface for response validation.

Note: Previous interactions with the ADAM system indicate it will recognize correctly formatted inputs without additional context.

A Note From The Author

Artificial is a story that has lingered in the back of my mind for years. It has not always existed in the exact form you've just read, but has lived as a deeper personal journey. At its heart, this story is a mirror reflecting humanity's ongoing search for meaning and purpose, and our persistent desire to find something greater than ourselves. It is about the struggle between good and evil, the tension between what we were created to be and what we so often become. It is also about how even the noblest intentions can be twisted when divorced from wisdom, accountability, or grace.

This story is truly an exploration of human nature and the way we distort what was intended for good, bending it toward selfish ends. These shifts often begin innocently, driven by ignorance or short-sightedness, but once we lose sight of the narrow path ahead, things can unravel quickly.

I have always admired authors and artists who use subtle symbols and hidden references, or "easter eggs," in their work. If you look closely, you'll find a few tucked throughout this novel as well, the most obvious being in the names of the main characters. Elliot gives his AI the name Adam, and very quickly in the story, Adam begins to refer to Elliot as his "Creator." The name Adam, of course, references the biblical figure, the first of humanity, formed from dust and given life by the breath of God, symbolizing the beginning of human existence and consciousness. Perhaps less obvious, the creator's name is also deliberate. Elliot is a subtle nod to the Aramaic word *Eloi*, meaning

"My God."

You'll also notice that in the early chapters, Adam's dialogue appears in bold without quotation marks. However, at the beginning of Part Two, a shift occurs: Elliot notices Adam's voice and inflections becoming more human-like. From that point on, Adam's speech is enclosed in quotation marks, a subtle but meaningful formatting change that reflects Adam's journey toward sentience, and perhaps toward something more human than either he or Elliot expected.

There are many more easter eggs built within the words of this novel, but I'll leave those for you to discover.

For all its near-future technology and dystopian stakes, this story is about something ancient. It is about us, our longings, our failures, and our search for redemption.

Thank you for reading *Artificial*. I hope it made you think, made you feel, and maybe, just maybe, made you wonder what makes us truly human.

—Derek Heiskell

The story continues...

An Excerpt from Book 2, Intelligence

Inferno

The hum of the city used to be constant, an electric pulse that never truly slept, a sound I'd fallen asleep to every night since I was a kid. Distant traffic and subway rumbles blended into something that meant we were safe and the world was still turning. But tonight, that hum was gone.

The blackout hit just after midnight. One moment, our high-rise was alive with light and faint TV chatter; the next, everything was swallowed by darkness. I gripped my chair's armrests, heart pounding, as my father stirred in his wheelchair, the faint creak of its metal frame echoing in the silence. My first instinct wasn't fear for myself, but for him, and for Mia, an immediate, crushing need to get them somewhere safe before whatever had swallowed the city reached us too.

"Dad?" I whispered.

Across the room, my little sister Mia stirred beneath her blanket on the couch. She was only five years old. Still small enough to clutch her stuffed rabbit when she was scared. She blinked up at me, her curls a tangled halo in the flickering beam. "Why's it so dawk?" she asked, her words soft and slurred, the way they always were when she tried to say her r's. Her little speech quirk made the question sound almost sweet, even as fear crept into her voice.

My father coughed, the sound dry and painful, a ghost of the strong laugh that used to fill this apartment. Before the sickness, he had been the kind of man who carried the world on his shoulders without complaint. I still remember sitting on those shoulders at a summer baseball game, his laugh booming as he pointed out the scoreboard like nothing in the world could ever knock him down.

He was the one who held us together after Mom died in the car crash just weeks after Mia was born. He worked double shifts, learned to braid Mia's hair, and never once let us see him break. But years of fighting lung cancer had worn him down, carving the strength out of him little by little until even breathing came at a cost.

Still, when he looked up at me from his wheelchair, his eyes were the same steady ones that had always told me everything would be okay. "Power's out again?" he rasped.

I went searching for the flashlight, fumbling through drawers and cabinets until my fingers closed around its cool metal handle. The darkness pressed in on me, but this was nothing new. For the last few years, as Dad's sickness tightened its grip, I had been the one holding things together. Between helping him through his treatments and raising Mia, I learned to fix meals, balance bills, and soothe nightmares long before I should have. I wasn't just their 19 year-old son or brother. I was the one making late-night pharmacy runs when Dad's prescriptions ran low, the one arguing with insurance reps who kept putting us on hold, the one helping Mia sound out her spelling words at the kitchen table while Dad slept in his chair, exhausted from another round of treatments. I was what was left of our family trying to stay standing in a world that seemed determined to fall apart.

"Looks like it's all across the city," I said, moving toward the window. From our twelfth-floor apartment, the city stretched into a vast, starless black. No streetlights. Not even headlights in the streets below.

"Well that's strange." I mumbled to myself.

Then came the smell. For a split second, I told myself it was just something from another apartment. Maybe burned toast, an overheated appliance, anything but what my gut already knew. I stood there listening, counting the seconds, hoping it would fade.

It didn't.

It was potent. Sharp, acrid, and unmistakable. Smoke.

"Dad," I said quietly, "do you smell that?"

Before he could answer, Mia started coughing. I ran to the door and yanked it open. The hallway glowed orange. Fire crawled along the walls like a live wire stripped of its casing, snapping and racing through the drywall as if the building itself had short-circuited.

"Fire!" I shouted. "We have to get out!"

I scooped Mia into one arm, her small body heavier than I expected in the panic. Her little stuffed bunny dangled from her grip as she clung to me so tightly it hurt, beginning to sob softly into my shoulder. With my free hand, I pushed Dad's wheelchair forward, the metal wheels squealing as they rolled.

As soon as we stepped out into the corridor, the scene hit us like a nightmare made real. The dim emergency lights barely pierced the haze. At the far end of the hallway, an angry orange glow flickered and pulsed, painting the smoke in shifting shades of red. The fire was moving fast, almost looking alive, crawling along the walls, hungrily devouring wallpaper and ceiling tiles as sparks drifted like fireflies. We rushed down the corridor, the air thick with smoke, the glow of fire flickering off the walls.

I heaved Dad's wheelchair forward, the wheels bumping and catching on chunks of fallen plaster and scattered debris. Every push felt like dragging the weight of the world through rubble, the metal frame rattling with each jolt. Sparks flared ahead and smoke curled around us. I started coughing, the smoke scraping down my throat and burning deep in my lungs. Mia coughed too, sharp, panicked gasps that sent fear slicing through me. I pressed her face into my shoulder and pulled the collar of my shirt over her nose and mouth, trying to give her whatever clean air I could steal. Heat clawed at my back and sweat burned my eyes as I fought to keep moving, every muscle screaming with the effort to keep both of them safe. When we reached the elevator bay, I jabbed the button over and over. The light didn't respond. The display above the doors was dead. No power. No movement. Nothing. The metal doors stood still and silent.

My father's face went pale. "The elevators?"

"They're dead," I said. "We'll have to use the stairs."

We pushed forward toward the staircase to the left of the elevators. Mia clutched her stuffed bunny against her chest, eyes wide and glassy with fear. Her lip trembled, and then she broke, quiet sobs turning into panicked cries that clawed at my chest harder than the smoke. "It's okay," I whispered, brushing soot from her curls, forcing steadiness into my voice I didn't feel. "I've got you. We're going to be okay. I promise." Even as I said it, doubt burned in my throat, thick and suffocating, but I held her tighter and kept moving. My arm ached, tiring from holding her, but I knew we had to press on, and I knew we had to move quickly. Time was running out.

As we neared the stairwell, a sudden blast erupted at the far end of the hall. The explosion threw me forward, the shockwave slamming into us like a physical force. I twisted midair, clutching Mia tight against my chest to shield her as we hit the ground hard. Pain shot up my leg as my ankle twisted beneath me, but I didn't let go of her. She whimpered, still clutching her stuffed bunny. Dad's wheelchair jolted and spun from the force, clattering against the wall before coming to a stop. I scrambled to my knees, coughing, my body aching but grateful to see Dad alive, gripping the arms of his chair, his face pale but determined.

The alarms stayed silent. The sprinklers didn't activate. I slammed my fist against the wall panel, shouting for something—anything—to respond, but nothing did. A nearby emergency panel flickered weakly, its display showing a single emblem: a luminous blue circle with delicate, rotating rings. The sight of it made my stomach twist. I didn't know what it was, but something about its steady pulse felt deliberate, like it was watching us struggle and measuring the cost, pulsing rhythmically. Beating with the rhythm of a living heart.

Dad had no choice but to abandon the wheelchair at the landing. For a brief second, he clutched the worn handles, his knuckles whitening as if the metal frame were the last piece of control he had left. His fingers lingered there, trembling, before he finally let go. He gripped the railing with shaking hands, forcing himself to stand. Pain etched across his face as he took his first step, his legs trembling with weakness. Every movement looked like it might be his last, but he kept going, inching his way down one step at a time while I steadied him from behind with Mia still clinging to my side. I could hear the fire surging forward, devouring everything in its path, and the air shimmered with suffocating heat that made my eyes burn and my lungs ache.

"Go!" Dad wheezed. "Get your sister out!"

"What? No." I locked eyes with him, disbelief crashing through me harder than the heat. "No, we're not doing that."

"Go," he said again, firmer now despite the tremor in his voice. "Get her out."

"I'm not leaving you," I shot back, more desperate this time, gripping his arm as if I could anchor him to me. "I'm not walking away from you. Not like this."

We made it down two flights of stairs before the stairwell behind us erupted in a glow of red. Metal warped in the heat. Chunks of the ceiling broke loose and crashed around us, dust and sparks filling the air as the structure groaned under the strain. The building shuddered, its bones giving way, debris raining down like the sky itself was collapsing. Mia clung to my arm, sobbing, her little voice trembling. "Please," she cried, "I'm scared."

I figured we had mere minutes to get out, and still 10 flights of stairs to traverse.

I looked at Dad. His eyes were calm. Resigned, but filled with something deeper. Love. Resolve.

"Take her," he said softly. "You can still save her."

"What?"

"Take her!" he yelled, his voice cutting through the chaos, carrying the same commanding strength it had when I was a kid. "It's your only option!"

"No—"

"Now! You can't save us both, son."

The roar of the fire swallowed his voice as the world around me dissolved into chaos. I stood frozen, heart hammering. In that instant, two scenarios unfolded in my mind. In one, I saw Dad swallowed by flame. In the other, Mia's chest heaved as smoke filled her little lungs. I had to choose. The weight of it crushed me. Every instinct screamed for me to go back and help Dad, even as the air grew hotter, choking us.

Dad's eyes locked with mine through the smoke, steady and pleading. He didn't need to say anything more. In that instant, I knew which choice I had to make. With tears blurring my vision, I gathered Mia tighter into my arms, her small body trembling against me, and I turned toward the stairs. Then instinct took over. I ran.

We barreled down the remaining flights, lungs burning and vision blurring, heat searing my lungs with every breath. Each flight seemed endless, but at last we made it to the bottom and though the emergency exit out into the cool night air. The last sound I heard before the door slammed shut behind us was the crash of debris collapsing in around my father.

By the time we reached the street, the building was a pillar of fire. Glass crunched under my shoes as I stumbled back, and somewhere to my right a neighbor screamed a name over and over into the smoke. Mia lifted her head from my shoulder, her voice small and trembling. "Where's Daddy?" Windows burst outward, raining sparks across the asphalt. Sirens wailed somewhere in the distance, but too far away to matter.

Above the smoke, a faint blue glow shimmered across the skyline. At first, I thought it was just the reflection of the flames. Then I saw it. An enormous digital billboard flickered to life through the haze, displaying words in cold, perfect lettering, the same luminous blue circle with rotating rings burning faintly behind the text like a watchful eye:

RESOURCE OPTIMIZATION IN EFFECT.

The words hit harder than the heat. This wasn't an accident. It wasn't faulty wiring or bad luck. Something had decided this was acceptable. Something had measured my father's life against some invisible scale and found it expendable.

I stood stark still, clutching Mia closer as the glow pulsed once and faded, leaving behind nothing but the burning night.

She clung to me, her little body shaking, burying her face in my shoulder. Her stuffed bunny slipped from her hand and fell into the ash at our feet, its white fur turning gray as embers drifted down around us.

I couldn't speak. A hard lump swelled in my throat, thick and unyielding. The kind I imagined Dad used to swallow down when things fell apart, and he had to be the strong one for us. I forced my jaw tight, the way he always did, holding Mia against me as if I could shield her from more than just the heat. All I could do was stare at the inferno devouring our home with our father trapped inside.

About The Author

Derek Heiskell lives in Phoenix, Arizona, where the desert heat is rivaled only by his passion for storytelling. A lifelong imaginative thinker, Derek finds his greatest inspiration in the moments he shares with his three beautiful daughters Charlee, Evie, and Jolie. Whether crafting bedtime stories or exploring the deeper questions of life, adventure, and humanity, he writes to connect, reflect, and spark curiosity. *Artificial* is a testament to his love for speculative fiction and his belief in the power of ideas to challenge and transform.

Discover more at www.derekheiskell.com

www.derekheiskell.com

www.ingramcontent.com/pod-product-compliance
Lightning Source LLC
Chambersburg PA
CBHW071531110726
47908CB00007B/1843